**With hatred running hot and molten
through his veins,**

Mateo de Montayas stared at the stately mansion across the street. The windows were aglow with light. Laughter and music spilled out to fill the night air. He shifted position under the shadowy oak tree hoping to catch sight of his quarry. The high and mighty English baronet who celebrated inside had destroyed his family.

Mateo slipped the miniature portrait from his breast pocket. A thin leather cord wrapped around his fingers as he gazed into the eyes of the laughing beauty pictured there.

"I couldn't help you then..." The pain of failure threatened to overwhelm him. He shoved it down, deep down into a dark place in his soul. He took a deep breath, fighting the anger that rose within. "I will make him pay for your death." His fingers closed around the small oval. "I swear it, Madre. I swear it."

Impetuous

by

Katherine Grey

Impetuous

Cover Art by *Rae Monet, Inc. Design*

The Wild Rose Press
PO Box 706
Adams Basin, NY 14410-0706
Visit us at www.thewildrosepress.com

Publishing History
First English Tea Rose Edition, 2011
Print ISBN 1-60154-959-8

Published in the United States of America

Dedication

Wendy, this book is for you.
You gave me faith because you believed.

Chapter One

London, 1812

With hatred running hot and molten through
his veins, Mateo de Montayas stared at the stately
mansion across the street. The windows were aglow
with light. Laughter and music spilled out to fill the
night air. He shifted position under the shadowy oak
tree hoping to catch sight of his quarry. The high
and mighty English baronet who celebrated inside
had destroyed his family.

Mateo slipped the miniature portrait from his
breast pocket. A thin leather cord wrapped around
his fingers as he gazed into the eyes of the laughing
beauty pictured there.

"I couldn't help you then..." The pain of failure
threatened to overwhelm him. He shoved it down,
deep down into a dark place in his soul. He took a
deep breath, fighting the anger that rose within. "I
will make him pay for your death." His fingers closed
around the small oval. "I swear it, Madre. I swear
it."

Tomorrow his cousin Eduardo would arrive in
London with the necessary papers that would give
Mateo entree into the Polite World. His lips quirked
at the term. From what he had learned about the
Beau Monde, polite was the last word he'd use to
describe them. A pack of vultures waiting to descend
on the weak was a more apt description.

He focused on the revelers making their way
down the stairs to the carriages lining the drive.
"Enjoy your happiness," he said under his breath,

"for it is about to come crashing down around you."
He looked again at the miniature he still held in his
hand. "Soon, *Madre*, soon."

With renewed determination, he pushed away
from the tree allowing the darkness to conceal him
as he made his way to the back of the townhouse. An
open window in an unattended room was all he
needed.

****

"You! What are you doing?"

Mateo dropped the sheaf of papers onto the desk
and slid the drawer closed. He edged toward the
French doors leading to a private garden.

The other man moved to block his path. Mateo
turned and sprinted out of the room. The sounds of
the ball were louder now. He raced toward them,
certain he could lose himself in the crush.

He ran into the ballroom and as if by magic, the
crowd parted. Stragglers darted from one side of the
room to the other. The music came to an abrupt halt
as everyone, musicians included, stared at him. He
scanned the room, taking in the rich velvet curtains,
glittering chandeliers, and ivory silk wallpaper. Gilt-
edged furniture shone brightly in the light of what
must have been hundreds of candles.

"Stop! Thief!"

The insult rankled. He'd never stolen anything,
unlike most of the English he'd met. If he found
what he was searching for, he would indeed become
a thief. But considering his attire of dark clothing
and mask, he couldn't blame the man for labeling
him as such.

Knowing his pursuer was close behind, Mateo
searched for the nearest avenue of escape. His
attention caught and held on a young woman
standing slightly apart from the rest. Soft honey-
gold curls framed her face. The dark blue of her
gown gave her skin a porcelain glow.

He closed the distance between them, grabbed her arm, and pulled her to his side. "Do not fight me."

The indrawn breath of the crowd caused him to loosen his grip just enough to ensure he inflicted no pain. "I mean no harm, I promise you," he said, his mouth close to her ear.

From the way all attention turned toward the door, he knew the man who'd discovered him in the study had entered the ballroom. But he also knew as long as he held a female captive, he was safe. This caused him more than a little chagrin. What would his noble father have said if he were alive to see his only son hiding behind the skirts of a woman? He pushed the thought away. His dead father's opinion mattered little now.

Mateo turned toward his opponent. "Welcome, my friend," he said with a flourish of his arm. "As you can see, we are in the midst of a grand ball. But you are indeed welcome."

Laughter filled the room as the crowd elbowed each other over the invitation since the ball was being held in the man's own home.

"Take your hands off her." Mateo's accuser pushed his way further into the room.

"Come now, Henry." An elderly matron moved to the edge of the mob. "Don't do anything rash."

"Yes, Wingate, don't do anything foolish. You don't want anyone to get hurt, do you?" a bearded gentleman yelled from the crowd.

The viscount gestured to Mateo. "Just him."

Mateo acknowledged this with a brief nod. From his position he could see almost the entire assemblage, but his back was to a small portion of the room. He had to get out of here before some fool decided to do something stupidly heroic.

"Am I surrounded by cowards and imbeciles?" Lord Wingate demanded.

A rustle of movement spread through the room, but no one moved to join him.

Mateo kept his hold on the woman and strolled closer to his means of escape with a nonchalance that belied his eagerness.

The ungodly scent of too many perfumed bodies made him long for a breath of fresh air. The oppressive heat of the room closed in on him. Sweat trickled from beneath his mask and ran down the sides of his face. He hoped the makeup he'd applied earlier to lighten his skin was still in place. He could feel it melting where his collar brushed against his skin.

Knowing he'd dawdled far too long, he forced himself into action. He pulled the woman toward the ornate double doors leading to freedom.

"You will not take Miss Darlington from this house," Wingate shouted.

Mateo halted mid-step.

Hushed voices rose and fell at this latest turn of events. By now, he had the rapt attention of the entire room. No one moved.

He gauged the short distance to freedom then turned to face Wingate. "Of course. As you wish."

Clicking his heels and sketching a small bow, he made a show of releasing his captive but then pulled her tighter into his arms.

Alarm flared to life in her eyes. "What are you doing?"

"I need a distraction so I can get away."

"I won't help you."

"Ah, but you will," he murmured and pressed his lips against her mouth. It was no more than a moment, but it had the desired effect.

A gasp escaped from the crowd.

Dazed by the turn of events, Teresa Darlington stared up at her captor.

"We shall meet again," he whispered and

disappeared into the shadowed hall.

Teresa raised a hand to her mouth trying to comprehend the sensations running through her. Her heart hammered in her chest; her lips tingled from the rough contact.

A hush fell over the crowd. She suddenly realized she held the attention of everyone present, horror and disapproval etched across their faces. Obviously, she hadn't reacted as was expected of an unmarried woman of quality, even if she was nearly on the shelf. Thinking fast, she did the only thing she could—she pretended to swoon.

"Teresa!" Lord Wingate knelt at her side, calling for help to revive her.

The babbling voices of the crowd grew louder. She struggled to maintain her composure. It wouldn't do to laugh and ruin the deception. Everyone spoke at once, each eager to voice his or her interpretation of what had taken place.

"Did you see that?"

"I couldn't believe it."

A female sighed from somewhere off to Teresa's right. "Wasn't he just dashing?"

"Dashing?" a male asked. "Audacious is more like it."

A vinaigrette was shoved under her nose while someone chaffed her wrists. She resisted the urge to push the offensive smelling pomander away. She fluttered her eyelids, making a great show of regaining consciousness, and hoped her acting was good enough to fool her eagle-eyed aunt.

"I want her moved somewhere quiet until she gets over the shock."

Teresa recognized the imperious tones with dismay. It seemed her aunt stood close by after all.

"Of course, Your Grace," Wingate responded.

In the next instant, she was lifted from the floor and carried into the library.

His lordship set her gently on the chaise and stepped back. "I must apologize," he began.

"I should say so," the duchess sneered. "What kind of man allows his guests to be accosted in so dreadful a manner?"

Teresa watched her aunt cross the room with a sense of impending doom. Wingate stood to the side, his face composed in grim lines. Curling her fingers into the satin material of her gown, she wondered who would draw first blood this time.

The viscount was a pompous, self-serving man matched in arrogance by her aunt, the Duchess of Perth, who made certain no one forgot her rank. Previous altercations between the two had taken on legendary status among the *Ton*.

"I'm fine." Teresa jumped into the silence as the two adversaries eyed each other with cold disdain. "It was just the shock." She attempted to placate her mother's sister before tempers flared. "You know I'm not prone to the vapors."

The duchess looked down her long patrician nose. "It's not every day you're subjected to such vulgar attentions." She turned to the viscount. "I do hope that wasn't part of the evening's planned entertainment."

"Of course not," he bit out. "Do you think I'd hire some slavering idiot to distress my female guests?" He clasped his hands behind his back and paced in front of the fireplace. "Especially Teresa of all people. You know I look upon her as my own child."

"I also know that you'd sell your own kin to stay in the *Beau Monde's* good graces. That nasty gambling loss you suffered a fortnight ago is more than enough to earn you the cut direct." The duchess smoothed a hand over her coiffure. "You have paid your markers, haven't you?"

She let the question linger in the air before settling her gaze on Teresa. "I'll send Sarah in with your wrap. We'll be leaving. I've had all the entertainment I can stomach." With that pronouncement, the duchess sashayed from the room.

"You must believe—" his lordship began.

Teresa held up a hand. "Don't apologize. I know you had as little to do with this as I did."

Wingate breathed a sigh of relief. "Allow me to extend the use of my box at the opera as a way to make amends. I know you don't get a chance to go as often as you'd like."

"Thank you."

"If you'll excuse me, I must see to the remainder of my guests."

"Of course," she murmured, watching him quit the room without a backward glance.

She sagged back on the pale green chaise, her fingers tracing the striped pattern. Who was the masked thief? What did the viscount have that was so valuable it would prompt someone to attempt a robbery during a ball? Had he purposely chosen to kiss her of all the other women present or was she just the most convenient? She traced her lips with a trembling finger.

And more importantly, would she see him again?

Chapter Two

Teresa entered the dining room surprised to find her aunt already seated. The duchess rarely left her bed before noon. Determined not to let the woman spoil her good mood, she helped herself to a cup of hot chocolate and a warm muffin.

She inhaled the rich scent of the fragrant liquid. "Good morning. I hope you slept well," she ventured, trying to gauge the other woman's mood.

The duchess looked up from sorting invitations into piles. "One always sleeps better in one's own surroundings."

Teresa was saved from responding by Lady Sarah's entrance. Dressed in a blue gown that matched her eyes, she swept into the room, dropped a kiss on her mother's cheek, and headed for the sideboard.

"Mmm. Everything smells wonderful. I'm absolutely famished this morning." She filled a cup with the steaming chocolate. "Our trip into the country yesterday must be the cause. Wasn't the day wonderful?"

"Sarah," the duchess said in a warning tone.

"Yes, Mother."

"What have I told you about your manner of speech?"

Sarah's sunny disposition disappeared as though a cloud suddenly passed over her. She gave Teresa a quick glance and swallowed. "A lady of my station doesn't chatter on like some hen-witted commoner."

Teresa sighed into her cup. She longed to come

to her cousin's defense but knew the duchess would repay her insolence by tormenting Mama. She gave the younger girl a commiserating smile.

Sarah helped herself to eggs, toast, and bacon. She stiffened at the sound of her mother clearing her throat. She set the plate down as if it might shatter at any moment.

"A large appetite is a sign of ill breeding," she recited. "A lady eats like a bird so she may weigh no more than a butterfly." With one last look of longing, Sarah placed a slice of toast on a clean dish and took her seat at the table.

At the sight of Sarah's down-bent head, Teresa itched to point out that Vivian's own plate overflowed with food. She clenched her teeth until her jaw ached, barely managing to keep a strangle hold on her temper.

The duchess slit open the first invitation of those deemed important enough to be considered. "How interesting. Lord Pendleton is having a rout in honour of a foreign guest—a Count de Montayas of Spain. We shall have to attend." She laid the sheet aside and continued on to the next.

"But Mother, you hate the Spanish. You said we should let Napoleon have them," Sarah said in a barely audible voice.

"So I did. Some things have to be tolerated to get what you want from life. This event could be very advantageous for you."

"Lord Pendleton is old enough to be my father," Sarah cried, near tears. "I don't wish to become betrothed to him."

Vivian looked up from the paper in her hand. "You will marry whom I choose. Do not worry yourself. It will give you wrinkles and who would want you then? Lord Pendleton is a wealthy man. He has close ties to the Prince Regent and more importantly, he has a son who will inherit his title."

"If I may, when is the Pendleton Ball?" Teresa asked in an effort to distract her aunt's attention.

The duchess cast her a disapproving look. "Three days from now."

"I'm afraid I'll be unable to attend. Please send my regrets."

"You will attend."

"I do not wish to go. I have accompanied you to three different soirees within the last fortnight. I even allowed you to drag me off to Brighton when I wanted to stay here with Mama and attend to my experiments."

Vivian's brown eyes snapped with anger. "How dare you take such a tone with me. You and your precious experiments. What do you think will come of them? I'll tell you. Nothing! Do you hear me? Nothing!" She slammed her hand on the table making the dishes rattle. "Do you think the *Ton* doesn't regard you as odd enough already?"

Teresa pushed away from the table. "No one will notice if I attend or not."

Silence filled the room as she stared at her aunt, unwilling to back down.

"Please. Please say you'll come." Sarah's whisper seemed loud in the tense air.

She met her cousin's pleading gaze and knew she would attend, if only for Sarah's benefit. "Very well," she said in a low tone.

Vivian gave her a superior smile and opened the next invitation.

Teresa dropped her napkin onto the table. "If you'll excuse me, I've lost my appetite."

She strode from the room, determined to ignore her aunt's smirk.

Heading up the stairs, she hoped the confrontation in the dining room didn't cause difficulties for Mama. She tried to control her temper but refused to allow the duchess to run roughshod over her. Swallowing the remnants of her ire, she followed the hall to the small suite of rooms at the back of the house.

Unsure if Lady Darlington would be up to visitors this morning, she gave a soft knock and waited. After a few minutes, she opened the door. "Mama?"

The silence of the room frightened her. She hurried through the sitting room. "Mama," she called, "where are you?"

Her heart in her throat, she flew across the small space to the partially closed bedroom door. Afraid of what she would find, she wavered for a moment then pushed the door open.

Relief swept over her as she took in the sight of her mother's slight form sitting on the window seat overlooking the garden.

"Mama, didn't you hear me call?" she asked.

Lady Darlington stared out the window, her fingers caressing a small leather bound book. "He broke his promise," she murmured.

"Who?" Teresa asked, already knowing the response she would receive.

"He said we would be together forever...and now he has left me here all alone."

Teresa kneeled and laid a tentative hand on Lady Darlington's knee. "I'm here, Mama."

Sophia Darlington looked down at her daughter as though surprised to find her there. "But I fear I am not. Without Robert, I feel as though I have lost the most important part of myself." She gazed out the window once more, pressing the book to her chest. "Loneliness is a long, slow, painful death."

Teresa touched her mother's cheek, brushing back the silver blonde hair that only accentuated her frailty. "Come out into the garden with me. You haven't left these rooms since Papa's funeral. I'd like you to see what I've been growing in the flowerbeds."

Sophia shook her head. "I must be here when he comes."

"Papa is dead," Teresa whispered, her voice breaking. "He's not coming back."

Sophia gave a wan smile. "He will come. One day soon, he'll come and we'll be together again."

"Mama, please don't say that."

"Do you not wish to see me happy?"

"Of course, but not that way. Not that way." Tears coursed down Teresa's cheeks. "I can't lose you both."

Sophia said nothing more, only turned to gaze out the window.

Teresa rose to her feet and dropped a kiss on the top of her mother's head. Brushing away her tears, she prayed for a little more time. Just a little more. There had to be a way to give Mama back the will to live. There had to be.

Chapter Three

"Relax, child. You're strung up tighter than a corset," Betsy complained. "I can hear your teeth grinding together from here."

The Pendleton rout was a mere two hours away. Teresa's head ached already, her body stiff with tension.

She watched the maid lay out a simple amber-colored gown on the bed, her plump figure leaning over the counterpane to smooth the silk material. Although Betsy had been employed as her personal servant for as long as she could remember, Teresa considered her a mother figure. Her own mother had been too wrapped up in her husband to become involved in the raising of a child.

"I can't help it. I hate these grand affairs. Aunt Vivian's sniping I can stand, but it pains me to see her throw barbs at Lady Sarah, especially in public. To be forced to endure it for a whole evening..." She trailed off, her words ending in a long sigh.

Betsy moved to stand behind her. "Maybe you can escape into the gardens. I've heard Lord Pendleton has an army of caretakers for the grounds alone." She picked up a hairbrush and began coiling Teresa's hair into an elegant twist.

"I fear it may be the only way I'll get through the dreaded affair."

She longed to beg off, but the image of Sarah's pleading face kept returning to haunt her, not to mention the horrible scene the duchess would create. She didn't feel up to dealing with her aunt's tantrums, so she would go and melt into the background as usual. At least she wouldn't spend the evening fighting off lecherous advances, as Sarah would have to.

****

All too soon, the footman helped her from the carriage. Alive with light and music, the entrance of the Pendleton townhouse was surrounded by guests jostling for position to enter the grand building.

"Come along, Sarah dear." The duchess' honeyed tones carried over the crowd.

Teresa rolled her eyes at her aunt's display of motherly affection. It was enough to make her cast up her accounts right there in the drive.

With leaden feet, she followed her cousin. She glanced at the trees on her left wondering if she could disappear behind one and hire a hackney to take her back to Perth House. Even as the thought formed, she dismissed it. Mama had paid dearly for her last act of defiance.

A portrait of Robert Darlington had suddenly gone missing from Sophia's suite of rooms. She'd been inconsolable at the painting's disappearance, begging Teresa to search the servants' belongings. Two days later, the portrait reappeared as mysteriously as it had vanished.

Although she couldn't prove it, she knew the duchess had taken the piece. As a way of keeping Teresa under her thumb, it worked well. She knew that as long as she threatened Lady Darlington, Teresa would obey her wishes.

With a sigh, she allowed her cloak to be taken and made her way to the ballroom. The instant she stepped into the room, she wanted to run in the opposite direction. The combination of overpowering warmth and too many people pressed into one place made her feel as if there was no air left to breathe.

Fighting the urge to back out of the room, she inhaled a shallow breath. The strong odor of sweat assailed her. The clamour of music and voices struggling to be heard blended into an unrecognizable cacophony of sound. Panic clawed at her each time someone bumped into her.

Lady Sarah materialized at her side, took her hand, and led her past the initial crush of guests. Teresa gave her a grateful smile. Now, that they were in the room proper, she felt slightly more at ease.

Large groups of people had a strange effect on her. She felt as if there wasn't enough air to breathe, as if everyone pressed in on her. She didn't understand nor could she control her reaction. Sarah tried to help her through the ordeal when she had no choice but to attend parties with larger guest lists.

Suddenly, the duchess cut between them, forcing Sarah to withdraw her comforting hold. "Sarah, be polite to this Spanish barbarian but do not encourage him." She turned to Teresa. "And you—you will not cause a scene as you did at the Wingate ball," she hissed.

"I have no desire to be the object of gossip."

The duchess raised her eyebrows. "As if a countrified little squab like you would even be noticed. Unless you throw yourself at a man like you did at Wingate's."

Teresa opened her mouth to retort that she had been an unwilling participant in that horrid little tableau but bit her tongue instead. She would *not* give her aunt the satisfaction of responding.

"Come along." Vivian swept Sarah back into the crowd.

Teresa searched for the terrace entrance. She skimmed over the guests, taking no notice of anyone in particular.

Columns of marble flanked each door leading into the enormous room. Cream-colored draperies framed the windows. Dancing couples whirled across the center of the floor while others filled various divans, chaises, and chairs set strategically about.

More to have something to do than any real sense of thirst, she went in search of a drink. With a glass of lemonade in hand, she made a slow circle of the room, her eyes locked on the open terrace doors and the freedom they offered. Just as it was in reach, a voice called her name. She stopped, prayed she wouldn't be asked to dance, and slowly turned around.

"Teresa, how are you? I fear it has been some time since I have called on you and your lovely mother. How is she?"

Realizing the speaker was Lord Pendleton, a smile came to her lips. Of all her father's friends, he had been the only one to try and stay in touch even though Mama continued to refuse visitors.

"She is well," she said, refraining from telling him the sad truth.

"That's good to hear." He drew her attention to the gentleman standing at his side. "I'd like to present the Count de Montayas of Spain. Montayas, Miss Darlington, the daughter of an old friend."

Teresa gave a small curtsey, her gaze never leaving the man's face. He stood a good foot taller than she. Sinfully handsome, he had hair as black as night, and his dark eyes were filled with an interested glint. They reminded her of polished onyx. With one quick glance, she knew the broad shoulders filling out the dark blue coat were his own.

"Miss Darling, did you say?" he asked in an accented voice.

"Darlington," she corrected.

He raised her gloved hand to his lips. "A pleasure, Miss Darling...ton."

His mouth brushed the back of her hand causing a jolt of electricity to burn its way up her arm. He released her with a quirk of his lips as though he knew the effect he had on her. She rubbed her hand on the back of her skirt, trying to wipe the strange feeling away.

"If you'll excuse us, my dear. So many more people to meet."

She tore her gaze from the count and gave Lord Pendleton a weak smile. "Of course."

She watched them walk away, then turned and hurried out to the terrace.

Depositing her unwanted lemonade on a nearby table, she headed down the steps leading to the solitude of the gardens. She would be safe as long as she didn't stray too far from the lights of the windows.

Unfortunately, she wasn't able to enjoy the true beauty of the flowers or the trees strung with small twinkling lights. Too many of the paths were filled with rakes and others seeking illicit trysts.

She sat on a decorative stone bench, feeling the tension gripping her fade away. She should be used to these events by now, but the panic was always there under the surface waiting to take hold of her. She'd tried to explain it to the duchess, but Vivian refused to believe her, insisting it was just another way for Teresa to try and cross her.

Refusing to dwell on her impossible relationship with her aunt, Teresa closed her eyes and inhaled the flower-scented air around her, finding the sense of peace she needed.

"Do you, as I, long to be free of this place?"

Teresa jumped from the bench and turned to face her unwanted visitor. The Count de Montayas tilted his head waiting for an answer.

"Why do you desire to leave?" she asked. "The ball is in your honor."

"I have grown weary of being sized up like a bull taken to market." He gestured for her to retake her seat.

She perched on the edge of the bench. "You don't like to be the object of attention?"

How odd that this man wanted to be overlooked when most of the men of the *Ton* considered the attention showered on them as their right by birth.

Montayas sat down beside her and looked at the townhouse. "I had not realized how many marriage-minded mothers, daughters, and widows would be in attendance," he said in a grim tone.

"You have no wife?" she asked in a careful voice. The last thing she wanted was to have him think she was one of the marriage hunters he mentioned. She shivered, remembering the strange sensation he roused in her simply by touching her hand.

He glanced at her, his eyes dark and unreadable. "No."

"Perhaps you will find one during your stay in our country." She wished she could call back the words the instant they were out of her mouth. For some reason, the thought of him marrying made her feel unsettled.

"I would not marry any of them." He flung his hand toward the glowing lights, his voice filled with anger. "They aren't interested in me—the man. They are interested in being the Condessa de Montayas. You English covet a title above all else." He turned, his gaze boring into her. "Some would even steal the birthright of another in their greed."

Shocked, Teresa stared at him. His eyes burned with hatred, his accent more pronounced than before. She had never come up against such animosity for a group of people.

She rose and moved away from him. "I must go back inside. I'll be missed soon."

It was a lie, but she no longer felt safe alone with him. She took a few steps away when his hand clamped onto her arm.

"Senorita, please." He turned her to face him,

muttering in Spanish under his breath. "I have offended you. I apologize for my lack of manners. Please stay."

Uncertain whether she should stay or go, she looked toward the growing crush of guests visible from where they stood. She shuddered, dreading having to brave the crowd again.

"You are cold." He removed his frock coat and dropped it over her shoulders. "Am I forgiven?"

"Why do you want me to stay?" she asked in a whisper, her fingers curling into the soft material.

He smiled, and she felt as though the moon had come out from behind a bank of clouds. It was ridiculous the way he affected her. His gaze roamed over her. The heat of embarrassment stole into her cheeks at his bold appraisal. Yet instead of being disgusted and offended, she felt as though flames surrounded her, sending their heat along her nerve endings.

"You are very beautiful."

"Me?" Her voice came out in a squeak.

"Come now, don't be coy. Every woman knows when she is beautiful and when she is not."

Teresa firmly believed she fell in the *not* category. Oh, she thought she was pretty in a passable fashion but definitely not beautiful. Lady Sarah was beautiful. "Have you met my cousin, Lady Sarah?" she asked.

"I don't remember and at this moment, I fear I do not care." He moved closer.

"My lord?"

The quiet voice drew his attention. Teresa didn't know if she was relieved or chagrined at the interruption.

Montayas turned toward the waiting servant. "Yes?"

"There is someone Lord Pendleton would like you to meet." The servant gestured toward the open

French doors and disappeared.

"Not another marriage seeker, I hope," Montayas muttered under his breath.

Teresa laughed at the sound of dismay in his voice.

He looked at her and smiled, his teeth flashing in the moonlight. "You find my predicament amusing, no? To show you I harbor no ill feelings, I wish you a quicker release from this tedious evening than I shall have."

She shrugged out of his jacket and held it out to him. "Thank you." She hesitated for a moment. "I fear I don't know how to address a count."

"Address?" he asked, puzzlement showing in his gaze.

"Yes, should I call you My Lord, or Sir, or Count?"

He took the frock coat, his fingers lingering over hers. "In my country, I would be called *Senor Conde*."

"Very well...*Senor Conde*."

He gazed at her for a long moment. "May I visit you in a few days? I'm afraid my time is not my own until then."

Teresa glanced away. In all the time she and Mama had resided at Perth House, she'd had no male callers. Of course her friend, Blaine Hobson, visited her on occasion. But while being a man, he roused no feelings other than sisterly affection. She took a deep breath and responded. "I will look forward to it."

"And so shall I. Good evening, *mi poco paloma*," he whispered, brushing his lips across the back of her hand.

Mateo tried to gauge her reaction. Had she recognized him from their previous encounter? Surely not. He had taken such pains to lighten his skin, wipe away any trace of his accent, and of course, to wear that dratted cloth tied about his head masking his features.

Without another word, he turned and strode toward the terrace. Now he would put his plan into place. Robert Darlington may have escaped his fall from grace by succumbing to an early death, but his family would still suffer. Suffer as the Montayas family had suffered.

Mateo looked back at the beautiful young woman standing at the edge of the garden. An unexpected pang of guilt assailed him. He would give her fair warning of what he intended. It was more than her father had done.

Chapter Four

Teresa looked out over the extensive gardens not really seeing them. A week had passed since the masked thief had accosted her at Wingate's ball, and yet she couldn't get him out of her mind.

"There you are." Lady Sarah slid her arm through Teresa's. "I can't believe we're really here. I'm so excited. Who would have thought that we'd be invited to Somerton House?"

"You are the daughter of a duke," Teresa said dryly, wishing some of Sarah's exuberance would rub off on her.

She smiled at her younger cousin, noticing how lovely she looked in the pale peach gown. Teresa glanced down at her own light green dress. When they stood together like this, she felt like the stem to Lady Sarah's blossom.

A small sigh whispered from her lips. She'd been in the doldrums since they'd arrived this morning.

Life at Perth House was becoming more difficult. The duchess barely tolerated her presence, treating her more like an unpaid chaperone for Lady Sarah than a member of the family. Not that she minded spending time with Sarah. She just didn't like being forced into situations where she felt uncomfortable or unwanted.

"But Somerton House. It's the grandest in all the area. Have you ever seen so many chandeliers in one place?" Sarah asked.

The question drew Teresa's attention away from her troubling thoughts. Her gaze roamed around the room. "It is rather daunting, isn't it?"

Heavy wine-colored drapes hung at the windows, furniture in the Rococo style crowded the room, and the gleaming marble floor all came together to give an impression of immense wealth.

Sarah tapped her cousin's arm with her ivory fan. "You sound as though you dislike all this grandeur. Oh, the dancing is about to begin."

Amid the rise and fall of chattering voices, the musicians could be heard tuning their instruments.

"I feel in need of some lemonade first," Teresa said, although she felt what she really needed was a glass of spirits. She let Sarah lead her away from the window.

There were fewer guests in attendance than expected. No one would class the gathering as the social event of the season. For that, she was thankful.

Viscount Linley intercepted them a few feet from the refreshments. "Good evening Lady Sarah, Miss Darlington."

"Good evening, Lord Linley," Lady Sarah said, her manner shy yet endearing.

"Good evening," Teresa returned as Sarah's cheeks flushed a becoming shade of pink.

She hoped the two would make a match. Though the viscount wasn't considered handsome by *Ton* standards, Teresa found his kind gaze and solicitous manner toward Lady Sarah comforting. Sarah had a difficult enough time with her mother; the last thing she needed was an overbearing husband.

Linley bestowed a smile on them and offered Sarah his arm. "I believe this dance is mine."

Sarah gave her cousin a pleading look. "If you'll excuse us?"

"Enjoy yourself." Teresa waved her away before crossing the wide expanse to join her aunt who held court in one of the corners of the room.

She veered off in another direction when she

recognized the other members of the circle. Mean, vicious gossips, the lot of them. She took a seat off to the side and searched for Sarah's twirling figure.

As one dance followed the next, Teresa gazed around the room, her attention focused on the male guests. Mentally, she measured each one against the man who'd burned his presence into her mind. It didn't seem possible that any of the gentlemen present could be the masked intruder.

After two hours of trying to decipher who he could be, she rubbed her forehead and gave up. She was driving herself mad and accomplishing nothing in the process. Claiming a headache, she said her goodnights and retired to the room she'd been given earlier.

Filled with a sense of relief, she closed the door. The sounds of the ball were muted here. A fire crackled in the grate, and the thick, white carpet felt luxurious under her feet after the hard marble floor of the ballroom. The tension of the evening drained away. She hated these overnight parties. She didn't like leaving Mama alone at Perth House. Admittedly, a house full of servants surrounded Lady Darlington, but Teresa worried nonetheless.

Why had the duchess insisted Teresa accompany them here? The woman had harped on what she deemed as Teresa's lack of proper behavior all the way home from the Wingate ball and continued to do so.

A rose-colored divan beckoned. Pushing away from the door, Teresa kicked off her satin slippers and curled up on the plush sofa, resting her chin on her hands.

She hated the way Aunt Vivian always made her feel as if she and Mama didn't quite measure up. True, Vivian had married a duke, but she was still her mother's sister, born into a family who worked in trade. Not that she would admit that to even her closest confidante.

If only Mama didn't continue to mourn Papa so. There had to be a way to make her happy again, to enjoy life again instead of watching it pass by from behind a window.

She shook her head, determined to put an end to her depressing thoughts. She left the divan and stood in front of the warm fire, her hands stretched toward the flames.

A light knock at the door brought her around. Expecting no one, she frowned and called out, "Is that you, Sarah?"

"No, it's Betsy."

"Come in, come in." Teresa hurried forward.

Betsy closed the door and set a branch of candles down on the mahogany side table, her plump figure casting a shadow on the nearby wall. "Why are you up here? The ball is a smashing success, at least that's the gossip below stairs." She clasped Teresa's hand and stared intently into her eyes. "Are you feeling poorly? I knew I shouldn't have let you talk me into helping you gather moss yesterday evening. You hadn't the proper boots for it."

Teresa squeezed her hand. "I'm fine. I just couldn't take any more inane conversations or false flattery. I only pleaded a headache as an excuse. And, I needed that moss to continue my studies on various types of plant life."

"You're sure?" Betsy asked, her blue eyes filled with concern. At Teresa's nod, her companion released her and delved into the clothespress. After a moment her muffled voice floated from its depths. "What do you mean false flattery? You're a lovely young woman."

Teresa snorted. "You only say that because you practically raised me."

"Pooh! If you spent a little more time with a looking glass instead of your experiments, you'd know I speak the truth."

Flopping backward onto the bed, Teresa stretched her hands above her head. "It doesn't matter what I look like truly. As soon as any potential suitors realize that I am interested in more than the latest round of parties and on-dits, they avoid me like the plague."

Betsy shook out a white lawn night rail and draped it over a chair. "You just haven't met the man who is your match yet."

"And I'm not looking either. I'm quite content with my studies. I won't make a fool of myself over some overbearing, arrogant male."

"That's because you haven't known a man's touch."

"Betsy!" Teresa covered her mouth and giggled.

"All I'm saying, child, is not all men like their mates to be empty-headed dolls to be herded about like one's cattle."

"Like your Albert," Teresa said in a soft voice.

"Yes. He was a man among men."

"Is that why you never remarried?" Teresa slid off the bed and hugged the other woman. "You're a strong woman, Betsy. I don't think I would have survived the loss of a husband and child in one senseless carriage accident."

"It's been ten years." Betsy stepped away and cleared her throat before continuing. "Come," she sniffed. "let's get you out of that dress before you have it creased beyond repair."

Teresa glanced at the small bedside table as she turned. "Have you seen my notebook?"

"If you mean that thing you're always scribbling in, no." Betsy moved to stand behind Teresa, her fingers going to the gown's fastenings.

At the touch of her hand, Teresa whirled around. "Wait. I must find my notebook. It has the latest journal article regarding Sir Isaac Newton's

Laws of Motion tucked inside. Where could it be?" She made a wide circuit of the room.

Betsy sat down on the bed with a sigh. "Shall I check your reticule?"

"No, I distinctly remember having it this afternoon when Lord Somerton took Lady Sarah and me on a tour of the house. I was making some notations about his books on botany. The library! I must have left it there when he allowed me to stay behind and look through his collection of antique manuscripts."

"Well, I'm glad you remembered. You can get it in the morning," Betsy said.

"I don't want to leave it there. What if one of the servants moves it and it gets misplaced?"

The maid pushed to her feet. "I'll fetch your notebook, then perhaps I can settle down with a nice pot of tea before the dawn breaks."

"I'll get it. First help me change, and then you can retire for the night."

Betsy stared at her, a shocked expression on her face. "You'll not be traipsing around in your night clothes. You're not at Perth House, ya know. Have I taught you nothing at all?"

"Who would see me? Everyone is still in the ballroom and will probably be there for hours yet."

"And if you're wrong? You'll be in the devil's own pocket then."

"Very well, I shall retrieve my notebook first. I guess I wouldn't want to run into Aunt Vivian in such a state of undress."

Betsy wrinkled up her face and shuddered. "It doesn't bear thinking about."

Teresa laughed. "While I'm gone, perhaps you can get your tea ready." Not giving her companion a chance to respond, she grabbed a candle and hurried from the room.

She leaned against the other side of the door.

One of these days her impetuousness would land her in trouble if she wasn't careful. Thank heaven for Betsy's steadying influence. Straightening her shoulders, she stepped away from the door. Now, if she could just find her way back to the library.

Remembering the room was on the second floor near the gallery, she turned in that direction. The halls had been left dark in this part of the mansion. Her hand cupped around the candle, she prayed the flame wouldn't go out.

As the entrance to the library loomed ahead of her, a figure materialized out of the darkness. She jumped back, losing her grip on the candle.

With a quick movement, the intruder caught it in mid-air. Before she could scream, a strong arm wrapped around her waist, pulling her against his chest and into the room.

He extinguished the candle with a breath of air that stirred the tendrils of her hair.

She shivered. Her heart beating out of control, she swallowed and fought back the panic that threatened to take hold. Teresa's gaze darted around the room for a means of escape. If she screamed, would anyone hear her over the noise of the ball?

Moonlight cast shadows along enormous bookcases lining the walls. The balcony doors stood open, the pale silk drapes fluttering in the breeze.

"Well, well, isn't this a surprise?"

Teresa stiffened at the sound of the deep, husky voice. She would know that arrogant tone anywhere. Her heart picked up speed. Slowly, she met his gaze. He wore the mask and clothes of black as he had done in their previous encounter.

He released her with an impudent grin.

Eager to put space between them, she crossed the room and stood with her arms folded on the back of a chair. "What are you doing here? This is too much to be a coincidence."

"I agree. Why do you always seem to appear where I am?"

"Me?" She gestured to herself in outrage. "I am a guest here. I have been a guest at every occasion that we've had the misfortune to meet."

"But why are you here and not in the ballroom with the others?" He moved toward her, gliding across the room like a shadow. "Perhaps, you were searching for me, eh?"

"And perhaps I took a knock in the cradle when I was a child," Teresa snapped. "Do you think me completely addle-brained? Why would I be searching for you when I didn't know you would appear like some wraith out of the mist?" Anger drained away her normal reserve around members of the opposite sex. She moved closer and stabbed him in the chest with her finger. "If I knew you'd be here, in this house, I wouldn't have come within a day's journey of it."

He grabbed her hand as she poked him again. "And why is that?"

"Because," she nearly shouted, "you cut up my peace. I can't concentrate on my studies. I've become completely muddle-headed. I even mislaid my notebook. I *never* mislay my notebook." Her mouth snapped shut as she realized what she'd said.

He pulled her closer, laying a finger against her lips. "Then perhaps," he whispered, lowering his head, "I have come in search of you."

He brushed his mouth over hers, a light touch that hinted at things to come. Teresa pushed at his chest. Propriety ruled her head for the moment but for how much longer?

He lifted his head. "I am taking liberties I haven't been granted, yes?"

"Yes, and I should appreciate it if you would not continue to do so," she said in the same tones Betsy had used to reprimand her when she was a child.

He smiled his wicked grin once more, bowed, and ran out onto the balcony. Without thinking, Teresa followed but stopped at the entrance wary of what he might do next. He turned and looked back for a long moment, then gave her a military salute, and vaulted over the side.

Knowing the great distance to the ground, she ran to the balustrade, visions of his lifeless body lying on the grass below running through her mind. Her fingers curled around the wrought iron railing.

There was no sign of him anywhere. She searched the darkness for movement.

Mateo stood in the shadow cast by the overhang of the balcony. She leaned over the edge, seeking him out. Her blonde hair shimmered in the moonlight, her pale skin glowing like a beacon calling him home. He pressed his lips together trying to feel her touch once more.

"Who are you?"

Her soft words floated down to him on the night air.

He ached to call to her but forced himself to stay in the shadows. He had no time to become entangled with a woman, especially this woman. He had to find the *Pequena* before it was too late.

The click of the French doors closing filled him with regret. What might have been had he not been bound by his vow to destroy her family?

He waited a little longer to be certain she had left, then with a flick of his wrist, released the black hook from around a spoke in the railing. Catching the heavy metal clasp, he coiled the black-dyed rope around his shoulder and made his way through the darkened garden.

****

Teresa rushed into her bedchamber and slammed the door.

"Heavens, you look as though you've seen a

ghost. What took you so long? I was beginning to worry."

"I...I got lost," Teresa stammered, her cheeks filled with heat as they always did when she lied to the woman who was the closest thing to a mother to her.

Betsy raised a disbelieving brow. "Lost? You look a little too ruffled to have just gotten lost. And where is your book?"

"My book? The notebook!" Teresa's gaze bounced around the room as she avoided looking at her companion. "I...I couldn't find it." At least that was true; she hadn't even remembered its existence much less to look for it.

Betsy moved to stand behind her. "You can keep your secrets," she paused and started unfastening Teresa's gown, "for now."

Teresa held her breath, praying she didn't look as confused as she felt. For the first time in her life, she hoped Betsy wouldn't linger after helping her change. She needed time alone.

A few minutes later, she stood before her maid clad in her nightclothes, all but pushing the woman out the door.

Betsy stopped, her hand on the door handle. "Are you sure there's nothing you want to tell me?"

Teresa blushed. "I...I..."

Taking the branch of candles with her, Betsy laughed and closed the door.

Teresa crawled into the large four-poster bed and pulled the quilt up to her chin, knowing she wouldn't be sleeping any time soon. With a feather light touch, she set her fingers against her mouth. Who was this man who made her forget everything but the sensations he aroused with his touch? Did he truly come to Somerton House to seek her out? She didn't think so.

She thought back over the evening's

entertainment. Had any one man paid her more attention than another? No, of that she was certain. She had danced only three times and each time felt as if she'd been asked out of duty rather than any real desire for her company. She sighed and stared into the darkness, finally succumbing to sleep as dawn approached.

Chapter Five

Teresa read the words written in crisp, bold strokes for the tenth time. The Count de Montayas would be unable to keep his appointment to call on her this morning and sent his regrets. As Betsy entered the bedchamber, Teresa dropped the vellum sheet of paper onto the writing desk.

The maid took one look at her face and began bustling around the room. "Well, let's get you out of that dress. Will you be wanting to wear your blue silk?"

"No, my gardening dress will do. As I won't be receiving callers, I'll work on my plant studies." She wandered to the window and looked out over the courtyard below. A jumble of carriages, curricles, and phaetons fought for space in the crowded drive. "Why isn't he coming? What caused him to change his mind?" The questions rose up inside her causing her to utter them aloud. It worried her how disappointed she felt.

Betsy laid a gentle hand on her arm. "I'm sure he had a good reason."

"They all do or so they claim. As soon as they find out I'm no great heiress and have interests outside of what they deem appropriate, the gentlemen of the *Ton* develop other engagements out of thin air." Teresa wandered away from the window.

"I think you're exaggerating a bit."

She stood in front of the looking glass, tilting it on the stand so she could view herself from head to foot. She trailed a hand over her reflection. "I haven't received a single caller in the last four years," she murmured. "It's happened many times before. I don't understand why I feel so let down."

Betsy dropped the brown dress onto the bed and took her charge by the shoulders, turning her around. "Now, you listen here. No fortune hunting fop or exotic looking stranger is worth doing this to yourself. The right man will come. I know it."

"You're right." Teresa gave herself a mental shake. She needed no one to make her complete even if she did, at times, become slightly jealous of Lady Sarah and her many visitors. "He'd better come soon though; I'm nearly two and twenty already." She left the mirror and moved toward the bed and picked up the dress. "Please help me change. My flowers await."

****

Teresa walked in and out of the shadows cast by the late afternoon sun. She moved from one plant to another, checking the soil, leaves, and color. Dropping her basket on the ground, she kneeled in front of a water aven. It didn't seem to be doing well at all. She checked the dirt around the stem. Maybe if she watered it twice a day. Although her book on plant life stated water avens flourished in marshy ground, she had hoped to grow it here in the shadowy area of the back garden.

Sighing, she rose and rubbed the small of her back. Too many hours of bending and pulling weeds had started to take its toll, but at least she had been able to keep her mind off the count.

She passed a hand over her forehead, brushing back the stray tendrils of hair that had come loose from her topknot and gazed over the blooming flowerbeds, a feeling of contentment settling over her. Her basket in hand, she walked up the path, picking a few flowers for her room.

"You are as beautiful in the sunlight as you are

in the moonlight."

She whirled around at the sound of the voice belonging to the object of her thoughts, uncertain if she'd conjured him from her imagination. But she knew in an instant, he was as real as she, from the blue-black sheen of his hair to his shiny leather boots.

Dismayed that he should see her in the drab, brown cambric of her gardening clothes, she fluttered a hand to her mouth. At the sight of her dirty fingers, she curled them into her palm, and dropped her hand back to her side. "What are you doing here?"

"I've come to apologize for not calling on you earlier."

Teresa continued up the path. "You needn't have done so. One can't be held accountable for what is said in polite conversation at a ball."

His gloved fingers closed around her wrist, bringing her to a halt. "You are angry with me." His voice held a sense of confused surprise. "Would it appease you to know that by being deprived of your company I took no pleasure in the remainder of the evening at Pendleton's?"

"I am not angry with you, sir." She shook off his hold. "You haven't said why you've come to my home."

"I've come in search of you."

Teresa stared at him as a similar phrase echoed through her mind. *"Perhaps, I have come in search of you."* It repeated itself over and over. She shook her head slightly, telling herself she was mistaken. The Count de Montayas spoke with a Spanish accent, the masked intruder didn't.

He continued as if he hadn't just set her world on end. "I would like to extend a dinner invitation to make up for not calling as we agreed." When she didn't respond, he grinned. "I've upset your English

35

sensibilities. I am being forward, taking liberties of a friendship I haven't been granted, yes?"

Those words, spoken like that, were almost exactly the same as those said by the masked intruder at the Somerton Ball. She felt the blood drain from her face, suddenly cold despite the warmth of the sun. The basket of flowers fell from her numb fingers.

Was it him? Could both men be one and the same? Not knowing what to do, she dropped to her knees to gather the blossoms.

He crouched beside her. "Will you join my family for dinner this evening?"

Teresa studied him. Could he be the thief? But why was he stealing from the members of the *Ton*?

Before she had a chance to decline, the duchess' strident tones filled the air as she marched toward them. "I think not. There will be no one to chaperone my niece as her lady's maid has other duties to attend to."

The count turned to face the duchess, a muscle pulsing in his jaw. "Miss Darlington will be adequately chaperoned. My aunt will be present among others. If you insist, I will bring her with me when I pick up Miss Darlington so you may meet her."

"You don't want to go, do you?" Vivian demanded.

She may not have wanted to accept the invitation at first, but now that Vivian dared her to defy her, Teresa found herself wanting more than anything to attend. She met Montayas' gaze. "I would be honored."

"Then we shall call for you at eight." He bowed, walked through the iron gate, and swung up onto a curricle. With one last nod, he started the horses down the drive.

Teresa turned to leave, ignoring the duchess.

"I'd like a word with you...about your mother."

Teresa froze, a sense of foreboding falling over her. She turned slowly to face her aunt. "Yes?"

"How is your mother today?"

"Fine. Surely, you didn't keep me here to discuss Mama's health."

The duchess sidled closer. "Oh, but I did. Everyone knows your mother belongs in Bedlam. Perhaps, I should look into just what that entails."

Fierce anger blasted its way through Teresa's body. "You leave Mama alone. Leave her alone! What kind of person are you? You torment your own flesh and blood to get what you want." Her fists clenched at her sides, she leaned forward until their noses nearly touched. "Oh yes, I know it was you who took the portrait of Papa. You even think about committing her or taking her things, and I will tell the entire world your precious secret."

Vivian stepped back, an eyebrow arched in question. "And what would that be?"

"I think the *Beau Monde* would be quite interested to learn that Lady Sarah is no more your daughter than I am."

"Who would believe you? Everyone thinks you're as mad as your mother, poking about in the dirt like some pig. Besides, you have no proof."

"With your circle of friends who delight in the slightest whiff of a scandal, would I need it?"

Vivian inhaled sharply, falling back a step.

Without waiting for a response, Teresa walked into the house. Once inside, she rushed up the stairs to her room.

She would never expose Sarah to such humiliation, but as a threat it might keep the duchess from persecuting Mama. She had never put any credence to the rumours she'd heard years ago, rumours that had been quickly squelched. But from her aunt's reaction, Teresa wondered if it was indeed true—Lady Sarah was a foundling brought secretly to the duchess in an effort to give her husband the will to live after a hunting accident.

She pushed the bedroom door open, spying her maid sitting on the divan waiting for her. "That woman loves to aggravate me." She paced in front of the bed with angry strides. "I don't understand why she has to make our lives miserable."

"Mayhap because she is herself," Betsy said softly. "I've arranged a hot bath in your dressing room. It'll help calm you." She pushed her charge forward. "Go on."

Teresa stepped into the dressing room and allowed Betsy to remove her soiled dress. She took a deep breath and held it for a moment, trying to find the sense of contentment she'd felt in the garden. Removing the pins from her hair, she stepped into the scented bath. She slid deeper into the steaming water and closed her eyes only to have Montayas push his way into her thoughts.

Could she be mistaken? She tried to imagine the two men standing side-by-side then mentally compared one to the other. They were similar in build and height, but that was all. The Count de Montayas had black hair and nearly the same color eyes surrounded by thick lashes. The masked intruder also had dark eyes, but his hair color was a mystery thanks to the cloth he always wore tied about the upper portion of his head. The fact that it had been dark each time she'd encountered him hadn't helped.

If she was right and they were the same man, what was he after? Why had he broken into at least three people's homes? Teresa rubbed her temples realizing the bath water had long grown cold. With no small amount of trepidation, she left the tub. Why had she let her temper goad her into agreeing to go to his home this evening? Why?

The question haunted her for the rest of the afternoon.

****

Was it too late to change her mind and send her regrets? Yes, she told herself as she watched a horse-drawn carriage pull to a stop.

"He's here," she announced to the empty room. "Betsy," she called and headed into the hall nearly colliding with the maid.

"He's here."

"I know, child, and now so does half the household. Will you be wanting your pelisse or your cloak?"

She looked down at her pearl-gray gown. "The pelisse. Unless you think I'll need the cloak?"

Betsy put a finger under Teresa's chin and lifted her face. "I've never known you to be indecisive. Don't worry, you look fine."

Teresa smoothed her hands over the silky material of the skirt, trying to gather her courage.

Betsy's mouth lifted in a small smile. "Come along then. We don't want to keep him waiting."

A few minutes later, Teresa found herself sitting next to the count, his *Tia* Elena seated across from them. No one spoke as the coach turned out of the drive. The silence grew longer the farther behind they left Perth House. She cast a quick glance at Montayas' profile, feeling more and more uncomfortable.

Unable to stand the tension any longer, she spoke. "Senor Conde, you invited me to join you, yet you say nothing."

"Tell me about your family," he commanded.

"My mother and I live with my aunt and cousin."

"You have no brothers or sisters?"

She shook her head, thinking that if she had maybe her mother would be less inclined to abandon the world.

"My father spent time in your country. He loved Spain," she volunteered.

"Ah, yes the baronet," Montayas drawled, his voice laced with sarcasm.

Teresa frowned. "You've been misinformed. My father wasn't a baronet."

His calculating gaze made her cautious. What was behind his curiosity about her family? She was certain it wasn't just an effort at polite conversation.

Finally, he spoke. "But your mother is called Lady Darlington."

"And I am Miss Darlington. My father was knighted. It's practically the same as a baronet except a baronet's title is inheritable whereas the title earned from knighthood is not."

She hesitated before continuing, not sure how much to divulge to this man who hadn't seemed like a stranger until now. "You see, my father served in the military for many years until a hip injury made it impossible to spend long hours in the saddle. He became an emissary to the king and traveled to different countries on his behalf."

"What of your aunt's husband, the duke?"

"I never met him. He died within two years of their marriage." Teresa leaned closer to him. "Though he died in a hunting accident—it's said— not in her hearing of course, that she drove him to the grave."

"What do you think of that?" Montayas asked.

"I think it's true."

He burst out laughing. "You are refreshingly honest compared to others in your social circle."

"I fear that's because many of them have constant plots brewing against one another. As neither you nor I have one, it's easier to be forthright."

"Yes, well," he said in an odd, rough voice.

A morose silence fell over the carriage and

lasted the rest of the journey.

Just as she decided she could stand it no longer, they pulled up in front of a townhouse in Grosvenor Square. The count stepped down from the carriage and helped the ladies alight. It was then that she noticed his aunt leaned heavily on a cane as she moved toward the front door.

"Madam," she hurried after her. "May I be of assistance?"

"She speaks no English."

Teresa turned at the sound of Montayas' voice. "What?"

He smiled. "Do not worry. She is more than capable of making herself understood. And she takes her chaperoning duties very seriously."

Teresa looked back at the house. The woman was nowhere in sight. "Then why has she left us alone?"

"She knows you are safe with me."

"Am I?"

"Here, among my family with its reminders of what I must do, you are most definitely safe." He gestured for her to precede him up the path.

She stood for a moment longer, wondering what he meant by the cryptic remark and why his eyes had become hard at the mention of his duties to his family. Hesitant to ask questions of him in his present mood, she turned and led the way to the door.

He reached passed her and opened it.

"You've no butler?" She asked, thinking this quite strange.

"No." He shut the door and took her pelisse from her shoulders.

He hung it in a closet cleverly hidden to look like a wall panel. As he shrugged out of his cloak, a dark-haired man entered the foyer. He questioned Montayas in rapid Spanish, who answered in kind before turning back to Teresa.

Fascinated by the interchange, she looked at the newcomer. He had the same dark hair and eyes as Montayas, but there the resemblance ended. Whereas he towered over her, this man was no taller than herself.

"May I present my cousin, Eduardo Casteo. Eduardo, this is Miss Darlington."

Teresa held out her hand to him. "I look forward to meeting the other members of your family."

Eduardo gave her hand a quick clasp before dropping it. "There are no others. You have met us all."

"I'm afraid I don't understand?"

"*El Senor Conde,* my mother, and myself are all that is left of the great family of Casteo," he said in heavily accented English.

Teresa shot a glance at the count.

"Come, let us not stand about in the hall as though we are unwelcome guests." He strode down the passage.

Eduardo guided Teresa toward the dining room. "He has been the unwelcome guest often throughout his life."

"But he is a count. Who would deny a nobleman entrance to their home?"

Eduardo stopped at the threshold of the room. "You'll find out soon enough."

He walked away, leaving her alone and wishing she hadn't come. She supposed it served her right for accepting out of anger and the urge to spite her aunt.

She gazed around the room, noticing the less than opulent furnishings. The carpet was slightly worn... The dining table and chairs were clean and serviceable, but hardly well cared for. She glanced up at the chandelier and counted at least four crystals missing from the design. Frowning, she took in the faded drapery and wondered about the noticeable lack of servants.

It didn't make sense. Why would Montayas rent a townhouse, here in Grosvenor Square of all places, which hadn't been properly tended? The answer came in an instant. He needed funds. Many men with inherited titles lacked the money to maintain their estates. That in itself accounted for the loveless marriages that flourished in the *Ton*. But, he said he'd no intentions of finding a bride in England. Then why was he here?

"Not quite what you expected, is it?"

She turned to find him watching her from the doorway, his face impassive. Not a single hint of his feelings revealed themselves in his dark eyes.

"I came with no expectations other than to enjoy a meal with your family."

"I'm afraid you're to be disappointed in that respect as well."

Before she could give voice to her confusion, the door to the dining room swung open. Eduardo entered bearing a tray of tea and sandwiches, his mother following close behind. He set the tray on the large table, bowed to Montayas, and left the room.

"I don't understand." Teresa watched the older woman settle herself in a chair and begin pouring out three cups of the steaming amber liquid.

"You'll not go hungry, but there is no grand meal awaiting you here."

"Then why did you invite me?"

Montayas crossed the room and leaned against the table. "It is time we discussed your father."

"My father?"

"Why am I here in England when I should be in Spain defending my country against Napoleon?"

"How should I know the answer to that?" Teresa snapped, losing patience.

"I am here to retrieve the *Pequena* from you.

Nothing more and I will accept nothing less."

"*Pequena?*" Teresa looked at his aunt for some sign of explanation, but the woman said nothing, continuing to stare at her over the rim of her teacup. "I can't give you this, this thing. I've never heard of it. I don't know what it is."

Suddenly the attention he paid to her at the Pendleton affair made perfect sense. Her heart cried a little as she realized his words and interest had been nothing more than machinations to retrieve something he believed she had in her possession. "You arranged our meeting at the Pendleton ball," she accused.

He shook his head and gave a sly smile. "That was a stroke of luck. Oh, I had planned to pay a visit to your father. But upon my arrival in England, I learned that he was dead. After I had gone to so much trouble to have documents forged stating *I* was an emissary of *my* king, seeking additional aid on his behalf." He gave a harsh laugh. "The king that no longer holds his throne thanks to Napoleon."

"Who are you?"

"No more than a mere Spanish peasant."

"A Spanish peasant? But you hold the title of a nobleman or is that a falsehood as well?"

"No, it's true. I am the Count de Montayas, but I have no great estate."

"What is this *Pequena* you speak of?"

"It's an heirloom stolen from my family by your father, a small jeweled box made of gold no bigger than your palm. The lid is encrusted with various gems: emeralds, sapphires, and diamonds. In the center, there is a ruby," he looked at her hands, "perhaps the length of your thumb."

"You can't believe my father would lower himself to thievery?"

"I'm sorry to shatter your precious illusions, but that's exactly what I believe. I was but a boy of eight when the *Pequena* disappeared. Twenty years ago I couldn't do anything. But, I can now."

"Twenty years! Have you proof my father is the culprit? Surely any evidence left behind by the thief has long since disappeared."

He inclined his head. "This is true, but I know two things." He held up one finger. "An English visitor greatly admired the *Pequena* and offered my father an enormous sum for it." He raised another finger to stand beside the first. "The man's name was Darling."

"But my family name is Darling*ton*."

"How hard is it to come to a new place and omit three letters from one's name? You, yourself told me that your family traveled all over the country."

"The similarity between my surname and your thief's is hardly reason to slander my father's reputation. He isn't even alive to defend himself."

Montayas pushed away from the table. "If he is innocent, as you so staunchly believe, then he wouldn't have to defend himself nor would you have to do it for him. Ask your mother about his stay in Spain, if he gave her any trinkets."

"I will not. I won't ask my mother anything."

Montayas crossed his arms over his chest. "You are just like your father. You do as you please without thought of how it affects others. My own father died a broken man because he failed in his sworn duty to safeguard the *Pequena*. He couldn't bear the shame of being an outcast of the church."

"What does the church have to do with a stolen jewel box?"

He slashed a hand through the air. "It doesn't matter. Because of Robert Darlington's greed, my family has endured hardship while you've been living a life of ease."

"Me?" She questioned in surprise. "I live in the house of a woman who can't stand the sight of me, who torments my mother with mean, petty tricks, and who is determined to keep everyone around her under her thumb."

He shrugged. "You have fine clothes, servants, need I continue?"

Her troubles meant nothing to him. She didn't know why she bothered to defend herself. "After Papa's death, much to my aunt's dislike, we moved into Perth House at the insistence of the current Duke of Perth, my uncle's nephew. Aunt Vivian had little choice but to take us in considering she and Lady Sarah stay in residence at the duke's indulgence. He stays at his estate near Bath, rarely coming to London."

"Excuse me if I do not feel sympathy for you. To live in such opulent surroundings must be a hardship indeed," he drawled.

Teresa ignored his sarcasm. "I would prefer a cottage for Mama and myself, but due to circumstances I won't discuss with you, Mama refuses to leave Perth House."

Terrified that the slightest breath of scandal connected to Robert Darlington would send her mother over the edge, she did the only thing she could. She threatened the one man who could destroy her family so completely. "You will stay away from my mother, or I shall renounce you and your forged documents."

"If you do, I will announce that your father is a thief."

"You have no proof."

He stepped closer. "Don't I?"

She stared at him, the connection between the masked intruder and the Count de Montayas clicking into place. He had no proof, or he wouldn't be breaking into houses all around London. Was he searching for the heirloom itself?

She leaned toward him. "No, I don't think you

do."

Teresa jumped back as *Tia* Elena's cane slashed the air between them. She'd completely forgotten the other woman was present.

"*Manten tu distancia!*"

Mateo responded in Spanish before turning back to Teresa. "She says we are standing too close to each other."

"I don't care. She's worried about propriety, and you stand there threatening to ruin my family." She left the room without another word, took her coat from the closet, and swept past an open-mouthed Eduardo without a second glance.

Slamming the front door behind her, she looked down the drive wondering how far she'd have to walk before she could catch a ride from a passing hackney.

Montayas stalked past her to descend the stairs. "The carriage is being brought around."

When the conveyance arrived at the front of the house, she hurried down to it, purposely ignoring his hand as she entered the vehicle.

As they set off, she maintained a stony silence. For the first time in her life, she wished she'd listened to the duchess. If she had, the whole disastrous evening would never have happened. *And you'd have no idea what Montayas was up to until it was too late*, a voice in her head mocked.

"I suggest you apprise your mother of what has transpired this evening. Perhaps, she will covet her social standing more than the *Pequena*."

Teresa met his dark gaze with more bravado than she felt. "As I said before, I won't mention your ridiculous accusations to my mother for any reason. She doesn't have your precious family heirloom."

He raised an eyebrow. "It must be quite tiresome to be so naïve."

"And it must be just as tiresome to pretend to be

what you're not. Or are you such an accomplished fraud that you believe your own lies?"

Mateo gave no sign that her barb hit home, but it did. He longed to give up the charade he'd been forced to play since his arrival in England. The lies he'd told and the need to be constantly on guard weighed upon his conscience. And then there were the women who chased after him not for who he was, but for his title and non-existent riches. He hadn't anticipated their single-minded pursuit when he'd planned his revenge.

"Why don't you give up this vendetta against my father and concentrate on filling your family's coffers? I might be able to help."

"Are you attempting to bribe me into keeping my silence? I'm afraid money would be the last thing to tempt me." He swept her figure from head to toe before letting his gaze settle on her breasts.

She pulled her pelisse tighter. "It's obvious you're in need of funds. I don't know why you have singled me out. I have no great wealth. Perhaps, you should be pursuing Lady Sarah."

"I have all the money I need to live quite comfortably for the rest of my life." *Provided I die within the next fortnight.*

As the carriage rolled to a stop in front of Perth House, Teresa slid from her seat. "I shall not thank you for the pleasant evening as it has been anything but, and I sincerely hope never to see you again."

"Give me the *Pequena,* and I will gladly disappear," Mateo drawled. He made no move to help her from the coach. She thought him ill mannered; he might as well allow the impression to continue. He watched her enter the house, then rapped on the roof and told the driver to take him home.

Mateo leaned back against the butter soft leather seat. He closed his eyes and concentrated on the rhythmic clip-clop of the horses' hooves, yet it gave him no release from the tension that gripped him.

With a grimace, he turned to stare out the window. How ironic that his beautiful temptress was also the daughter of his most hated enemy. His hand fisted on his thigh. Regardless of who she was, he would not be swayed from destroying her family. He would do whatever was necessary to avenge his parents' deaths even if he ended up swinging in the wind at the end of a rope.

He had given her a chance to hand over the *Pequena*. Earlier he'd decided that if she did so willingly, he would spare her but if not...at least she would have the knowledge of what was coming. And be able to prepare for the ruination of her family's name and reputation. Mateo shifted position realizing the carriage had stopped. He leaned forward just as the door opened.

Thanking the footman, he stepped down from the carriage and sent the driver on his way. He would have to speak to Eduardo about getting his own means of transportation. Borrowing Pendleton's coach was an inconvenience to them both.

As he made his way to the front door, he tried to calculate how much he and Eduardo had already spent. Passing one's self off as a rich nobleman was not only tiresome but damned expensive.

Taking the stairs two at a time, he rushed through the front door. "Eduardo!" he called, pulling at his cravat.

His cousin sauntered out of the parlor, a slab of bread and cheese in one hand, a plate in the other. "Yes, *Senor Conde*." Mischief danced in his eyes.

"Don't call me that. I am no more a count than you are," Mateo said in a weary voice.

"You play the part well. What do you need that has you yelling my name at the top of your lungs?"

"First, help me out of this damn thing." Mateo pointed to his cravat. "I feel like it's strangling me."

Eduardo lay his meal down on the round hall table and set to work trying to untangle the once perfectly tied neck cloth.

Mateo breathed a sigh of relief as the material slid down his neck. He was glad to be home even if it was only a temporary one. Here he could speak his native tongue and not have to watch every word he said. Here there were no pretenses. His cousin knew all there was to know about him.

Eduardo stepped back. "Let us hope everything we must accomplish will be as easy as unknotting your cravats."

"I don't think anything about our stay in England will be easy. I need to purchase a carriage of my own." Mateo followed his cousin into the parlor.

"And this is a problem?" Eduardo dropped down onto a velvet settee, propping his booted feet on the small table in front of him.

"Yes. Have you forgotten we have limited funds?"

Eduardo took a bite of his bread and chewed slowly.

Mateo's irritation rose with each passing moment. He reached out, snatched the sandwich, and dropped it back on the dish. "How can you sit there and do nothing? Didn't you hear what I said?"

"Of course I did. My ears work fine even when you aren't shouting." His cousin rose and stretched before heading out of the room. "Follow me," he called over his shoulder.

Mateo followed him out the back door. There, in the small courtyard, stood a black coach gleaming in the moonlight. He ran his hand over the dark paint, opened the door, and peered inside. Deep burgundy curtains hung at the windows and matched the leather seats.

Stepping back, he looked around. His cousin seemed to have disappeared. Seconds later, he heard the sound of horses and hurried down the short path to the stables.

Eduardo met him halfway, leading two magnificent horses as dark as the midnight sky. "I realized if you were to play the role of the rich nobleman, you'd need your own carriage."

Stunned, Mateo could only gape at the other man. "How?" he finally managed to croak.

"While you were informing our baronet's daughter about the sins of her father, I was procuring all this." Eduardo grinned. "You have your talents, I have mine."

"They're not stolen, are they?"

"No." Eduardo scowled. "You're the master thief, not me."

"Only by necessity." Mateo clapped him on the shoulder. "And I seem to remember there isn't anything you can't get your hands on."

"I will do whatever is necessary to avenge our family name." Eduardo said, turning serious. "Remember that, Mateo. Anything."

Mateo dropped his hand to his side. "As will I, cousin. As will I."

Chapter Six

Mateo shifted his weight on the narrow ledge and eased the casement window open. He pushed the curtain aside and pulled himself through the opening. Gaining his feet, he melted into the shadows, his vision adjusting to the dim room.

Moonlight flooded through the window doing little to dispel the eerie stillness. Glancing around, he realized he was in a dressing room. The information he'd received from Eduardo proved wrong once again. With a growl of frustration, he pushed the mask he wore onto his forehead and wondered how much money his cousin had squandered bribing the servants of the house only to be told lies and half-truths.

Now, he'd have to search the house to find the room that Teresa used for her studies. He'd learned she kept anything she deemed of value under lock and key in her workroom. He sincerely hoped at least that was true.

With a pang of regret, he pulled the mask over his eyes and moved to the door. He'd wanted to avoid searching her house although he refused to examine his reasons too closely. Yesterday, he'd been confident she would hand over the *Pequena* as soon as she learned it was stolen. Instead, she'd become indignant and refused to even acknowledge her father's part in its theft.

He wanted to believe she was an innocent party to the destruction of his family, but until he had the jeweled box in his possession the entire Darlington family was suspect.

He moved into the next room and closed the door behind him with a quiet click. Instead of entering the hall as he expected, he found himself in a bedroom. His heart quickened at the thought that it could be Teresa lying in the bed surrounded by satin sheets and goose down quilts.

Forcing himself to concentrate on the task at hand, his gaze passed over a lady's dressing table and three overstuffed chairs grouped together as though they waited for the latest exchange of gossip before settling on a large credenza filled with framed portraits. A candle flickered among them casting ghoulish shadows on the faces immortalized in paint.

Curious, he moved closer. The wick sputtered, trying to survive in a sea of molten wax. He poured it off into a nearby glass, and the flame flared to life. Inspecting the paintings, he noticed they were all various poses of the same man. A man whose face he would never forget. Sir Robert Darlington.

Did his daughter mourn his death so much that she had created a shrine to him? Mateo moved to the bed. He held the candle higher as the sleeping woman turned toward him. It wasn't Teresa. This woman was older, frailer, misery evident in her face. She clutched a man's shirt to her breast even as she slept. Lady Darlington. It was she who mourned the death of the black-hearted thief.

He returned the candle to the credenza. Perhaps, it wasn't too much of a loss to have stumbled in here. It explained Teresa's reaction when he told her to confront her mother over the theft. He took one last look at the woman and slipped from the room. Standing in the darkened hall, he grinned. First, he would search the workroom, and then since he was here, he might as well pay a visit to Miss Teresa Darlington.

Masquerading as the intruder she'd kissed so

warmly in the past, he had nothing to lose and everything to gain. Squashing the impulse to whistle, he continued down the hall.

****

Betsy removed the last of the flowers and ribbons that had decorated her mistress' hair and dropped them on the dressing table. She plucked the pins from the coiled tresses and laid them in their ivory case. "Are you sure nothing's bothering you?"

Teresa looked into the mirror and met the older woman's pale blue eyes. "You've asked me that same question at least a dozen times today."

"I know, but you keep feeding me one sham after another. Something is wrong; I can tell. You've not gone near the greenhouse all day, and you've been unable to settle to anything else. You've become withdrawn and tense just as you were after your father's passing."

Teresa turned away from the mirror and took Betsy's hands in her own. "I'm in trouble...no—the family's in trouble. I don't know what to do."

"Trouble? What do you mean? Does this have anything to do with that encroaching mushroom of a count?"

She couldn't help but smile at her companion's words in spite of her worries. "I'm afraid he's much more than a social climber." Her smile faded. "I've always trusted you as I have no other. I must have your word that what I'm about to tell you will go no further than this room."

"You have it."

She gestured for Betsy to sit and quickly related the horrible scene that had taken place at Montayas' home the night before.

The maid jumped to her feet, indignation in every line of her body. "How dare that odious man cast aspersions on Sir Robert's character?"

"Betsy."

"Wait until I see him. I'll give him a dressing down he'll never forget."

"Listen to me. It won't do any good. Unless the heirloom is returned to him, he said he will announce to all who'll listen that Papa was little more than a common thief."

Betsy slumped onto the bed. "There has to be something we can do."

"There is. I just haven't figured it out yet."

Teresa stared at the flames crackling in the grate. If she concentrated hard enough, she would come up with a plan. She had to. Her family's reputation depended on it.

Lost in thought, she was dimly aware of the hall clock striking four. The maid still sat on the edge of the bed, her mouth turned down at the corners.

"Betsy," Teresa called softly, "why don't you go to bed. It's almost dawn. There's no sense in both of us staying up all night."

The older woman nodded. "I'll retire to my room, but I don't think I'll be sleeping much."

Teresa followed her to the door and watched as she wandered away, muttering to herself.

Turning back toward the bed, she removed her robe and dropped it on a chair as she passed. She didn't expect to sleep but blew out the candle and crawled under the soft sheets.

How could this have happened? Rolling onto her side, she tried not to think what the scandal would do to Mama.

A cold draft filtered into the room. Teresa scrambled into a sitting position unable to shake the feeling she was no longer alone.

A pale shaft of moonlight shining through a gap in the heavy curtains turned the room into a mysterious place full of light and shadow. Certain it was only her imagination playing tricks on her, she left the bed to close the drapes.

From a darkened corner, a figure detached itself from the blackness and stepped into the pool of light. Teresa grabbed her wrapper and held it in front of her.

Dressed in black once more, he stood perfectly still, his eyes following her movements.

"Why are you here?" she asked.

"A poor man's longing for a glimpse of heaven once more."

"As much as I like Perth House, I've never once considered it heaven."

"I meant you."

Flustered, she tried to control her racing heart. Mesmerized by his innate grace, she made no move to escape as he closed the space between them. He reached out and brushed a gloved hand down her cheek.

Fighting the urge to rub her face against the soft kid leather, she stepped back. "You shouldn't be here. If anyone sees you, I'll be ruined."

"Very well, I will leave, but only if you give me one sweet kiss to dream of."

She considered him for a moment. Anything to get rid of him, she told herself, ignoring the small thrill of anticipation coursing through her. She inched forward, stood on tiptoe, and pressed a quick child-like kiss on his jaw.

"You call that a kiss? It's no wonder you are unmarried."

Stung, she marched to the door. She saw him for the first time not as her romantic masked intruder, but as the Spanish count bent on bringing scandal upon her family. "Leave now or I'll scream and bring the entire household running."

He inclined his head. "As you wish."

Surprised that he gave in so easily, she moved away from the door, certain he was up to something. Feeling his dark gaze upon her, she took refuge near the fireplace.

"Good night, my lady. I hope you sleep better than I will." He headed toward the door.

"Good night, *Senor Conde de Montayas*," she said softly.

His stride faltered for a mere second then he continued on as though he hadn't heard her. He opened the door, glanced right, then left, and slipped into the hall.

Teresa rushed forward and slammed the heavy oak door. If she hadn't been watching for his reaction, she would never have noticed it. That brief moment when he checked his movement confirmed her suspicions. She hoped she hadn't been foolish by letting him know she knew his identity.

She stared at the closed door as his words echoed through her mind. *A poor man's longing for a glimpse of heaven once more.* A tiny corner of her heart wished his words were true. But her rational side told her not to believe a word of it. Obviously he didn't believe she knew nothing of the whereabouts of his family's heirloom. Unless he thought she was so empty-headed that he could persuade her to his will with flattery. Little did he realize she had no illusions of great beauty.

She dropped into an overstuffed chair, tossing the satin dressing gown onto a nearby stool. Why else would he have broken into Perth House?

Broken into Perth House! "That's it." She jumped up, grabbed her wrapper, and rushed from the room.

She pushed her arms into the dressing gown sleeves as she ran over the carpeted hallway and down the stairs. Rounding the corner, she hurried to the back of the house toward the servants' quarters. She gave a quick knock on Betsy's door then burst into the room without waiting for a response.

"I know how we can stop him." Excitement raced through her.

Betsy yawned and lit a small candle on the bedside table. "What?" She blinked sleepily as light filtered around the room.

"I know how we can keep Montayas from spreading his horrible accusations. All we have to do is find the jewel box first."

Betsy sat up and gestured for Teresa to join her on the bed. "Pray tell, how would we do that?"

"He's been entering some of the homes of the *Beau Monde*. I think he was searching for the jewel box each time."

"He's been what?"

Teresa told the other woman of her encounters with the intruder and her suspicions about the count, careful to leave out any mention of their meeting a few minutes ago. "So, you see if I can find it first, I can give it to him on the condition that he keep his accusations against my father to himself."

"I understand." Betsy rubbed her hands together. "Sort of like blackmail. He gets his precious treasure so long as he keeps his mouth shut."

Teresa winced at the older woman's words. "Don't make it sound so vile. All we're doing is giving him what he wants in return for what we want."

"It's one and the same if you ask me. But if even he doesn't know where it is, how do you plan on gaining possession of it?"

"That's where the difficulties set in. I have to work out the particulars such as which houses he has searched. I think he's working his way through Papa's circle of friends who reside in London. Perhaps he believes one of them has it." Teresa jumped up from the bed and began to pace. "He's already searched Wingate's and Somerton House. I'm sure he's searched Pentleton's townhouse as well. I just need to figure out who is next on his list, then I can get there before he does."

"Get there? You mean you plan to warn his next victim?"

Teresa smiled. "Oh no, I plan on doing much more than that." She looked around the room, leaned closer, and whispered, "I'll search the house, but I'll need your help."

"Have you gone mad?"

"I have no choice. It's the only way to keep him from ruining Papa's name."

"But you know nothing of thievery or how to go about entering another's home without detection." Betsy hesitated for a brief moment, a speculative gleam in her eye. "Or do you?"

"Of course not. Thankfully, I know nothing of that side of life and count myself lucky to be able to say so. How could you think such of me?"

"Well, you forever have your nose stuck in a book on one subject or another," Betsy mumbled, her face reddening in embarrassment. "And some of them the most unladylike subjects too."

"You think anything other than gardening, painting, or sewing is unladylike." Teresa tried to hide her smile. They'd had this conversation so often, she swore she could quote her companion's arguments verbatim.

"Then you cannot truly mean to go on with this...this idea of yours. If you get caught, you run the risk of being jailed until you are an old woman. You could," Betsy choked on her next words, "you could hang."

Teresa swallowed with difficulty. She hadn't considered the consequences of being found out. Jailed. She'd heard terrible stories of those held in Newgate or Old Bailey. The beatings, lack of food, the foul, fetid air that permeated the cells. She shivered and clutched her robe closer to her throat.

"I have no choice," she stated again. "I will do anything to keep scandal from touching Mama's memory of Papa. She barely clings to life from day to day. It would kill her." Teresa looked up at the ceiling. "And I'm certain Aunt Vivian would make sure Mama knew of the gossip."

Betsy reached for her hand and clasped it in her own. "The scandal arising from you being sent to prison or worse would kill her too."

"Then I shall have to make certain I'm not caught," Teresa said. The enormity of what she was about to undertake settled around her like a lead blanket.

The older woman gave her hand another squeeze. "I'll help you any way I can. And if, heaven forbid, you are captured, we will hang together."

Teresa pulled free. "I can't ask that of you."

Risking her own life was one thing, but she couldn't bear the weight of another's, especially the woman who had all but raised her.

"You asked me to help and I agreed. Whatever the outcome, we'll face it together. If you deny me in this, I will tell all to the duchess."

"Very well." Teresa blinked back the tears that threatened to spill over and enveloped her friend in a fierce hug.

She could not fail. She would not let this woman who had watched over her for the past eleven years, caring for everything from scraped knees to the bruised emotions of her first foray into the Polite World, die at the end of a rope.

Wiping the dampness from her eyes, she sat back noticing her companion was teary-eyed as well. "Now," she sniffed, "can you arrange a meeting with Freddie?"

"Freddie!" Betsy exploded. "That ungrateful jackass nearly lost me my position. I finally convinced the duchess to give him a place, and he resorts to stealing the first chance he gets."

"That's why he's the perfect choice."

Chapter Seven

Teresa cast a furtive glance around the darkened garden. Now that it was time to put her plan into action, she wished she were any place but here. Had she finally allowed her impulsive nature get her into something she couldn't get out of? And what of Betsy? Would she pay for Teresa's impetuous mistakes with her life?

Determined to silence the fears clamoring within her, Teresa forced herself to go over all Freddie had taught her in the last week. She checked her pocket for the stub of candle she grabbed earlier. A hand went to her hair. She hoped the black cloth tied around her head was enough to hide the light-colored strands. With one last prayer, she hoisted herself up and through the window.

A surge of adrenaline flowed through her as she realized she was in one of the two libraries the Marquess of Kingsbury kept well maintained. Elated that her memory had served her correctly, she wandered around the room, her hand trailing over the many bookshelves. If she could remember the layout of each townhouse on her list as well as she did this one, getting in and out of the houses would be one less worry.

Her hand on the doorknob, she took one last look at the window. Once she left this room, escaping without detection became even more dangerous.

The handle turned beneath her hand. Stifling a startled cry, she backed away from the door. *Hide!* her terrified mind screamed. She raced toward the window.

As freedom loomed in front of her, a hand clamped around her arm and dragged her back.

"What the hell are you doing here?"

Her body went limp with relief as Montayas' deep tones filled the room. Yanking her arm free with a nonchalance she didn't feel, she moved closer to the window. "I'm trying to protect my father's reputation just as you are here trying to ruin it."

"What are you talking about?"

"Don't play the fool with me. I know you're searching for the *Pequena*. How can you threaten to expose my father as a thief when your property isn't even in his family's possession?"

Montayas glanced toward the door. "Be quiet."

"You'll not silence me. I want the answers I should have demanded when you first voiced your ludicrous accusations."

He clamped his hand over her mouth. "Someone's coming," he whispered, pulling her into the shadows of the heavy brocade curtains. He glanced out the window and then back at the door.

Voices. Teresa heard them now. Still indistinct but louder.

Montayas gave her a warning look then removed his hand from her lips and positioned her in front of the window.

She struggled against his grasp. "What are you doing?" she whispered.

With one quick shove, he pushed her through the opening.

Barely suppressing a scream, Teresa fell through the air and landed on her knees with a soft thud. The short fall stole her breath. Thankfully, the thick grass of the formal garden had acted as a cushion.

Seconds later, the count joined her on the lawn. He grabbed her hand and ran toward a small copse of trees. In the leafy shadows, he turned to face her.

"Are you trying to get me killed?"

"Me?" she shrieked. "I didn't just push you out a window."

"Lower your voice. Someone may decide to search the grounds if they see the open window."

Thoroughly incensed over his ill treatment of her, Teresa ignored him. "I can't believe I ever thought you a gentleman. You're nothing but a—"

"Shut up." He scanned the yard.

"How dare you speak to me like that."

"If you don't shut up, I'll—"

"You'll what? Put your vile tasting glove over my mouth?"

"I'll do much more than that. Now be quiet!"

"I don't think anything could be worse than that," she sniffed.

"How about this?" He pulled her into his arms and kissed her.

What started out as a way to keep her quiet became so much more. Desire flared to life inside him. He pulled her closer, his hands gliding down her back.

Teresa wrapped her arms around his neck, savoring the feel of his hard body pressed against the softness of her own. His tongue traced the contours of her mouth before slipping between her lips. When she met it with her own, he groaned deep in his throat, his hands sliding down to rest on her hips, urging her closer.

The movement had the effect of a bucket of cold water. Confused by the rushing swirl of emotions threatening to overwhelm her, she broke free. Taking a few stumbling steps backward, Teresa stared at him, unable to believe this man had set off such powerful yearnings inside her.

"I guess it worked. I don't hear a sound."

She took one look at his smug expression and couldn't believe he had been so unaffected by the shattering kiss. Anger and humiliation warred within her. Anger won. Not for the first time, she wished she had been born a man. A man could defend his honor on the dueling field or with fisticuffs. And right now, she would love to blacken his eye. Instead she did the next best thing. She kicked him in the shin.

"Ow! Can't stand the silence, eh. Just like a woman, always chattering like birds."

"I think I hate you," she said and turned on her heel.

Mateo laughed and watched her stomp away, muttering to herself all the while.

"I can't believe I let him kiss me. I must be going mad."

Her first words floated back to him but the rest were lost as she lengthened the distance between them. He smiled and rubbed his bruised leg. Now was probably not the best time to tell her how beautiful she looked even with her honey-colored hair dull and dirty from the ashes she had rubbed into it to disguise the color.

She disappeared through the old wooden gate that led out to the street. With a soft chuckle, he started after her. This hunt for the *Pequena* might not be such a hardship after all.

Stepping into the narrow alley, he wrinkled his nose at the smell of rotten vegetables and stale urine. Teresa stood some yards ahead next to a hackney. He shook his head in wonder. How could a woman so slight in stature have such a courageous heart?

How many others would have stood up to him giving insults as good as those she received? Would any other member of the *Ton*, male or female, have dared to break the law by entering the Marquess of Kingsbury's townhouse? And now, she stood alone in a dingy, foul smelling alley as though it was no more dangerous than a stroll in the park.

With a quick glance around, the object of his thoughts tossed something up to the driver and stepped inside.

Alarm bells went off in his head. Had she no sense at all? Hadn't she heard of unscrupulous drivers who would deliver unchaperoned women to procuresses of some of the most depraved brothels in London? No, she couldn't be that naïve. Even he, who came from another country, knew the dangers. She could disappear into the teeming cesspool of London's slums never to be seen again.

He rushed forward, grabbing the horses' bridles. "Wait, I wish a ride."

"I already got a passenger."

Surprised by the youthful voice, Mateo looked up at the driver. Hunkered down and nearly swallowed by a black cloak, it was impossible to judge the man's age much less his size. "I'm willing to share if the lady is."

"How you know it be a lady?"

"I saw her enter your coach."

"How do I know it ain't you she was trying to get away from?"

"Was she running?" Mateo inched his way around the side of the horse.

A snort of laughter filled the air. "Ha! Tess don't—" The youthful voice died abruptly as though he realized he'd said more than he should have.

The carriage door flew open; Teresa's slim form filled the space. "Why are we—?"

Mateo left the horse and grabbed for the door.

She caught sight of Mateo and frantically tried to close it. "Go, Freddie. Go!"

Mateo heard the snap of the whip and the cry of the driver. The horses lunged forward. Running alongside the carriage, he gauged the distance and dived through the opening, knocking Teresa to the floor.

He lay there trying to catch his breath. "Are you unhurt?" he managed to gasp.

"I'd be just fine if you'd get off me." She pushed at his chest with both hands.

Rising, he braced one hand above his head and offered her the other. Darkened hulks of buildings flashed by the window. Teresa ignored him and scrambled onto the worn leather squabs.

"Haven't you had enough entertainment at my expense, that you risk life and limb jumping into a moving carriage?" She pulled off the black cloth covering her hair and tossed it on the cushion beside her before grasping the window ledge in an effort to keep from being thrown from her seat.

"What if you didn't make it?" She closed her eyes and turned away as though she couldn't bear the mental image.

Mateo put a finger under her chin and turned her face to meet his gaze. Did she feel the unexplainable bond that seemed to grow stronger each time they met? "Would it have mattered?"

"How can you ask that? Yes, yes it would have mattered."

At her unhesitating response, some part of him, some part he thought long dead, began to glow in the embers of his soul. Was it possible to escape the past? "Why?" he asked.

"Your injuries would have been my fault. I was angry at you and your continued slander of my father. I wanted to get away from you, so I told the driver to go."

Her words were like shards of ice, each one sent to splinter what was left of his heart. Self-disgust rose up like foul-tasting bile. When would he learn? When? Her father was heartless enough to take the one thing that mattered most to Mateo's family. He had to remember she was her father's daughter.

In an effort to gain control over his growing anger, he rapped on the roof. "Slow down!" he bellowed.

The driver peeked through the opening. "Tess?"

She nodded. "He's right. You should slow down before the horses get hurt or the hackney overturns."

"Make sure you closes the door, too." Freddie gestured to the door banging wildly against the side of the carriage.

"It's a wonder we haven't been thrown ourselves considering the breakneck pace we've been traveling." Teresa scooted further into the corner.

As the horses slowed, Mateo leaned out the opening, grabbed the swinging door, and pulled it shut. "Too bad you didn't get rid of me while you had the chance." He flung himself down in the opposite corner and stared out the window.

"And what is that supposed to mean? I've already told you I'm glad you weren't injured."

"Only because you don't want me haunting that high and mighty conscience of yours." He rubbed his jaw, feeling the rough whiskers that signaled he needed another shave. "But once you got over your initial guilt, I'd wager you and your family would throw one hell of a party."

Confusion and something else he couldn't identify flashed across her face. "I would never take joy from another's death," she whispered.

"Even mine?"

"I don't understand you. You hate my family and believe I hate you in return. I know nothing about you or what happened twenty years ago." She bit her lip then continued. "Perhaps you could explain it to me?"

"Are you admitting that what I say is true, that your precious father was no more than a thief who coveted something that didn't belong to him? And by taking it, destroyed my family and our lives as we knew them?"

"I admit nothing of the sort," she flared. "I don't know why I bother. It's obvious you have no intention of listening to anything I say, yet you refuse to explain why you believe the things you do."

She glared at him then turned to stare out the window. Such anger had burned in her gaze that Mateo expected the passing scenery to burst into flame. She was an awesome sight when she was mad.

The color of her eyes changed to a deep fathomless brown, her cheeks flushed with color. It was all he could do not to sweep her off the seat and into his arms. The fact that she was currently garbed in men's clothing did nothing to deter his desire. Black breeches clung to her hips and thighs outlining her shapely figure. She wore a matching black wool shirt tucked into the waistband. The fabric pulled taunt against her full breasts. Mateo curled his fingers into his palms in an effort to resist reaching out and touching her.

Did he dare tell her of his past and her father's part in it? Would she draw back in horror at the things he'd done to keep body and soul together? And why did it matter so much?

He brushed his fingers over her sleeve just as the carriage rolled to a stop. She turned to him, her face devoid of expression. The door opened, and Teresa slid toward it.

"Wait." He tightened his hold, aware of the driver watching him.

"You all right?" the driver asked.

She glanced at the young man. "I'm fine, Freddie. Will you give us a few minutes of privacy?"

With a belligerent glare at Mateo, he nodded. "I'll be right outside here." He closed the door and began to whistle.

Mateo resisted the urge to strangle the young

buck. Instead, he released his hold on Teresa and sent a swift prayer toward heaven to help him do the right thing for once in his miserable life. He didn't hold out much hope. God hadn't been there when he needed Him in the past. He doubted He'd help now.

Mateo took a deep breath and plunged ahead. "Would you meet me tomorrow night at the McNaughton rout? I will answer any questions you have then."

"I won't be attending. I didn't receive an invitation. The duchess and Lady McNaughton aren't on speaking terms."

"Then you shall come as my guest. No one would dare deny the great Count de Montayas the right to bring a guest," he said, his lips curled in self-mockery.

Seeing her hesitation, he stroked her hair off her cheek and leaned closer. "Please, *mi pico paloma*, say yes," he murmured, drowning in the scent of her so close and yet so far away.

She leaned back and scooted toward the door. "That's the second time you've called me that. What does it mean?"

"My little dove."

"Don't call me that. You insult my family and then attempt to flatter me. Please call me by my proper address: Miss Darlington."

"I'm doing nothing of the sort." He rubbed his thumb back and forth over her wrist. "Do you wish to fly away from me then?"

She pulled her hand free. "Why does it seem as though you are two different men? At times you're a hard, angry man bent on revenge and then, at other times you are..." Her unspoken words hung in the air.

Mateo sat back against the cushions. "I am what circumstances force me to be." He wouldn't apologize for being the man he was. Not when it was her father who was responsible.

She opened the door and stepped out calling to the driver. "I'm ready."

"About time too. It's late. You don't wanna be gettin' caught."

"Yes, I know. I'll be more careful."

Mateo heard the anxiety in the driver's voice and waited to hear Teresa's reply before following her into the street.

"Why does he call you Tess?"

Her lips formed a mischievous smile before she glanced away. "I have secrets as well. Good night, Senor Conde."

She walked down the narrow side street, the hackney driver beside her. They stopped in front of a towering brick wall that ran the entire length of the alley. The driver bent and gave her a leg up, to boost her high enough to reach the top of the wall.

Jealousy ripped through Mateo as the other man's hands grasped Teresa's buttocks, thighs, and then her calves in his attempt to lever her upward. He jerked forward, jealousy burning in his heart. He had no claim on her. It was obvious this young man named Freddie did.

He turned, eager to be away. Once he arrived home, he would drink himself into a stupor and maybe, just maybe, he would be able to forget about his beautiful temptress for a little while. He took one more look back. He couldn't help it. Teresa was nowhere in sight, and the driver was headed back to the hackney.

Mateo slowed to a stop. If he could persuade the man to join him for a pint, or two, or three, it would provide ample opportunity to learn more about the youth and Teresa. Nothing induced a man to loosen his tongue like alcohol. He smiled what Eduardo called his devil's unholy grin, and with his hands stuffed in his pockets, strolled toward his prey.

Chapter Eight

Mateo blinked and tried to concentrate on what Lady Somebody or other was saying, having forgotten her name long ago. His gaze kept straying to Teresa. She stood alone near a marble column sipping lemonade and watching the dancers swirl around the floor. He learned no more about her last night than he'd known before.

Only one bit of knowledge had come from his prowl with her friend. Freddie, a tall, gangly youth of seventeen, could drink his weight in ale and show no ill effects.

He, however, had woken with such a violent headache; it was all he could do to crawl out of bed when the hour approached noon. Having Eduardo witness this humiliation did nothing to improve his mood. Even now, his head throbbed with each beat of the music.

He made a noncommittal reply to his unwanted companion's latest question and wondered how his evening had come to this. Teresa had arrived on his arm; a vision dressed in a gown the lightest shade of green he'd ever seen. Trimmed with darker green accents, it drew the eye to her small waist and full breasts without the brazen effect of putting her assets on display. They had barely entered the ballroom before she'd excused herself to say hello to an acquaintance. She hadn't come near him since.

At Lady Somebody's sudden indrawn breath, Mateo dragged his gaze away from Teresa. The room had grown quiet only to erupt in whispered murmurs that grew louder as everyone began talking at once.

Following the direction of the stares, he noticed a man dressed in a plain brown jacket and buff-colored trousers standing at the entrance to the ballroom. He wasn't someone Mateo recognized from previous social engagements, but it was obvious everyone present knew who he was. Even more unusual, the stranger had created a stir among the jaded members of England's elite.

One or two of the men separated themselves from the crowd and greeted the newcomer. Soon he was surrounded by a bevy of women, young and old. Despite his gaggle of admirers, he craned his neck to survey the room.

Intrigued, Mateo nodded an acceptance of his companion's hurried excuse as she practically ran across the room, squeezing her not insubstantial frame to the front of the group. She fluttered her eyelashes and giggled like a young girl, but the stranger barely noticed her. His attention was riveted on someone across the room, a grin spreading over his face.

Mateo looked over his shoulder to see Teresa staring back at the stranger, a brilliant smile turning her already lovely features into incomparable beauty. The man pushed his way through the crowd and headed in her direction while she moved to meet him.

"Blaine!" She greeted him with a quick hug, stepping back to prevent whispers of impropriety but allowed him to retain hold of her hands.

Mateo cocked his head, trying to hear the man's words, but they were lost in the babble of other conversations now that the novelty of the stranger's appearance had worn thin. Who was this man Teresa welcomed like a long lost lover? The question ate at him. He found himself developing an irrational hatred for a man he'd never met.

He moved forward to make it known he was Teresa's escort this evening. He'd gone no more than a few steps, when she allowed his new adversary to sweep her out onto the dance floor.

He lifted his glass and took a long swallow, watching Teresa smile up at her partner as they moved in time to the music. Did she have to look like she was enjoying herself so much? Meanwhile, he was stuck listening to one mother after another extol the virtues of their paragon daughters.

As the dance ended, he gave a pained smile to the latest debutante shoved beneath his nose and made his way through the crush of guests. He ignored those who would have detained him, trying to reach Teresa's side before the music began again.

"Are you enjoying yourself?" he asked, placing a solicitous hand on her wrist, resisting the urge to drag her away from the man standing opposite.

"Very much so," she responded, her eyes dancing with laughter.

"Tess always enjoys herself in my company."

Teresa made a face at her companion and turned to Mateo. "I'd like to introduce my friend, Mr. Blaine Hobson."

Mateo inclined his head toward the other man taking in his startling blue eyes and dark brown hair that hung just below his shoulders. No wonder the women swoon over him, Mateo thought cynically. The man looks like some dark knight out of the past.

Teresa turned to Blaine. "This is Count de Montayas. He is visiting from Spain as an emissary of his king."

Mateo bestowed a smile on her. "I'm merely here to thank your king for his military help in my country's fight with Napoleon."

Blaine's face tightened into cold disdain. "Then you are speaking to the wrong man." He turned on his heel and disappeared into the crush of guests.

"You'll have to forgive him. His mother's family is French. He was pressed into service with the infantry. When he refused to fight on behalf of the English, he was imprisoned."

Mateo looked at the man who stood knee-deep in admirers with newfound respect.

"He managed to escape," she continued, "and make his way to the Prince Regent's bedchamber where he pled his case to Prinny himself."

"It's a wonder he didn't end up dead." Mateo realized he and Blaine Hobson had more in common than he would have guessed.

"The Regent spared his life on two conditions. Blaine can have no contact with his mother's family until the war is over, and he must be chaperoned by one of his majesty's guards at all times."

Mateo shifted his gaze to the beefy looking man lounging against a pillar just far enough away from Blaine's circle of women to be unobtrusive. "To ensure he isn't a spy for the French?"

Teresa gave a slow shrug. "I'm not sure, but I believe that is the reason."

He transferred his attention to the woman at his side. "Tell me, how did you come to know a man who would risk his life to steal into the Prince Regent's bedchamber?"

She gave a small laugh. "When the news made the gossip rounds, everyone claimed to know him. It gave him the attention he's always tried to avoid. Before he was known only as a minor poet, good— but no one of consequence. Now, he's one of the most sought after people in London." She sighed. "Too bad, no one wants to get to know the real man."

"Do you know the real man?" Mateo asked as jealousy surged through him once more.

"Yes. His father served as an assistant to my father during his military career. Papa sent him to deliver a rather sensitive document to his superiors.

Blaine's father was killed. It was never determined who the murderer was. Papa felt so guilty, he moved Blaine and his mother into a small cottage on our estate."

"So you look upon him as a brother," Mateo surmised, relief flowing over him.

Teresa gave him a coy look. "Are you jealous, Senor Conde?"

"Sorry to disappoint you." Eager to change the subject, he placed her hand in the crook of his arm. "Would you like to take a walk in the gardens? We have yet to have the talk I promised you."

"Yes, I think I've waited long enough for my answers," she said, her gaze growing serious.

Making their way around the edge of the room, Mateo led her out to the terrace. A short flight of stairs led to the flagstone path winding its way through the geometric designs of the formal gardens. They walked in silence as though each was hesitant to break the air of camaraderie between them.

"Why do Mr. Hobson and the carriage driver from the other night call you *Tess*?" Mateo asked.

Teresa met his gaze and wondered why the nickname seemed so important to him. "It's a remnant of my childhood. Nothing more."

"Then why do men who claim you as a friend call you by such an intimate name?"

"Intimate?" She wasn't sure she liked what he was implying. "What exactly do you mean by that?"

"I only meant that I have never heard Lady Sarah address you as such. If I have offended you, I apologize. Sometimes my command of your language is not all I wish it to be."

Teresa thought his command of the English language more than adequate. She wondered about his motives once again. Why couldn't he just be the person he seemed to be on the surface instead of having so many hidden layers that she sometimes compared their conversations to the peeling of an onion?

"I would like permission to call you Tess," he murmured.

Breaking free of her contemplation of his secrets, she looked at him. "Why?"

"I do not want to call you Teresa...it doesn't suit you."

"Teresa is a fine name. After all if it's good enough for a saint—"

He cut her off, laying a finger against her lips. "But you're no saint, are you?"

She backed away. "You could call me Miss Darlington as is proper."

"But I am hardly proper, don't you agree?" He gave her a devilish grin.

The slightly antagonistic, formal relationship between herself and the Count de Montayas suddenly merged into the exciting and dangerous relationship between herself and the masked intruder. How did he manage to switch from one personality to the other so quickly? She walked a fine line between the two, the count on one side and the exciting intruder on the other.

She moved across the path under the guise of examining a decorative border of greenery. "Very well, you may call me Tess. But it's no great compliment."

"Why do you say that?" He stepped in front of her.

She blew out a breath of air in frustration. "I earned the name from Betsy, my lady's maid and companion. As a child, I often found myself in one scrape or another. Betsy would claim that I was sent from God as a test of her patience. Test...Tess. The nickname evolved from there." She fingered the leafy plants. "My father indulged my curiosities more than he probably should have."

"It doesn't seem to have made you into one of the spoiled, self-centered debutantes I've met this evening."

"No, it made me into something much worse."

"I don't understand."

She gave a small sigh. "I fear I am a blue stocking."

"Blue stocking?" His brow furrowed in confusion for a moment, then he stepped forward and lifted the hem of her gown.

"What are you doing?" Teresa shrieked, trying to pull free of his grasp.

"I've never seen blue stockings before. You claim to have them, yet these," he pointed to her legs with his free hand, "are white."

She smoothed her skirt back into place. "I didn't say I was wearing them," she snapped. "I said I am one."

"One what?"

She shook her head, wanting to reach out and shake him. He couldn't be that thickheaded, could he? She didn't think so, not given the knowledge of the English language he displayed earlier. No, he was just being difficult. "A blue stocking," she said between clenched teeth.

"How can one be an article of clothing?"

"Are you being deliberately obtuse?"

The instant the words left her mouth, his whole demeanor changed. He flinched, his body stiffening as though preparing for a blow. His face became an expressionless mask.

Teresa reached out a hand. "Have I offended? I didn't mean to. I seem to lose my temper whenever I'm around you."

"Offend? How can a great lady of society be concerned over the feelings of a mere Spanish peasant, much less offend him?" His dark eyes no longer reminded her of polished onyx. Now they burned with anger—hard, dark, and dangerous.

"I'm sorry."

With a brief nod, he turned on his heel and strode down the path.

"Senor Conde. Please wait."

He halted, then turned around slowly. "It is best I do not stay. Long ago, I learned the hard way to control my temper. I fear I do not have control of it now."

She saw his struggle to speak perfect English and knew he was far angrier than she had guessed. "You would harm me?" She couldn't keep the fear from her voice.

"With every word, you insult me more." He gave a harsh laugh. "What am I to expect, eh? I come to ruin your life. In your eyes, I'm no man of honor." With each word his accent became more and more pronounced.

"I didn't mean—"

He waved her off as though she was no more than a bothersome insect, leaving her standing alone in the darkness.

How had a conversation regarding her nickname dissolved into such a terrible mess? He had gone from his thief persona to that of the angry count with terrifying suddenness. She had been rude and insulting. That would have been enough to make any man furious. Trying to apologize had only made things worse. Perhaps if she tried again.

She hurried up the path. Her skirts held above her ankles, she ran up the stairs leading to the terrace, nearly colliding with Lady Sarah and Viscount Linley at the top.

"Teresa, are you well?" Lady Sarah asked, concern marring her features.

"Yes, yes. I'm fine." Teresa tried to move around them.

"Are you certain?" The viscount stepped into her

path. "You look upset." He gazed out over the gardens. "No one has been less than a gentleman to you, have they? Tell me his name. I shall call him out on your behalf."

"No! No, I was alone." She gave a brittle laugh. "I guess I just got frightened. It was foolish of me to wander about alone, but I couldn't resist a peek at the gardens. If you'll excuse me." With a flurry of skirts, she pushed past him and rushed into the ballroom.

The heat, lack of fresh air, and the number of people slammed into her as soon as she stepped inside. She would never be able to make her way through the crush. Feeling as though she couldn't breathe, she leaned against the wall, her eyes searching the room. Damn this stupid fear of large crowds. How would she ever find Montayas? It was all but impossible.

"I'm afraid your escort left."

"Left?" She turned to see Blaine holding out a glass of champagne.

"Here, you look as though you need this more than I do."

"You mean he's gone? He left me here? Wonderful. As soon as it gets out that the great Count de Montayas deserted me, I haven't a prayer of avoiding the vicious tongues of the gossips." She took the glass and drained it.

"Easy. Keep that up and they'll be saying you're a drunkard."

"How do I get into these situations?"

He put an arm around her waist and urged her out onto the terrace. "I imagine it isn't so hard. You had quite a knack for getting into trouble as a child."

"But now I'm an adult. You'd think I would have learned how to avoid it." She moved to the balustrade, watching couples move about the garden.

"There's nothing for you to worry about tonight. When I saw Montayas storm out of here, I casually mentioned to a few people that he asked me to see you home. I think we can safely assume they'll spread the word to all and sundry. See, no harm done." He stroked her cheek with his knuckles. "It was a hell of a row, wasn't it?"

She glanced at him. "Not really."

Blaine turned her to face him, his eyebrows lifted in disbelief. "If your friend looks like that after a small disagreement, I'd hate to see him angry."

"Oh, he was angry, furious in fact. I insulted him by questioning his intellect. I'm sure I hurt his feelings, not that he would ever admit that. And then, to top it all off, I questioned his honor."

"No wonder he left you here."

"Thanks. I can always count on you for sympathy."

"I'll have my carriage brought around and take you home. I've had enough fingers pointed at my back tonight." Placing a hand on her waist, he guided her toward the ballroom entrance.

"How do you stand it? All the whispers and stares."

"I didn't do anything to be ashamed of. I stood up for what I believed in. If that gives people who think they're my betters something to talk about, who cares. As long as I can still look at myself in the mirror, nothing they say or do matters. Besides if they're busy gossiping about me, then they're leaving some other poor fool alone."

Teresa laughed. "Even as children, I always thought you had a unique outlook on life. Me, I hate being the object of gossip."

He stopped suddenly, the crowd surging and flowing past them. "You're stronger than you think."

She wasn't so sure. If Montayas carried out his threat to expose her father as a thief, there would be no avoiding a scandal. How could she have let her temper get the best of her? As if he didn't have reason enough to hate her, she'd added fuel to the fire. No doubt, he'd be more determined than ever to destroy her family. She had no choice now but to continue with her plan to find the *Pequena* first.

****

Teresa gathered the ends of the sheer white drapes and put them out the window to flutter in the breeze as a signal to Freddie that all was going according to plan. She knew he was out there in the darkness but couldn't see him. He hadn't thought she would be able to get inside the Earl of Leighton's townhouse. Ha! She'd gotten inside so easily; it would put him to shame when she told him.

The problem was she had no idea where to start searching. If the earl had been married, his wife's jewelry would have been the obvious place to start, but the man had been a widow for some years now.

Feeling her way along the dark hall, she'd gone no more than a few feet when her questing fingers found the edge of a door casing. A surge of adrenaline fired through her. Was this what Montayas felt when he crept through the houses of the *Ton* in the middle of the night?

The door handle turned with a slight squeak. Holding her breath, she listened for footsteps. She waited a minute more before slipping inside. She fished a small candle out of her pocket, lit it, and made a quick circuit of the room. Books lined one wall while a large desk dominated the far end. Two chairs faced a fireplace, their backs to the rest of the room. A strange mask from some primitive country hung on the wall near double glass doors leading to a small stone terrace.

Teresa crossed to the desk. She stared at the paper-strewn blotter. No, the desk would be the last place the *Pequena* would be hidden. She tried the top right-hand drawer anyway. Locked. Just as she knew it would be. Her gaze roamed around the room before fastening on the bookcase. She'd read about hidden rooms and books that looked like books but were in fact clever hiding places for one's valuables.

A beautiful vase standing atop a tall pedestal caught her eye. She moved around it, looking at it from one angle then another. *What are you doing?* she scolded herself. *You're here to look for Montayas' jeweled box not to admire the furnishings.*

Crossing the room, she stood in front of the rows of books. She ran her fingers over the leather bindings, hoping for some obvious title like "The Hidden Treasure" that would give the hiding place away. She focused on anything unusual or of an odd shape. Her brow wrinkled in concentration, she stooped to examine the books on the lower shelves.

"What the hell do you think you're doing?"

Chapter Nine

Her heart hammering in her chest, Teresa
whirled around to face the Earl of Leighton standing
just inside the room. His eyes glittered in the light
from the branch of candles he held in one meaty fist.
The flame cast menacing shadows over his features.

"Answer me, boy. Did Smitty send you?"

Teresa shook her head, not sure if her voice
would give her away. She touched the black cloth
she wore in the same manner as Montayas and sent
up a prayer that she'd had the foresight to braid her
hair and wrap it around the top of her head before
donning the mask.

"If he has sent you, he'll regret it." Leighton
turned and set the candelabra on a nearby table.

The instant his back was turned, Teresa darted
toward the door.

A hand curled around her arm, dragging her
back. For a man two years past his fiftieth summer,
the earl moved with surprising speed and agility.

"Oh no, you're not going anywhere. Smitty gave
his word I could have three more days to repay the
debt."

Teresa tried to twist away from him. His fingers
tightened around her collar.

He spun her around to face him. "Is this some
type of threat, or has he become impatient and
decided to have you collect my valuables to pay my
gambling losses?" Spittle formed at the corners of
Leighton's mouth as his anger mounted. "Answer
me," he shouted, shaking her violently.

She grabbed his forearms, digging her fingers

into his linen shirtsleeves. "No, sir."

Leighton stilled, his gaze disbelieving. "No, you say? Yet you've broken into my home. Shall I turn you over to the watch?"

Teresa stayed silent, her fear strangling her as effectively as the noose from which she would hang if the watch got their hands on her.

The earl ran his fingers down the length of his goatee. "No. No, I don't think that will give Smitty a moment's pause. You will take a message to him."

For the first time since he entered the room, a frisson of hope blossomed inside her. She nodded, unable to believe he was going to let her go.

"Or should I say, you will be that message."

Before she realized what he intended, he struck a lightning swift blow to her cheek.

Her head snapped back and she fell to the ground. A cry of pain and shock escaped her unnoticed. Cupping her face, she stared up at him through tear-filled eyes. She felt the warmth of her blood oozing over her fingers.

He advanced toward her. Teresa scrambled out of reach. She jumped to her feet, searching the room for an escape. Her cheek throbbed with each beat of her heart.

"Come here, you little bastard," Leighton roared, giving chase to her desperate flight around the room.

Passing by the desk, she grabbed a small bronze statuette, hurling it at her attacker. He quickly sidestepped, the statuette bouncing harmlessly on the plush carpet.

The double glass doors loomed to her left. She turned in that direction.

Leighton was further away than she. She was younger, quicker. She had to reach them first.

Scooping up the inkwell, she threw it at him and ran toward freedom. He sputtered and cursed behind her. Unable to help it, she glanced behind her.

His face dripping with black ink, he lunged forward.

They crashed into the French doors. The panels rained down in a shower of glass as Teresa and her attacker fell to the floor.

She kicked at him, pulling her body free of his grasp inch by inch. Shards of glass pricked her arms and legs. She headed for the pedestal holding the vase she'd admired earlier. Using it for leverage, she pulled herself up.

She took a shaky breath. Then he was on her, knocking her head into the wall.

He closed his hands around her throat, his grip unrelenting. "You tell him the next time he tries threatening me to send someone who can carry out the task not a mere boy."

He tightened his hold on her neck.

Teresa clawed at his hands. She felt her windpipe being crushed with each squeeze. Her lungs burned. Spots danced in front of her eyes. She couldn't gather the strength to fight back. Her legs buckled.

Throwing out an arm in an effort to hold herself up, her fingers brushed over the vase. With the last of her ebbing strength, she curled her fingers around the rim and brought the vase down on Leighton's head.

He groaned and slumped to the floor. Teresa fell to the carpet in a crumpled heap, coughing and choking. Air rushed into her lungs. Gasping, she crawled a safe distance away from the earl's still figure.

"Tess!"

Cradling her throat with her hands, she looked up. The French doors hung drunkenly on their hinges. Freddie stood between them looking like an avenging angel. His black cloak all but concealed him.

"Oh, God." He bent down next to the earl.

"Dead?" she croaked.

"No. We have to leave. Now!" He whipped his cloak around her and lifted her into his arms. "I have to get you to a doctor." He hurried around the side of the house, keeping to the shadows.

Thankfully, the hackney wasn't far off. He looked at Teresa and winced. She'd taken a horrible beating. Guilt tore at him with each step.

He slipped through the side gate and opened the door to the coach. Gently, he laid her on the floor, rearranging his cloak around her. "Tess?"

Her eyes fluttered open then slid closed. "No doctors."

"You need care. I have to get help."

"Betsy," she croaked.

It would be impossible to take her to Betsy like this. Not when she wouldn't be able to enter Perth House under her own power. He had to take her somewhere; he knew nothing about doctoring.

Her breathing had settled into shallow rasps of air. Freddie closed the door and jumped up into the driver's box. He opened the trap and looked down on her once more, then whipped the horses into a gallop. She was right, a doctor would ask questions. Questions that couldn't be answered.

Paying no heed to the carriages filled with various revelers and partygoers returning to their homes, he raced through the streets as if the demons of Hell chased him. But there was no way to outrun the demons in his mind. Guilt ate at him, bringing tears to his eyes that no self-respecting man of seventeen would own up to. He'd nearly gotten her killed.

When she'd come to him for help, his ego swelled with self-importance. How could he have thought that he, a lowly street urchin, could know enough about the *Ton* and their ways to keep her from harm? He brushed at his watery eyes with the sleeve of his coat, blaming it on the wind, and drove on.

The carriage careened around the corner, and Freddie jerked the horses to a halt. With a skill that belied his age, he maneuvered them into the cramped opening of a nearby alley. He leaped to the ground and swung open the side door. Tess lay still in the darkness. Fear tightened its grip on his heart.

With as much gentleness as he could muster, he lifted her into his arms and ran down the alley. He gave one last glance over his shoulder. His unattended coach and horses were an open invitation to the next thieving soul passing by. It was the first honest work he'd done since the death of his parents' eight years ago. At least he knew how to survive on the streets if they were stolen.

He skidded on a patch of wet cobblestones and nearly slid into the door he'd been seeking. Shifting Teresa firmly against him, he rapped on the wooden door. When no answer came, he pounded on it. Flakes of peeling paint filled the air. He leaned forward, listening, certain he heard the sound of approaching footsteps.

The door was wrenched open. The sight of the man glaring at him disconcerted Freddie, and he wondered for the first time if he'd made a mistake coming here. The stranger wore blue breeches, shiny boots, and a loose flowing shirt gathered at the cuffs. His hair was slicked back and was as black as his eyes. A small thin mustache completed the rakish look.

"We take in no beggars," he said in heavily accented English.

"I'm not a beggar. I need to see Montayas."

The guardian of the door looked Freddie up and down as though he was something he would scrape off the bottom of his highly polished boot. "I think not. El Senor Conde does not converse with those beneath his station." He started to close the door.

Realizing he was losing his only chance to get help, Freddie snarled, "The hell he doesn't," and barreled past the uppity butler. Suddenly the skills he'd acquired living on the rougher side of London didn't seem quite so bad. They were certainly coming to good use tonight.

"Montayas," he shouted, striding down the dark hallway.

A hand clamped on to his shoulder, spinning him around. Before he had time to regain his balance, the butler's fist connected with his jaw, sending him sprawling. Frantic, he tried to protect Teresa from the impact, taking the brunt of the fall himself. He felt her flinch from the jarring motion.

Freddie scooted away from the other man. He looked around for something to use as a weapon. As a door slammed at the far end of the hall, his stomach filled with dread. If he couldn't defend Teresa and himself against the butler, how would he fare against others?

"Eduardo!"

Freddie's attacker ignored the caller, his legs planted in a boxer's stance, his fists ready to strike another blow.

Freddie looked around the man's legs. Montayas. He was never so relieved to see someone in his life.

A spate of rapid fire Spanish passed between the two men as he slowly rose to his feet. His jaw throbbed, his arms ached despite Teresa's slight weight. A low moan came from within the folds of his cloak serving to remind him he had suffered nothing compared to her.

He cleared his throat, unsure of his welcome. "Montayas, we need your help." He shifted the bundled form in an effort to ease the burning in his muscles.

The cloth slipped downward revealing his burden.

"Teresa!" The count stepped around his cousin. "She lives?" he asked in a hoarse voice.

Freddie nodded.

"What happened?"

"Say you'll help her first an' I'll tell you."

"*Si, Si*, I will help. Come." Montayas opened a door to his left. "There is a settee inside. Put her down there." He turned toward Eduardo who watched the proceedings in sullen silence. "Get Tia Elena quickly."

Eduardo responded to the order, his voice taking on an argumentative tone.

Montayas snapped off a single word in his native tongue. It echoed in the hall like the crack of a whip and sent the other man stalking up the stairs muttering what Freddie was sure were epithets not meant to be said in the company of ladies. He turned and followed the count into the room.

Freddie crossed the threadbare carpet and laid Teresa on the settee, unwrapping the cloak from around her. He pulled the last of the heavy cloth from her body revealing an expanse of shapely leg where her trousers had been torn. His ears burning from the betraying heat of embarrassment, he grabbed the material and folded it closed. He looked up to find Montayas watching him with hooded eyes.

"Was she attacked?" Mateo forced himself to ask.

"Hell, yes. You don't think I did this to her, do you?" Freddie demanded, his hands forming fists at his sides.

"No. No, I mean was she... How you say—?" Mateo struggled to find the English translation for the word that pulsated in his brain like a living beast.

Freddie seemed to grab his meaning instantly.

"No! Not that," he exclaimed, a horrified expression on his face.

The clicking of a cane on the marble floor of the hall preceded Elena's entrance into the room. Mateo hurried forward and led her over to Teresa's inert form.

He looked at the bruised and bloody face of the woman who'd come to mean more to him than she should. He couldn't deny it any longer. "Tell me what happened."

"I helped her into the Earl of Leighton's townhouse. He weren't supposed to be home. Tess insisted I wait outside. Said it'd be safer." Freddie brushed his fingers over her hair. "Safer. He nearly killed her."

Teresa opened her eyes. "Freddie?"

"It's okay, Tess. I got help." He gestured to Mateo and his aunt.

Mateo crouched down beside her. "Tia Elena will tend to your injuries." He reached out to touch her but changed his mind and stood. If he touched her now, he didn't know if he'd be able to let her go. And that was the one thing he had to do.

Eduardo returned, dropped a cloth and bowl of water on the side table, and left the room without a word. Elena dipped a corner of the material into the bowl and began washing Teresa's face with gentle strokes.

Mateo sighed knowing he would have to deal with his cousin's disapproval later. He let his gaze roam around the room trying not to dwell on the deep purple bruises marring the white skin of Teresa's throat, or the dried blood on her cheek.

Each time he looked at her, murder raged in his soul. The earl may have had the advantage over a small woman, but soon he would learn what it was like to face a man. A man bent on vengeance. A man with nothing to lose because it had all been lost years ago.

He glanced down at her. "You were searching for the *Pequena*." He didn't have to ask. He knew exactly what she had been doing even after he'd tried to warn her of the dangers involved.

"Yes, though I wasn't very successful." Her hand fluttered against her throat.

Her voice reminded him of the hoarse, raspy voiced woman who lived on what remained of his estate in Spain. A woman who had spent her life drinking spirits to chase away her sorrow. "Did he take you for a thief?"

Teresa waited until his aunt turned away to dip the cloth into the water before answering. "Yes, but he believed I was there to collect on a debt owed to someone named Smitty."

"Smitty!" Freddie's exclamation filled the room.

"You know this man?" Mateo asked.

"He's a money lender what resorts to violence when he doesn't get his blunt."

Elena turned to Mateo and spoke in Spanish, gesturing to Teresa.

"What's she sayin'?" Freddie asked, anxiety clouding his eyes.

"She says we must leave the room so she can examine the lady properly." He headed for the door, gesturing for the younger man to follow. "We'll wait in the hall."

They had no more than crossed the threshold before Elena closed the door behind them.

"Tell me the rest."

Freddie quickly related the night's events leading up to his and Teresa's arrival. "I don't know what made me go 'round the back of the house. I kept having the queerest feelin'. That's when I saw the earl and Tess crash into them fancy French doors. By the time I reached her, he was knocked cold, and Tess was on the floor." He hesitated for a moment and contemplated the closed parlor door. "Them marks on her throat, I think he was trying to squeeze the life out of her."

Mateo paced the length between the door and an ornately carved table that had seen better days. The scenario would explain her injuries. He shuddered and expelled a deep breath. Thank God, she'd been able to fight the bastard off. He would never forgive himself if she died because of her foolish quest to find the *Pequena* before he did.

He stopped, turned, and looked at Freddie. How much did he know? "Did she tell you why she is looking for the...this item?"

"Yes. But after this, I think she was shamming me."

"Shamming you? What does that mean?"

"I think she was lyin'."

"What makes you believe she lied to you?"

"Because nobody'd kill for a worthless jewel case even if he was afraid of goin' to Newgate for stealin'."

"If it's of no value, why does she risk her life for it?" Mateo contained his surprise. She hadn't betrayed him or his search for the jewel box after all.

Freddie shoved his hands in his pockets. "That's what she won't tell me."

The parlor door opened, and Elena ushered them into the room, explaining the extent of Teresa's injuries.

Seeing Freddie's worried expression, he quickly translated. "All is well. Teresa suffered cuts and bruises on her arms and legs as well as her cheek. My aunt believes a ring may have caused the cut on her face. As for her throat, it will be sore for a few days, and her voice will take time to return to normal."

He met Teresa's shadowed gaze. "She is lucky. This time."

Teresa looked away and released a shaky

breath. "Freddie, will you take me home now?"

"We will both accompany you home. There are plans to make if your reputation is to survive your night's adventure," Mateo said, not giving the younger man a chance to respond.

Within minutes the threesome were ensconced in Freddie's hackney while Eduardo took over the reins. He glanced up at the ceiling then out the window as they headed toward Perth House.

"Do not worry. Eduardo may not like his present task, but he won't take it out on the horses." Mateo stretched his legs across the small space, inadvertently bringing his booted feet in contact with Teresa's.

She quickly shifted position, moving her feet away and inching closer to Freddie.

Mateo gazed at her profile as she stared past her companion and out the window. He squelched the feeling of loss that ran through him at her withdrawal. Now wasn't the time to dwell on his foolish protective feelings toward her.

Instead, he focused his attention on her companion and the idea forming in his head. "How well do you know Perth House?"

"Well enough."

"Do you think you can get to the servants' quarters, rouse Teresa's maid, and tell her you have delivered the lady home safe?"

The lad shrugged as only a seventeen-year-old could. "Of course," he snorted. "Should Betsy go to Tess' room?"

Mateo directed his gaze to Teresa. "I assume the household believes you retired for the evening long ago?"

She stared at him, anger snapping in her eyes. "Yes."

"Then there's no reason to do anything that will cause questions to be asked. The maid's sudden appearance in her mistress' room at this late hour is bound to do just that."

She gave him a mutinous look. "Send her to me, Freddie."

"No," Mateo bit out. Why did she have to do the opposite of everything he said?

Freddie looked from one to the other, his uncertainty of whom to obey showed in his expression.

She crossed her arms over her chest. "I said, 'yes'."

Mateo reached up and rapped on the trap door. "Stop the coach." He leaned forward. "You will either obey my wishes or Eduardo and I leave you right here to face the scandal that will surely result from your late night arrival with a young man," he inclined his head toward Freddie, "and no suitable chaperone in sight."

She pressed back into the worn leather squabs, compressing her lips into a thin line. "Fine," she snapped.

He sat back with a sardonic smile. "I thought you'd see it my way." At his knock, the hackney began to move.

Freddie tucked her hand into his. "It's best we does as he says. Montayas is right. We've no good excuse for bein' out and together."

Mateo clenched his fingers into a fist, resisting the urge to rip their hands apart. He looked at the other man closely. What was it about the young man that Teresa allowed him such liberties yet she pulled away from a mere accidental touch of his boot against hers?

"After I seen Betsy, what do I do?" Freddie asked.

Mateo shook away the traitorous thoughts and concentrated on the task at hand. "Teresa will need a mount saddled and waiting for her early in the morning."

"I can do that. I worked in the stables a few months, before I got the sack. I still got friends there who owe me a favor."

"I don't think riding is the best idea," Teresa broke in. "Already my body aches from the earl's less than gentlemanly behavior."

"Less than gentlemanly behavior? You English have a strange way of describing the vicious act of beating a woman."

"I wasn't beaten," Teresa said.

"No?" He gave her bruised throat a pointed look.

"No. I came out the victor, didn't I?"

Freddie grinned and gave him an expectant look.

Mateo quirked his lips into a half smile. "So you did."

The hackney rolled to a stop.

Seconds later, Eduardo pulled open the door and let down the steps. "We have arrived, El Senor Conde," he added the title in a sarcastic tone.

Freddie stepped down then turned and helped Teresa out of the coach.

Mateo exited and glared at Eduardo. "You may return to the townhouse."

"And how should I do that? We have no carriage of our own."

"You're speaking English. Either you're trying to impress the lady, which I doubt, or you're trying to worm a ride back to Grosvenor Square in Freddie's hackney."

"I'm doing neither," Eduardo snapped. "I am merely pointing out the obvious."

Mateo slipped a hand into his pocket then flipped a coin in his cousin's direction. "Then hire another coach, not this one. Or better yet use your feet. Perhaps the walk will cool your temper."

Eduardo snarled a response in Spanish, spun on

his heel, and left.

Mateo watched him disappear into the misty fog filtering around them. With a shake of his head, he turned to find Freddie and Teresa staring at him.

"Not intending offense, Sir, but you needs to get better servants," Freddie volunteered.

"Eduardo is more than a servant. We were forced into an alliance by a legacy of loss and betrayal...the same way others are bound together by that same legacy."

"Yet you send him away without a proper conveyance." She gestured toward the street. "Aren't you worried he may be attacked by footpads or ruffians?"

"He's a very resourceful man. He'll be fine."

Mateo led the way down the narrow street, stopping before a stone wall covered with vines. He opened an iron gate that seemed to magically appear from within the forest of ivy. He waited for the others to pass through, then took one last look down the alley, and closed the gate behind him.

Freddie glanced around. "How'd ya know about the gate? I come here lots of times without the duchess knowing, and I never found it."

"A well-informed person suffers fewer nasty surprises. I hate surprises. Go to Teresa's companion and the stables as we planned, then you may go home. I'll be in touch with you tomorrow."

The younger man nodded. "You can count on me. I'd never let Tess down." He walked away, his dark clothing blending among the shadows in the garden.

Teresa broke the stilted silence Freddie left behind. "Thank you for helping me tonight." She began to move away.

Mateo caught her arm and pulled her to a stop. "I don't dismiss as easily as your servants. I will see you inside before I leave."

She yanked free of his hold. "Freddie isn't a

servant."

"Perhaps not," he conceded. "But his loyalty to you allows you to manipulate him whether you mean to or not. How else can you explain his willingness to help you break the law?"

"You speak to me of breaking laws? You have admitted to holding forged papers from your king. You've broken more laws than I ever will."

He looked away, hiding a smile. His admiration for her grew with each encounter. Never had he met a woman who fought with words, who could voice her opinions and arguments so forcefully without once resorting to tears and the other emotions many of her gender relied on to get their way.

"I suppose you are angry now that I've spoken the truth."

He tilted his head to the side and looked at her. "No. I was just thinking how beautiful you look."

Teresa stared at him with a skeptical expression. "You're doing it much too brown. If you don't mind, it's been a long night. I would like to get inside before the sun rises."

"Do I not deserve a kiss for rescuing you tonight?" He knew he risked her temper, but couldn't resist baiting her once more.

"*You* didn't rescue me. Freddie did. And I would no more kiss you than I would eat a bucket of chitterlings."

Mateo raised his eyebrows. "Really? Then I leave you with one last thing to think about as you lie in your bed."

"And that would be?"

"A man driven to desperation will do almost anything to achieve his aim."

Chapter Ten

"Freddie gave me your message last night. Heaven knows why you would want to go riding this morning after being out until the wee hours last night."

Teresa squinted against the early morning light as Betsy opened the drapes.

The maid turned, took one look at her charge, and rushed to the bed. "Oh my God, what happened to you? What happened? I'll kill Freddie."

"I'm fine. I know it doesn't look it, but I am." Teresa swallowed with a painful grimace. Her voice sounded terrible even to her own ears. "Don't blame Freddie. If it wasn't for him, I might be in bigger trouble than I already am."

Betsy reached out and stroked Teresa's throat with gentle fingers. "You don't sound fine, and you certainly don't look it. I would guess this is the reason I found a pot of theater makeup outside my quarters this morning. I think you should forgo your ride this morning."

"I can't. I was nearly caught last night. It was Freddie who took me to safety and then to Montayas for help. This ride is all part of Montayas' plan to pass off my injuries."

"I knew this hare-brained scheme of yours to find the jewel box first would come to a bad end. But I said I would stand by you and I will." Betsy left the bed and began laying out Teresa's brown velvet riding habit. She stopped suddenly, clutching a pair of riding boots to her chest. "Should I expect a visit from the Bow Street Runners?"

"No, the earl believed I was a lad. We shouldn't come under suspicion if we're able to fool the *Ton* into believing my bruises come from a riding mishap."

"Then you best get out of that bed and start eating the toast and tea I brought you." Betsy gestured toward the small table next to a pale yellow chaise.

Teresa pushed aside the quilt and slipped from the bed. Her body ached in places she didn't know existed. A shaky feeling started in her legs and traveled through her entire body. She sat back down with a plop. How was she going to manage getting on a horse when she felt like she'd been trampled by one?

She had to rest several times as Betsy helped her into the riding habit. Finally, she sat at her dressing table contemplating the toast waiting her. She took a small bite and immediately regretted the action. The crusty bread scraped her already sore throat raw. Eager to ease the pain, she grabbed the teacup and nearly drained the contents.

She refilled the cup and poured another for the maid. Between sips of the warm tea that soothed her throat, Teresa closed her eyes while Betsy styled her hair into a sleek coil at her neck.

A short time later she emerged into the early morning sunlight. On her way to the stables, she wondered how Montayas would stage her riding accident. Though if she continued to feel as terrible as she did now, he wouldn't have to stage anything. Staying on her horse was going to be quite an accomplishment.

She rounded the corner in the flagstone path and found him waiting for her. Montayas stepped away from the post he'd been leaning against.

"Good morning." He glanced at the groom who stood nearby with her mount. "I hope you slept well,

Miss Darlington."

"Yes, thank you."

"Then shall we take our horses to the park?" He gestured for the animals to be brought forward.

Her groom set a mounting box in place. Teresa pulled herself into the sidesaddle, watching with envy as Montayas swung onto his horse with ease.

She walked the mare forward as he angled his mount next to hers. Teresa looked behind her. Her groom was ready to accompany them at the required discreet distance.

Feeling Montayas' gaze, she turned back.

"Your lady's maid did well in covering the bruises on your face and throat."

Teresa touched her cheek. "She's more than a mere maid."

"Can she be trusted?"

"With your life."

"My life? She has no hold over my life."

"She knows all you told me when you accused my father of stealing your precious jewel box."

"She knows—"

"That you're a fraud? Yes." She kicked her horse into a trot leaving him behind.

He caught up with her soon enough. "I want to apologize for what happened to you last night."

She slowed to a walk. "Why? You weren't even there."

"Yet, I feel responsible. If I had confirmed my suspicions about your father or if I'd located the *Pequena* before confronting you, you wouldn't be risking your life trying to prove me wrong."

"I'm not trying to prove you wrong. I'm protecting my father's reputation."

"It's one and the same, is it not?"

Teresa sighed. "Yes, I suppose it is. Are we staging my accident soon? I don't think I can ride much longer."

Montayas checked the distance between them and the groom. "Do you think you could manage a gallop until we get around the hedge up ahead? It'll provide cover for a few moments."

She nodded.

He gave her a hard look. "Are you sure? We can find another way."

"No, I can do this."

"Then go now. Hurry," he urged, pushing his stallion into motion.

Teresa spurred her horse forward.

They raced passed the barrier of the hedge neck and neck before coming to a stop.

He jumped from his horse and grabbed the reins of her mount. He looked over his shoulder then whisked her from the saddle. Turning the horse, he slapped it on the rump, sending it flying back the way they came.

Teresa lay on the soft grass just as the groom came into view. Montayas dropped to his knees beside her.

"She's been thrown. Send for help," he shouted at the man.

Teresa resisted the urge to turn her head toward the sound of the groom's retreating hoof beats. Instead, she cracked an eye and looked at Montayas. He too was watching the departing groom.

Satisfied the man had gone for help, he whipped a snowy handkerchief from his pocket. Helping her into a sitting position, he held the linen cloth to her mouth. "Spit on this."

She pushed it away. "A lady doesn't spit."

"A lady doesn't steal into the homes of members of the *Ton* either."

She pulled his hand closer and spit on the material, wishing it was his eye instead.

He wiped the handkerchief across her cheek.

She batted his hand away. "That's disgusting."

"It may be so, but I haven't any water so this will have to do. Will you stop fighting me, or the groom will be back with help before we are ready."

Teresa submitted to his ministrations unable to keep from wrinkling her nose each time the cloth touched her face. "Why are you washing off the stage makeup? I thought it was to keep the duchess, among others, from knowing about my bruises."

"I have no intention of revealing those on your throat. They would be impossible to explain. If you have a visible injury, they may be more inclined to believe you have no others." He pulled a small vial from his breast pocket and carefully shook a few drops of the greenish liquid onto a clean corner of the linen square.

"I hope you're right." She wondered not for the first time what his past had been like. What would cause him to know so much about deceiving others? Why had he had to learn these methods and where had he learned them?

He pressed the cloth to her cheek. When she started to pull away, he placed his free hand behind her head preventing her from moving.

"It stings," she said with a wince.

"I'm sorry." His dark eyes filled with sympathy.

He was so close; she had only to lift her hand to trace his mouth with her fingertips. The stinging sensation receded as other confusing emotions came to the surface. She stared at him, biting her lip as she tried to understand the sudden longing to touch him.

"It will make the cut and bruise look fresh as though they were sustained during your fall from the horse." He met her gaze, the handkerchief slipping to the ground unnoticed as he caressed her cheek with his fingers.

Moving closer, he gathered her into his arms, his mouth a mere breath away from her own. Desire burned in his gaze. She leaned toward him, a silent invitation to his kiss.

"Teresa," he breathed then shook his head. "Much to my regret, we have no time for such pleasures, but I shall collect them later." He pushed to his feet and helped her rise.

Teresa started to give him a well-deserved set down but changed her mind. She had wanted his kiss. She couldn't deny it, but he didn't have to be so smug. "Perhaps, perhaps not."

Lifting her onto his horse, he smiled at her. "I will enjoy your kisses again just as you will enjoy mine." He swung up behind her, his arms closing around her to take the reins.

"Are all your countrymen so insufferable?"

Montayas laughed, a rich deep sound that vibrated through her body. "Only those of us who are enticed by women with honey blonde hair and brandy-colored eyes."

****

Teresa pushed away the scientific journal Betsy brought her that morning and flopped back onto the pillows. Most of the articles were still unread. She was bored. Bored. Bored. Bored. She'd end up in bedlam if she had to spend one more day in bed.

Her voice was almost back to normal, sounding only slightly husky at times. Betsy had let it slip to the rest of the household that Teresa suffered from a cold. It was the only thing they could think of to explain the sound of her voice. The bruises on her neck were growing fainter with each passing day. Soon she'd be able to dispense with the theatrical makeup altogether.

A visit to Mama's suite of rooms seemed like the perfect way to ease back into her normal routine. Slipping from the bed, Teresa quickly donned an old gardening dress. Perhaps, after her visit with her mother, she would check on the gardens. It'd been too long since she'd spent any time with her plants. Surely, Betsy wouldn't object to a walk around the grounds.

Pulling on a pair of half boots, she opened the door leading to her chambers and took a quick look around for the woman who had hovered over her from the moment Montayas had carried her into the house. A sad smile pulled at the corners of her mouth. Besides Lady Sarah, Betsy had been the only one who had come to visit her during the time she'd been confined to bed.

Had Montayas washed his hands of her? Worse yet, had he found the jeweled box and was now on his way back to Spain? Something twisted painfully in her heart. She didn't understand it. She should be glad she'd been spared his overwhelming presence, his arrogance, and snappy remarks, but instead she found herself missing their verbal battles, his overly familiar manner, and the sound of his voice as it whispered in her ear.

After a careful knock on the door, Teresa let herself into her mother's room. "Mama?" she called heading toward the bedchamber.

Lady Darlington was curled up on the window seat, holding the same lonely vigil she did day after day. Teresa took in her mother's fine silk day dress and fashionable coiffure at a glance. A picture of Robert Darlington sat at the other end of the green striped cushion.

"Hello, Mama."

"Hello, dear. Have you recovered from your accident?" Teresa tried to control her sudden start of surprise but apparently not well enough.

"Lady Sarah came to visit while you were recovering. She told me you had been thrown from one of Vivian's horses." Lady Darlington shuddered. "Nasty beasts, horses. I never did understand your fascination with them."

"Why didn't you come to see me?" For the past three days, she had explained away her mother's continued absence from her bedside with the excuse of ignorance. But Lady Darlington had known of the incident and hadn't come. Not once.

The older woman patted her hand. "I would have, but what if Robert finally came for me and I wasn't here? I've waited so long; I couldn't risk not being here. You understand, don't you dear?"

Teresa wanted to cry out no, she didn't understand. That her father was dead and never coming back. How could her own mother not care enough to see that she hadn't been seriously injured? Instead, she withdrew her hand and stepped away. "Of course, Mama," she murmured, fighting back tears of bitterness.

With a sigh, she left Lady Darlington looking out the window for the husband who would never return. Closing the door behind her, she headed for the stairs hoping to slip outside unnoticed. She needed the quiet solitude of the gardens more than ever.

"Teresa!"

She cringed at the sound of her name in her aunt's imperious tones. Straightening her spine, she turned to face the duchess.

"I see you've decided to stop playing the invalid."

"One would hardly call being thrown from a horse an act to gain sympathy."

The duchess raised an eyebrow. "Perhaps, but we all know you would do just about anything to capture a man's attention and rescue you from becoming a spinster."

Teresa took a deep breath and released it slowly in an attempt to hold on to her temper. "I do not care if I'm a spinster, considered on the shelf, or any of those other thoughtless terms used to describe an unmarried woman older than the latest fashion."

"Really?" The tilt of her head and disbelieving tone said all that her aunt had not.

"If you have no other reason to detain me, I see no cause to stand here any longer. We both have known for a long time that we care little for each other so your opinions mean less than nothing to me." Teresa turned toward the staircase.

The duchess grabbed her arm, spinning her around. "I've watched you when you think no one is looking. I've seen the way you flaunt yourself whenever that foreign count is present." Her face contorted with fury. "Just remember, if you bring shame to yourself, you bring it to my household as well."

After nearly getting herself killed, Teresa knew all too well the consequences of her actions. "I've done nothing to be ashamed of. I've danced with the Count de Montayas only a few times and accepted his company on outings on even fewer occasions. I've done no more than Lady Sarah has with Viscount Linley."

"Do not even attempt to compare yourself to a titled lady. You are little better than a commoner's daughter. Remember that the next time you are tempted to reach beyond your station."

Teresa wrenched her arm free. "Have you forgotten that you're a commoner's daughter? Would still be one if you hadn't reached above *your* station by marrying a sickly member of the aristocracy?"

The duchess looked down the hall towards Lady Darlington's rooms. "How is your mother lately?" she asked, malice burning in her eyes. "Is she missing any of her precious portraits?"

"No, and I don't expect her to. Has Linley asked for Lady Sarah's hand yet?"

"Why do you ask? Surely, you have no hopes of snaring him for yourself. He wouldn't look twice at a drab little mouse like you."

"I'm only trying to make myself clear. If anything belonging to Mama should happen to disappear or be mislaid perhaps—"

"Are you threatening me?" the duchess interrupted.

"Not at all, I'm just wondering how eager the viscount will be to marry Lady Sarah when he finds out her true parentage or perhaps I should say her lack of it." Teresa hurried down the stairs and out into the gardens. She hated resorting to her aunt's means of controlling people through threats, but if it made things easier for Mama, she had no choice.

Skirting the formal path, she headed across the lawn to the small greenhouse tucked away at the edge of the grounds. She'd taken no more than a few steps when Betsy's voice sounded behind her.

"Where do you think you're going?"

Biting back a smile, she turned around. "The greenhouse? I can't stand to stay cooped up in that room a moment longer."

"Then it's a good thing you have a visitor."

"A visitor?" Excitement clamored in her chest. "Is it Montayas?"

The maid shook her head. "Mr. Hobson. Why don't you change into something more presentable than that horrid gown, and I'll see him into the salon."

"You don't like my dress?" Teresa teased. They'd had more than one argument over the old gardening dress with each one ending in Betsy's threat to burn it or give it to the rag collector.

"It's good enough for gardening, I suppose, but it does nothing to emphasize your beauty."

She linked her arm through Betsy's and walked up the path. "And why are you suddenly concerned with showing off my 'great' beauty?"

"You shall have to marry sooner or later," Betsy lowered her voice, "and I think Mr. Hobson would make you an excellent husband." She gave Teresa's shoulder a quick squeeze and walked toward the front of the house, leaving her charge staring after her, her mouth open in surprise.

Giving herself a mental shake, Teresa made her way up the staircase and into her bedroom. Lady Sarah's maid came out of the dressing room at the same instant carrying a mauve day dress with pale rose piping along the bodice and sleeves.

"Hello, Molly. Has Betsy roped you into helping me change?"

"Yes, you don't mind, do you?"

"Not at all." While she submitted to the maid's ministrations, Teresa wondered how the timid little woman had lasted so many years under the duchess' domineering manner. True, she did serve Lady Sarah, but Teresa was certain the duchess had a lot to do with how her daughter was presented.

In no time at all, Teresa hurried down the stairs, eager to see Blaine. Shedding her lady-like decorum, she lifted her hem and ran lightly down the long hall. Outside the door, she took a deep breath and smoothed her skirts into place. After checking that her hair hadn't slipped free of its pins, she stepped into the room.

Blaine stood in front of the long windows overlooking the gardens. She noted his flowing dark hair, elegant clothes, and highly polished Hessian boots. She waited for her heart to speed up or the sudden pulse of excitement that always overtook her whenever she was with Montayas. Nothing. Not even a tingle. She felt nothing more for Blaine than admiration for a good looking gentleman and the love one would have for a family member.

Clearing her throat, she walked toward him, her hand extended in greeting. "Blaine."

He turned and smiled. "You're looking as beautiful as ever despite your recent malady."

She accepted his compliment with a brief inclination of her head and a grin. "Surely, you didn't come all the way to Perth House just to turn my head with flattery."

His smile faltered just for a moment before he pulled it back into place. "You're right. Will you walk with me in the gardens?"

"Where's your guard?"

He rolled his eyes. "He's waiting for us outside."

Teresa led the way to her favorite stone bench and sat down. "Is something wrong?"

He sat down beside her. "How could anything be wrong? I'm sitting beside one of the loveliest women I know in a garden that would make Eve herself jealous."

"Now I know you're in some kind of trouble. When we were children, you always made the most outrageous statements to keep people from seeing the way you really felt." She took his hand in her own. "Tell me, please."

He withdrew his hand and handed her a package she hadn't realized he carried until now. "I brought you a gift. Why don't you open it so you can admire my impeccable taste?"

She gave him a long look then pulled the string from the tightly wrapped brown paper bundle. Carefully removing the paper, Teresa gave a gasp of surprise at the title of the slim leather bound book she had revealed. She touched it almost reverently. "Galileo's theories on science and the universe. How did you know I was interested in Galileo?"

He chucked her gently under her chin. "There's not much I don't know about you. Don't forget we've known each other a long time."

"I could say the same about you." She set the gift and wrappings aside. "Please tell me what's wrong."

He stared at her in silence before leaving his seat on the stone bench. "I...I'm going to France." He ran an agitated hand through his hair.

"France? Now? Why?" Teresa jumped to her feet, her gaze flying to the guard who stood a few yards away talking to one of the maids. "You can't go to France now. Not with the fighting going on. The Prince Regent will have you executed."

Blaine clasped her hands in his. "My cousin and his family need me. I have to help them. They've been accused of spying for England."

"But what can you do? You have no proof that they aren't."

"They would no more spy for Prinny than I would for Napoleon."

Teresa threw herself into his arms, tears springing to her eyes. "Please don't go. I couldn't bear it if anything happened to you."

"Pardon, I see I am interrupting."

She knew that condescending voice anywhere. She looked over her shoulder at the Count de Montayas, his mouth a thin, tight line. Disapproval emanated from him in waves.

Chapter Eleven

"Not at all." Blaine set her from him. "I was just leaving."

"Wait. Don't go. There has to be another way." She reached out to clutch at his arm, but he stepped away with a rueful smile.

"I'm afraid there isn't." With a brief nod to Montayas, he turned and walked across the lawn.

"Blaine, come back. I'll help you figure it out," Teresa called, her voice cracking with emotion.

But he never turned around, never even looked back. As he walked out the side gate, she couldn't help feeling he'd just walked out of her life. "Why won't you let anyone help you?" she whispered.

"Has he decided he hasn't the blunt to offer you carte blanche?"

Teresa spun around to face her tormentor. "That man," she pointed toward the gate, "is the closest I'll ever come to having a brother, and he came only to bring me a gift." She snatched the book from the bench but not before he saw the title.

Expecting it to be a book of poetry, he raised his eyebrows in surprise. "Books on mathematical principles are the way to your heart? Most women are happy with a bit of frippery."

"If you've come to insult me, you've accomplished it quite well. Good day." She turned on her heel and walked away, her angry strides eating up the short distance to the house.

Filled with self-loathing, Mateo muttered a particularly vulgar epithet. Why did he let his jealousy rule his tongue? He'd come to see how

Teresa was faring because he couldn't get the image of her, battered and bruised, out of his head. It haunted him during the day and tortured him in his dreams at night. And in the space of a heartbeat, he had all but accused her of being a whore.

He looked up at the windows he knew to be her rooms. Was she there right now raging over his behavior, or was she crying over the departure of Hobson? Did it even matter? He could scarcely afford to keep her in the style to which she was accustomed. There were times in his life when he considered himself lucky to have two coins at once.

Shoving his hands into his pockets, he made his way back to the carriage. After giving orders to the newly hired driver to return home, he leaned against the cushions and wondered if this entire trip to England was nothing more than an exercise in futility. He was no closer to finding the *Pequena* than he was when he arrived. The relationship between him and Eduardo was changing. And he lusted after a woman who saw him only as a threat to her family.

He looked out at the passing sights. Fashionable women promenaded about on the arms of well-dressed gentlemen. Others were patronizing expensive shops, dressmakers, and jewelers. His life was so different from all she knew.

From the moment the *Pequena* disappeared, he'd been forced to make decisions no child should have to. She believed he owned all the riches and vast estates that would accompany a title. How would she feel to find out that his great estate consisted of a ramshackle house and a mere five acres of land that he'd sell his soul to retain?

The coach rolled to a stop. He exited the carriage before the driver had a chance to open the door. Entering the townhouse, he headed for the study. Eduardo should have disposed of most of the Earl of

Leighton's valuables by now. Mateo smiled to himself. What better way to avenge Teresa's beating than to take from her attacker that which he prized above all else?

When he'd first entered the earl's residence under the cover of night two days ago, he was consumed with anger and blood lust. But upon making his way to the bedchamber, Mateo noticed the house was filled with riches. Instead of attacking the earl, he stole as many of the valuable items as he could carry in the sacks he'd fashioned from the brocade drapes in the parlor.

Mateo stopped in the doorway. The room was nearly empty of the treasures that had covered every surface just a short time ago. Eduardo stood by the window, the curtain gripped in one hand as he looked out. His sullen expression told Mateo they had not regained the easy relationship they'd shared most of their lives.

"I see you've been busy," he said, moving toward the bottle of whiskey and glasses that stood on a side table.

"I still do not understand why we have to risk our lives because you have some strange sense of honor over the Darlington woman," Eduardo replied in Spanish.

Mateo switched to his native tongue as well. "If you get rid of the earl's belongings in your usual fashion, no one will be able to trace it to us."

His cousin waved away the compliment and turned from the window. "Have you forgotten why we are here? The woman you chase after is nothing more than a means to retrieve the *Pequena*. Her father is the bastard who destroyed our families. He took not only what belonged to us, but he took the lives we should have had."

"I have forgotten nothing," Mateo said in a deadly tone, his hand tightening around his glass.

"You forget I have lost far more than you. Do not think to remind me of the losses the Montayas families have suffered."

"Yet you know nothing more about the *Pequena's* whereabouts. I am tired of this country and its insipid women." Eduardo crossed to stand behind the desk they shared.

"Don't be so certain of what you think I know. I've learned a lot by chasing after the Darlington woman," Mateo drawled.

"Have you found the jewel box?"

"No, but I'm close."

"How close?"

He sent the other man an irritated glance. "Close enough."

"If you spent less time climbing under a certain lady's skirts, it would be back in our possession by now."

Mateo swallowed the last of his drink, set the glass on the desktop, and leaned his hip against the side of the desk. "Not that it's any of your business, but I haven't been under a woman's skirts since we arrived in England."

A brief flash of disbelief crossed Eduardo's face before he spoke. "Perhaps I should try my seduction skills on her. I might have better luck and an enjoyable night for my trouble as well. Women have always preferred me to you."

Mateo lunged forward, smashing Eduardo against the nearest wall. The force of contact jolted through his body. "If you touch her, I will kill you, cousin or no," he ground out. "Stay away from her. I don't want you in the same room with her. Do you understand?"

Eduardo managed a slight nod.

Mateo released him and shoved away from the wall.

"So it's as I suspected." Eduardo rubbed the

back of his head. "You want her for yourself."

"I don't care what you think you know. Heed my warning or you'll wish to hell you had."

"Do not worry, cousin of mine. She is all yours; just remember why we are here." Eduardo turned on his heel and strode from the room.

****

Teresa entered her bedchamber with a sigh of relief. The light supper she'd shared with her aunt and cousin had been more tedious than usual. As they were attending a musicale this evening, Teresa was left to her own devices. And she had already decided what she would do.

She touched her throat, remembering what happened the last time she'd stolen into someone's home. Now was not the time to become one of the delicate, fragile women the *Ton* was so enamored with. She would protect her family's name at all costs.

Her gaze skimmed over the bed to the clothespress where her dark trousers and shirt were carefully hidden, then back to the bed. There, sitting in the center of the pale yellow satin striped quilt was a small package wrapped in paper. Curious, Teresa approached the bed and perched beside the package. She knew she hadn't put it there. Maybe it had come in the day's post and Betsy had brought here.

Removing the wrapping with care, she uncovered a well-worn book; the gold lettering stamped in the leather cover was faded and difficult to read. The pages themselves were dog-eared and well thumbed. She flipped through the book, realizing the words weren't written in English. Upon closer examination, she determined the language to be Spanish. She looked around the room, waiting for the tingling feeling that overcame her whenever Montayas was near, but it didn't happen, and he didn't materialize out of the shadows as he was wont to do.

Confused, she ran her fingers over the title. Why would he give her a book that was obviously precious to him? Was it a means of apology for his odious behavior this afternoon? She would never understand him. With one hand he pushed her away and with the other he beckoned her near. She worried her bottom lip with her teeth as she contemplated the gift.

"You sent for me?"

Teresa looked up as Betsy bustled into the room. "Yes. Would you let the staff know that I've a headache and will be retiring early?"

"You're ill?" The maid rested her hand on Teresa's forehead. "I'll call the doctor. It might be a relapse. I told you not to overdo it today."

Teresa caught her arm as Betsy started to leave the bed. "I'm not ill. I need everyone to believe I'm abed—"

"Oh, no. You are not playing the thief any longer. Have you forgotten you nearly lost your life the last time?"

"Believe me I haven't forgotten. I must do this, surely you of all people understand why." She glanced down at the book in her hands. "Montayas and I exchanged words this afternoon. I'm afraid he may be more determined than ever to bring scandal down on our heads."

Betsy clucked her tongue and shook her head. "When will you learn that sometimes holding your tongue is the better part of valor? I suppose I only have myself to blame for encouraging you to form your own opinions and to be able to debate them logically."

Teresa tried to smother a grin. "I'm afraid logic has nothing to do with Montayas. He has a way of arousing my anger with a minimum of effort."

"Accusing your father of being a thief certainly wouldn't put you on the friendliest of terms."

"And that's why I must go tonight. Lord and Lady Sexton are to attend the evening's entertainment with the Duchess and Lady Sarah. I will be able to search for the jewel box without incident." She hesitated for a moment then asked in a quiet voice, "Have you heard from Freddie?"

The maid gave a slow nod. "He still refuses to help. He said he wouldn't lead you to your own death."

"I guess I'm on my own."

"Please reconsider. Would it matter so much if Montayas found the box? He has nothing to prove that your family had anything to do with its disappearance."

"You've forgotten the *Ton* lives for scandal whether unfounded or not. If I can find it first, I can use it to buy his silence." She slid from the bed, leaving the book behind. "Will you let me know when Aunt Vivian and Sarah leave?"

Betsy released a long sigh. "Yes."

****

Teresa stood in the Sexton's garden. The trees and bushes took on sinister shapes in the dark. She suppressed a shiver and looked up at the heavens. The moon and stars seemed to have fled, leaving the sky as black as the cover of her notebook. Even the surrounding streets were still and silent as though they held their breath, as though they too knew of the danger of what she was about to undertake.

Moving forward on leaden feet, she skirted the side of the house and tried the first window she came to. When it slid open, she took it as a good sign and pushed back the curtain.

The image of Leighton's face as he tightened his hands around her throat flashed through her mind. Teresa stepped back from the window and pressed her fingers to her neck. *I can do this. The house is empty except for staff which will all be asleep by now.*

She covered her mouth with her hands and took a steadying breath then swung one leg over the windowsill and entered the house. Standing in the shadows of the room, she lit a candle and took stock of her surroundings.

Leather chairs faced a hearth where dying embers glowed in the darkness. A thick carpet covered the floor while a settee and lady's writing desk took up much of the empty space in the room. A vase of flowers sat in the center of an ornately scrolled table.

Teresa guessed she stood in Lady Sexton's drawing room. Gathering her courage, she left the corner near the window and crossed the room. She curled her fingers around the door handle and gave it a quiet turn. Releasing a pent up breath, she stepped out into a marble floored hall and closed the door behind her. A wall sconce left burning near the front door illuminated the foyer.

Blowing out her candle, she moved toward the staircase leading to the gallery and the bedchambers. Her black satin-slippered feet made no sound as she mounted the stairs, making her glad she'd had the foresight to wear them instead of her half boots.

As she gained the top step, she stopped for a moment taking in the many paintings of Sexton's ancestors lining the walls. She took one last look behind her and started down the gallery. The eyes of the portraits seemed to follow her as she passed. In her mind she heard their whispers as they told stories of the past.

She stopped in front of the master bedchamber, her hand reaching for the door handle when a door opened further down the hall. Without stopping to think, she rushed headlong into the room. Panic raced through her. She ran for the closest window. Pulling the heavy drapes aside, she pushed open the window and climbed out onto a narrow ledge.

Teresa looked up at the sky. Rain began to fall. What else could go wrong? She stepped to the side, her hands pressed flat against the rough bricks of the building, hoping against hope she was out of sight.

The sound of the interior door opening sent her climbing up over the gables and onto the roof. It was raining harder now, leaving the roof slick with water. She hurried along the slates in an effort to reach the far side. She prayed she would be able to climb back down to the ground. The rain pelted her skin, soaking her clothes.

Suddenly, her feet slipped out from under her. She landed on her stomach, sliding toward the edge of the roof. Her fingers scrabbled for anything to hold on to. She bent her legs, trying to gain purchase.

It wasn't working. *God, I'm going to die.* The thought flashed through her mind and was gone in an instant.

Down, down she slid. Teresa caught the edge of a broken slate and dug the tips of her fingers underneath it. She held on with all her might, stopping the downward momentum. Her hips were braced against the edge of the roof, her legs kicking the air.

Her heart thundered against her ribs. She looked at the ground below and a wave of dizziness crashed over her. With a shaky breath, she moved one hand to another shingle and began the painstaking process of pulling herself up the side of the roof. At the top she collapsed in fear and exhaustion, resting her cheek against the cold slates. A whimper escaped her unheeded, as her tears mingled with the rain.

She didn't know how long she lay there but knew it had been too long. Drawing her legs beneath her, she shivered from a combination of fear, exhaustion, and the icy rain. The longer she stayed on the roof, the more dangerous it became. But how to get down?

Inching to one side, she looked over the edge into black nothingness. Teresa pressed her lips together and gathered the tattered remnants of her courage. Her fingers clenched in her lap as fat drops of rain continued to splash around her. Absently, she allowed her gaze to follow the path of the water as it ran down to the rainspout where it swirled and eddied before disappearing from sight.

The rainspout! She almost dismissed it as a possibility but instead grabbed hold of it, turning it over in her mind. It might work.

And if it didn't... She wouldn't be alive to notice.

She twisted around until her back faced the spout. Gripping the slates, she slid her legs from beneath her body and prayed her cold-numbed fingers would hold her weight. With agonizing slowness, she backed down the roof until she was able to reach the edge.

Her heart hammered in her chest after what seemed a lifetime of climbing. She eased down a supporting pillar to the balcony. Teresa landed on the floor on her hands and knees, taking in great gulps of air, thankful the worst was over.

Now, she had to find a way to reach the ground level. She couldn't go into the house. Her sodden clothes and slippers would leave too many telltale clues that someone had broken into the Sexton townhouse. Teresa looked through the railing spindles, remembering Montayas dressed as the masked intruder as he leapt over the side of the balcony at Somerton House and disappeared into the night. At this moment, she would have given almost anything to know how he accomplished such a feat.

She came to her feet and ran her hand across her forehead. The rain softened into a silvery mist. The moon came out at last to illuminate the garden with pale shafts of light, changing ominous shapes to ordinary trees and bushes.

She leaned over the balustrade and tried to gauge the distance to the rolling green lawn. She could jump to the ground. After all, she'd survived being pushed out a window without a scratch. Giving herself no time for second thoughts, she climbed over the side and stood on the narrow ledge that dropped off into thin air. She rested against the railing for a moment, drawing a deep breath, then cast one final glance at the glass doors leading to the balcony.

Wrapping her hands around the ends of two spindles, she stepped off the edge and hung by her hands then let go. She landed in a crouch on the wet grass. Her hand rasped across a rough surface, but she didn't stop to examine the object. Leaping to her feet, she sped across the yard. Gone was the care to stay in the shadows to avoid being seen. Her first thought, her only thought, was to get back to her own rooms as quickly as possible.

She ran past a misshapen tree that looked like it had lost too many battles against Mother Nature and the gardener's clippers.

A hand clamped onto her shoulder, pulling her backward.

Chapter Twelve

Panic and fear spurred Teresa into motion. She whirled on her captor, striking out with her hands and feet.

"Stop. Ow." Mateo muttered an oath as her fist connected with his jaw. He gave her a slight shake while trying to dodge the blows. "It's me, Montayas."

Teresa stilled. "Montayas?"

"Yes, my brave one."

She rested her forehead on the crisp linen of his black shirt. "It's hard to be brave when one is frightened out of her wits."

Mateo gave a soft laugh and folded his arms around her. His heart still thudded in his chest. He didn't think he would ever forget the sight of her dropping down from the roof to the balcony and finally, to the ground. How she'd come to be in such a predicament, he didn't know. Wasn't sure he wanted to know.

She shivered and snuggled closer, pressing herself against him. As much as he wanted to believe it was desire behind her boldness, he knew in reality it was the cold and her wet clothes that pushed her to seek his warmth. He lifted her hand intending to press it to his lips. Feeling a sticky wetness, he turned it over. Blood oozed from a scrape along her palm.

She sucked in her breath as he ran his fingers over the cut. He reached up and pulled her mask from her head.

Teresa grabbed for it, a sound of protest escaping her. "What are you doing? What if I'm seen?"

Her hair was coiled around her head. The light breeze blew the loose strands free causing them to snake down the side of her neck.

"You won't be." He wrapped the cloth around her hand.

"How can you say such a thing? I've no coach to ride home in to keep from being seen."

Mateo removed his own mask and tied the length of material around his neck.

Teresa smiled and flicked the drooping cloth with a finger. "I've never seen a sorrier cravat in my life."

He twined a loose curl of her hair around his finger and gave it a slight tug. "And I've never seen a more interesting coiffure."

She ran her hands over her hair. "Yes, I'm certain I look quite ghastly. But the style works well under a cloth tied about one's head."

"Ghastly is not a word I would use to describe you."

She gave him a coquettish look. "I can well imagine the words you'd use."

Mateo raised his brows. "Can you? Hmmm, I shall have to put that to a test very soon. But now, as much as I am enjoying this dalliance, you shouldn't be standing about in wet clothes, and we must go before we're discovered."

She shook her head as he put an arm around her waist and guided her toward the gate. "How like a man. Always looking for an excuse to have a woman disrobe."

Mateo's shout of laughter floated away on the night air.

****

Eager to see Teresa after her roof top adventure of the night before, Mateo questioned a stable boy as to her whereabouts. Learning she was last seen on the terrace, he handed the ribbons of his phaeton to the boy and thanked him.

He knew he should present himself at the front door but walked around the side of the enormous townhouse instead. He had to find a way to keep her safe, to convince her to stop her insane attempts at house breaking before she got herself killed. But how to approach it was the problem. The lady allowed her feathers to be ruffled all too easily. It took but the slightest word from him to set her off in high dudgeon.

"Look out!"

Mateo jumped back just as a small sphere hit the ground near the toe of his boot. He picked up the orb, noting the depression in the earth caused by the impact. Closing his fingers around the object, he looked up at the balcony. Why was he not surprised to find Teresa standing there?

"Are you hurt? I'm terribly sorry," she called before disappearing from view only to reappear a few minutes later at the doorway leading to the terrace.

Mateo tossed the ball into the air and caught it. "I'm afraid if you were trying to do away with me, you shouldn't have shouted a warning."

"I wasn't trying to do anything of the sort. Heavens, why would you even think such a thing?"

"I've threatened your family's reputation or perhaps I've stolen one kiss too many." Her eyes narrowed, and he quickly changed the subject. "What were you trying to do?"

"Just this afternoon, I finished reading a paper on Galileo's experiments. I wanted to try them myself."

"What type of experiments?" Mateo grinned. He couldn't help himself. "How to crush a man's skull from a great distance?"

"If that were the case, I'd have used my bandbox filled with as many stones as I could find—not a small silver ball." Her light brown eyes danced with laughter.

"Then I shall be forever grateful that you could not find enough stones. Now, won't you tell me what you were really trying to do?"

"It is said Galileo dropped metal balls of different weights from the Tower of Pisa to show that regardless of their weight, they all fell at the same speed. I was attempting to recreate the experiment to see the results for myself."

"Do you spend all of your time reading scientific journals? Don't you read just for the pleasure of enjoying a good tale?"

"Is that why you gave me your book? I'm afraid I can't read it. I don't know how to read Spanish."

Mateo reached out and took her hand, rubbing his thumb across her palm. In the daylight, the cut she sustained really was no more than a scratch. "The book is *Don Quixote*. It is Cervantes' great work. Have you not heard of it? I'm surprised as you seem to do nothing but surround yourself with books."

Teresa pulled her hand free. "I spend time doing other things."

"Ah yes, how could I have forgotten? You also try to get yourself killed on a regular basis." He threw the orb into the air once more.

She reached out and snatched it before it could fall back into his palm. "And you are to blame. I wouldn't be in this position if it weren't for your cork-brained belief that my father stole your precious family heirloom."

For the first time, Mateo became aware of various servants milling around the area. Gardeners were busy pruning, cutting, or weeding everything in sight while members of the kitchen staff hurried to and fro with supplies from the storehouse. There were far too many ears straining to catch a tidbit to be spread as gossip later for him to broach the subject of her dangerous escapades.

Instead he gave a slight bow. "I would be honored if you would ride with me in the park."

Her suspicion of his motives was all too easy to read in her expressive face. "We'd be unfashionably early. One doesn't go to Hyde Park until late afternoon. It is where one goes to see and be seen."

"I am not interested in being seen. I wish only a few minutes of privacy with you. We have matters best not discussed in such surroundings." He drew her attention to the staff.

"We have no carriage at our disposal. The duchess and Lady Sarah have taken the only one to visit the modiste."

"Fetch your bonnet and I shall await you in the drive. My phaeton is more than adequate transportation." He turned and headed back to the front of the house.

He'd barely retrieved the vehicle from the stable boy before Teresa descended the stairs wearing a straw hat crowned with small pink flowers. She had also changed her dress and now wore a delicate green walking gown. Without a word, he handed her up into the carriage and took his own seat. With a flick of the ribbons, they were off.

Neither spoke as they headed toward Hyde Park. Perhaps this was not the best idea he'd had lately. Yet he felt compelled to ensure she stopped her search for the *Pequena*. Not so much for his sake, but for her own.

He turned into the park and slowed the horses to a walk.

Before he could say a word, she turned to him and spoke, "I believe I know what you intend to say. I will not stop looking for the jewel box."

"Surely it isn't worth your life."

She tilted her head to look at his face. "But you

deem it worth yours."

Mateo ground his teeth and struggled to maintain his temper. "Don't be a fool. It is all I have of my family's legacy. It's time you faced reality. You will never win this ridiculous game you're playing. You haven't the skills necessary to find the damn box without getting yourself killed in the process."

"However big the fool, there is always a bigger fool to admire him," she said in a smug voice.

"Now you are calling me a fool?" Mateo went from anger to amusement in the span of a few seconds.

Teresa folded her hands primly in her lap. "I am merely quoting Nicholas Boileau-Despeax. He was a seventeenth century French poet. You may make whatever inferences you like."

He pulled off the path and brought the horses to a stop, composing his face into a serious mask. He enjoyed sparring with her almost as much as he enjoyed her kisses, but this topic was no laughing matter. With a heavy sigh, he took her hand and held it in both of his. "You must stop putting yourself at risk. Neither your father's memory nor his reputation is worth it."

Teresa met his gaze. "I fear I cannot. You are determined to destroy my family. I won't, I can't, stand idly by and let you do so."

Mateo released her and ran a hand through his hair in frustration. "I swear I'd like to strangle you at times. Must you always be so stubborn?"

"A fly, sir, may sting a stately horse and make him wince; but one is but an insect and the other is a horse still." She glared at him. "That is a quote from England's own Samuel Johnson. Your threats will not deter me."

Mateo raised his brows. "The devil cites scripture for his purpose." He folded his arms over his chest and waited for her response.

"You have read Shakespeare?" She stared at him in wonder.

He gave a slight nod. "I fear I have given myself away with that quote from *The Merchant of Venice* so I can only answer in the affirmative. Why are you so surprised? Does my less than noble upbringing preclude me from such pleasures?"

As though afraid she offended him, she laid a hand on his arm. "I gave no thought to your childhood or education. It's just that so few people, other than scholars, have taken the time to study his works much less be able to quote them."

Deciding to take advantage of her momentary distraction, Mateo lifted her hand and pressed a kiss into her palm. "Won't you reconsider and let me continue the search alone? You are far too beautiful to die at the end of a rope or worse."

"What could be worse than hanging at Newgate?" Teresa curled her fingers inward. "Like you, I would sacrifice anything," she said. Her voice trembled despite her efforts to control her emotions.

He dropped her hand back into her lap. "Then we have nothing left to discuss." He gave the reins a shake and guided the horses back in the direction they had come.

"Are we returning to Perth House?"

He gave her a brief glance. "I think it's for the best."

Teresa watched him a moment longer. He was back to being the autocratic count. She felt a sense of loss she couldn't explain. When he wasn't hating her for her father's supposed crime, he was all she found appealing in a man. His teasing manner combined with the warmth of his gaze always had a strange exhilarating effect on her. But when he became stiff and formal with her, she knew he was angry.

Wishing she could bring back the persona of the masked intruder, she kept quiet during the short ride home. Perhaps he would regain his good humor by the time they arrived. If so, she would invite him to take refreshments with her on the terrace.

As they entered the drive and came closer to Perth House, she noticed another carriage present. In the space of an instant, she knew something was wrong. The carriage belonged to Doctor Watley.

"Something's happened to Mama," she cried, trying to exit the phaeton without waiting for it to come to a halt.

Montayas grabbed her with one arm locked around her waist to keep her from tumbling to the ground.

"Stop. You must stop. Something's happened to Mama." Without waiting for help, she scrambled off the seat and rushed toward the house. Teresa rushed to the top of the stairs. She kept telling herself it was nothing serious. Mama just had a slight cold. She was fine this morning when they had breakfasted together.

Catching sight of the duchess hovering near her mother's chambers, Teresa came to a dead stop causing Montayas to crash into her. His arms shot out to steady her.

Vivian met her gaze then cast an anxious glance at Sarah. "I did nothing. I swear it."

With an arm at her back, the count guided Teresa down the hall.

"What's wrong with her?" she whispered.

Lady Sarah came forward and took Teresa's hands in her own. "I don't know. I came to bring her a book she wanted to borrow and found her collapsed on the floor. I sent for the doctor while the footmen helped her to bed."

"She keeps insisting Robert is there with her," Vivian said softly.

"Oh, God. No." Teresa pushed past them. She reached for the door handle.

It pulled out of her hand as it opened from the other side. Doctor Watley stood on the threshold. He ushered her away from the door and closed it behind him. One look at his grave expression and she began to tremble.

He laid a kind hand against her cheek. "I'm sorry, my dear. It appears as though her heart gave out."

"No." Teresa backed away from him. "You're mistaken. I must see her."

The doctor shook his head. "I'd advise against it. It's better to remember her as she was not as she is now."

"No. No. She's not dead. She's not dead." Teresa covered her mouth with her hand.

Her legs crumpled beneath her. She fell to her knees. Tears streamed down her face as she wrapped her arms around her suddenly cold body. "Mama, how could you leave me?"

Mateo lifted her into his arms and looked about the hallway.

"In here." Lady Sarah opened the door leading to Teresa's bedchamber.

"He can't go in there. Send for Betsy," the duchess ordered. "I won't have Teresa's reputation sullied."

"Mother, please." Lady Sarah rolled her eyes. "He is hardly likely to ravage her now."

"Sarah!" Vivian stared at her aghast.

Mateo ignored the interchange and carried Teresa into the room. He approached the four-poster bed and gently set her on the light blue counterpane.

She clung to him, burying her face in the crook of his neck. Her tears soaked his shirtfront.

"I'm alone. I'm all alone," Teresa repeated over and over.

Mateo pulled her onto his lap. Propriety be damned. He rubbed his chin against her hair as he made soothing noises. "You're not alone. I'm here."

She lifted her head and stared at him with dark, haunted eyes. "Are you, Mateo? Are you really? Or do you deem this the perfect time to take your revenge upon my family?"

He ignored the stab of pain her question caused. Did she think so little of him that she believed he would take advantage of her loss? Instead he savored the sound of his name upon her lips though he was certain she wasn't aware of addressing him by his given name. He wanted to ask her to repeat it again and again just to hear the word roll off her tongue. But now was not the time to indulge his wants and needs.

Never had he seen his feisty lady so overcome. He felt at a loss as how to comfort her. Her anguish tore at him as if it were his own. He'd felt this helpless only once before, and he liked it less now than he did then.

A few minutes later, Betsy entered the room. Her eyes were red rimmed, a well-used handkerchief clutched in one hand. She cleared her throat and, in a shaky voice, thanked him for his kindness.

She sat down next to Teresa and stroked her arm. "It'll be all right child, you'll see."

Mateo slid from the bed and gave Teresa's hand a squeeze. "Please call on me if you should need anything." He looked at the maid. "I do mean anything."

Locked in her own pain, Teresa barely acknowledged him. He turned and left the room but not before he took one last glance at her tear-ravaged face.

Lady Sarah stood in the hall waiting for him. "She'll be all right, won't she?"

"I'm sure she will be fine in a few days. Our Miss Darlington is a very strong lady." He hoped his words sounded more reassuring to the young woman than they did to himself.

They descended the stairs and walked to the front door. "You will let me know the funeral arrangements?"

Lady Sarah nodded.

"Thank you." Mateo slowly made his way to the phaeton. For the first time in twenty years, the search for the *Pequena* seemed trivial indeed.

Three days later, Lady Darlington's family gathered at her grave. Mateo stood behind Teresa willing her his strength. When the reverend began to speak, she leaned back against Mateo's chest as though she could no longer stand on her own. He kept a firm clasp on her arms, afraid she would collapse.

While she didn't shed a tear, her pale, drawn face told him far more than any words could. Her black mourning gown only accentuated her pallor. She was suffering and filled with guilt. It was a situation he could well identify with. He had been racked with self-doubt upon his own parents' deaths, feeling as though there should have been something he could have done to prevent it.

Chapter Thirteen

Mateo rolled to his side in the vast bed, his eyes probing the darkness of the bedchamber. Something, some sound, had awakened him from his restless slumber. He quieted his breathing and listened for it again.

The creak of the door as it opened had him reaching for the pistol he kept on the bedside table. By now, he'd become accustomed to the dark and easily picked out the figure entering the room and closing the door.

He shifted to a sitting position and aimed the gun at his midnight visitor. "One more step and you're a dead man."

"That would be quite something considering I'm a woman."

"Teresa?" He set the pistol aside and lit a candle. "What are you doing here?" Concern and something close to fear raced through him.

Although she had dressed in black, she'd left her hair uncovered. The blonde strands had been scraped back and wrapped in a tight coil at the base of her neck. With the moon shining and her hair gleaming like spun gold, she could have been seen and noticed all too easily. Since her mother's death, she seemed to have no regard for her own well-being. It pained him to think that his pursuit of revenge had pushed her to this point.

She stood at the foot of the bed. "I've come to give you what you want in exchange for my family's honor."

"You cannot bargain with something you do not

have."

He settled the thin sheet closer to his waist where it'd fallen. He left his shoulders and chest bare but wished for the dressing gown draped over a nearby chair. For the first time in his life, he felt uncomfortable with his own nudity.

It wasn't a pleasant experience. He was at a loss to understand the sudden wish for modesty. At any other time, he would have enticed into his bed any woman bold enough to steal into his sleeping quarters without a second thought. But now, all he could think of was the damage Teresa's reputation would suffer if they were discovered in such intimate surroundings.

She moved to sit on the bed near his hip. "True, I haven't found the jewel box, but I have something else."

Mateo slid a few more inches of space between them under the pretense of shifting his position. "And that would be?"

"Me."

"You? I don't understand."

"You want me. You've told me so yourself. I will give myself to you if you swear not to besmirch my family's reputation."

Mateo nearly choked on his tongue at her words. Never had he expected such an outrageous proposal. Not from this fiery temptress who could slay a man with mere words.

"What?" His voice sounded strangled even to his own ears.

Teresa smiled then. A small, sad smile. "You've changed your mind."

"No! No, I haven't. I still find you desirable, but I know you too well." He laid his hand over hers. "This isn't in your nature. To offer the use of your body like a common whore."

"I fear I'm not myself any longer. Since you've

come into my life, I've done things, said things I would never have dreamed of. But now... Either I can strike this bargain with you, or I can continue to try to find the *Pequena* on my own. And we both know I will be far more successful in getting myself killed than anything else."

"Just because you feel you have a choice doesn't mean that either of them is the right thing to do."

"Perhaps not." Teresa scooted closer. "But this one is by far the better." She leaned forward, set her hand on his chest, and pressed her lips to his.

He grasped her arms, pushing her away and ending the kiss before it had a chance to begin. He stared at her in the flickering light of the candle.

Her eyes were dark, the pupils large. In the dim light, he could barely detect where her irises ended and the pupils began. Was it fear or desire that caused the effect? Though he was surprised by her bold intrusion into his bedchamber, he wagered the answer to his question was fear.

He ran his hands down her arms. If he led her to believe he'd accepted her bargain, perhaps he could frighten her into withdrawing the offer. Far better for her to change her mind than to think he rejected her. And she would, no matter how gently he worded it. She had to see that this bargain was no bargain at all. It would strip her of her self-respect and leave her with nothing.

Having decided on his course of action, he cupped her chin and ran a thumb over her bottom lip. "Are you sure you want to do this?"

Teresa shivered at his touch and met his gaze. Could she do this? Could she offer her body to a man who had no feelings for her other than as a means to achieve vengeance on her family? It seemed much easier this morning in the greenhouse when she'd come up with the plan. The Darlington name was the only legacy her parents had left her. She wouldn't see it dragged through the mud regardless of the cost.

But if making love to him would keep her family's reputation from harm, wasn't it worth it? For, on her part, it would be making love. Somehow, her feelings for the notorious Count de Montayas had strayed from antagonism to something deeper. An emotion she was afraid to put a name to or even voice aloud when she was alone.

Taking a deep breath, she was finally ready to answer his question. "I know what I'm doing."

Skepticism flashed in his eyes. "You would sacrifice your virginity for a dead man's honor? What of your future husband?"

Teresa shrugged. "I have no plans to marry so I'm not depriving a future husband of his right to a pure and untouched bride."

"Very well, then." Mateo drew her alongside his length and kissed her eyes, the tip of her nose, her cheeks, and finally her mouth.

Teresa forgot her momentary misgivings as he touched her. He drank from her lips as though he could never get enough of the taste of her.

He pulled her closer. His hands trailed down her back to the small waist and finally to the curve of her buttocks. He released her lips to press kisses to her jawline and down the sensitive cord in her neck.

She reveled in the feel of his naked chest beneath her palms. Her fingers roamed across the muscled expanse. She followed the line of dark hair down his stomach to where it disappeared under the thin cotton sheet.

Mateo shuddered and grabbed her hand preventing her from exploring further. Shifting to lie between her legs, he groaned at the feel of her against him. His arousal was strong and fierce. He wanted nothing more than to take action and lead them to the inevitable conclusion. But he couldn't.

He would hate himself just as surely as she would hate him afterward.

Breaking the kiss, he sat up. "We have to stop," he rasped.

"Why? Did I do something wrong?"

How could he answer that when it was all he could do not to pull her back into his arms?

Teresa turned her head away. His kisses always left her feeling weak and filled with longing. But it was nothing like this. With each touch of his mouth and hands, a desperate ache blossomed and grew. "You make me feel wanton," she whispered.

"*Wanton?*" I do not know this word. It means?"

Teresa bit her lip and stared at him as she tried to decide the best way to explain the term. Her instincts told her to use words, but her body was telling her other things. She wanted to know if she affected him the way he did her. Making up her mind, she moved close and rubbed against him.

A jolt roared through his entire body when, with a boldness he would never have guessed she possessed, she slipped her tongue past his lips and into his mouth. He gave into the sensations for a brief moment before his tarnished sense of honor reasserted itself. His chest heaved as he fought to control his body's unruly desires.

"I like *wanton*," he said with a devilish grin, "but not here and not tonight."

Mateo moved to sit on the side of the bed. He reached for his robe, thrust his arms into the sleeves, and tied it at his waist. "If we don't stop now," he ran a shaky hand over his face before looking at her over his shoulder, "we'll do something you will regret for the rest of your life."

"I won't regret it." Teresa crawled to his side and ran her fingers down the side of his face. "Ever."

He caught her hand, brought it to his mouth and kissed the soft skin of her palm. "You are encouraging me to do things I shouldn't."

She gave him a flirtatious grin. "When have you ever needed encouragement?"

He laughed. "Never when I am near you."

"Perhaps it is only when we are together that our true natures appear. Why do you think that is?"

Mateo knew she was right. When he was with her, his obligations didn't seem so important, so burdensome, but her presence should have brought them into focus not the opposite. "We both have nothing to lose. You know my secrets, and I know yours."

"As you say, we have nothing to lose," she whispered.

He caught her hands and leaned toward her until their breath mingled and the hair's breadth between their mouths became sheer torture. "Make no mistake Teresa, I want you. But only when you desire me for myself, the man that I am and not for my word of honor or a promise to keep your family's reputation intact."

Teresa pulled away and left the bed. She moved into the shadows hoping the darkness would hide her burning cheeks. Humiliation writhed within her like a living thing. How could she have been so naïve to think that she could strike such a bargain? She, who chased away some of the most eligible men of the *Ton* every time she opened her mouth.

She curled her hand against her heart and felt warm skin. Embarrassment flashed anew. He had managed to loosen the fastenings on her shirt, and she hadn't even been aware of it, so lost in the swirl of sensations that flooded over her. With fumbling fingers, she hurried to button it.

Funny. He was right after all. She would have regretted it if he'd taken her at her word and bedded her. Oh, she still wanted to make love to him, but she wanted him to do it for the same reasons he stated to her—because he wanted her and only her, not just the chance to bed a willing virgin.

"Teresa?"

She turned to look at him. In the time it had taken to straighten her clothing, he'd dressed in breeches and a clean linen shirt.

"Regrets already?" he asked quietly.

She gave a wan smile. "Perhaps."

"Come." He held out his hand. "I'll see you home, and you can tell me how a woman such as yourself knows the meaning of the word *wanton* and I, a man of the world, do not."

She giggled. It slipped out before she could control the burble of laughter. He had taken an awkward situation and defused it completely with his question.

She crossed the room and took his hand. "It is amazing what one can learn from books and study."

He looked down at her, a frown appearing on his face. "I don't think I want to know what one does to learn about this subject."

Teresa laughed again. It felt so good to be happy again even for a short time. Since Mama's death, sadness and loss weighed on her like a wet wool cloak. She hugged his arm. "Perhaps there is an experiment or two I'm willing to share on the journey to Perth House."

"Really?" Mateo leered at her. "Then I think we shouldn't linger here. He clasped her hand more firmly and led her into the hall.

After a few steps, he came to a halt. "Did I ever tell you I was a very eager student when I was a lad?"

Chapter Fourteen

With a languid stretch, Teresa opened her eyes and took pleasure in the stripe of sunlight that lay across her bed. She had tumbled into bed the night before without giving a thought to closing the drapes. The warmth felt like a caress on her skin. Her lashes fell closed, and she curled into the blankets, letting her thoughts drift.

Suddenly the memory of last night came back with startling clarity. She turned onto her back and, with a groan, clasped a hand to her forehead. How could she have done something as shameful as offering her body to Montayas? She'd never be able to face him without feeling the sting of embarrassment. What must he think of her? She wished for all the world that just once she had better control over her impetuous nature.

In her mind's eye, Montayas' sheet-clad figure floated tantalizingly. All of the glorious sensations aroused by his mouth and hands came rushing back. A disturbing knot began to form in her stomach as she ran a finger over her lips.

She yearned to feel his touch just as she longed to learn the hard contours of his body. Her eyes snapped open. "Mad. I have gone completely mad," she muttered, tossing the blankets aside.

Pulling the cord to summon Betsy, she paced back and forth. Would Montayas avoid her now? Why couldn't she be more experienced in the ways of men? She'd always prided herself on her ability to reason through difficult situations. And now, there seemed to be no way out of her present predicament.

A knock on the door sounded as she turned and began her trek toward the window once more.

"Come in," she called, still mulling over the problem of facing Montayas in the near future. She turned to retrace her steps and came to an abrupt halt.

It wasn't Betsy who leaned against the closed door. The Duchess of Perth eyed her with an unreadable expression. Disquiet tightened Teresa's nerves. Surprise was the last thing she should have felt. She'd expected this visit long before now.

"Aunt Vivian," she acknowledged the woman with a nod.

"There are things we need to discuss."

Hoping to forestall the inevitable, Teresa gestured to the bell pull. "Betsy is on her way up."

"We won't be interrupted. She's been given orders to stay below stairs until I send for her."

"She is *my* maid." Teresa felt her temper begin to rise.

Vivian arched a brow. "And she lives in my home."

For how long? Teresa had expected her aunt to make it known that she would have to find new living quarters within days of Mama's death. Now, nearly a fortnight later, it seemed the duchess had come to do just that. In an effort to conceal her agitation, Teresa turned to the clothespress and perused the contents as if she had no other concerns than which dress to wear.

"I'm must say I'm surprised to hear you refer to her as a mere servant. You allow her too much familiarity."

Teresa allowed the comment to pass unnoticed.

When she failed to respond, Vivian cleared her throat, her annoyance at Teresa's lack of respect filling the air.

With a sigh Teresa sat on the bed. This was the

last thing she wanted to deal with this morning.

The duchess advanced into the room. "I've come to offer you a bargain."

Teresa cringed. That was one word she didn't want to hear ever again. A flush heated her cheeks at the memory of last night's disastrous outcome of her own attempt at bargaining.

Vivian took a seat on the divan, smoothing her skirts into place. She looked at Teresa from under lowered lashes. "One that is in both our best interests."

A hysterical laugh threatened to escape Teresa. The duchess never did anything to benefit anyone but herself. "I'm listening."

"As you know, upon your father's death, I allowed your mother and yourself to move into Perth House."

"I believe it was the current Duke of Perth who allowed us to live here just as he allows you and Lady Sarah to do the same."

The duchess tightened her lips into a frown of displeasure at being reminded of the fact.

"But now," Teresa continued, "that Mama has died, you feel no remorse in casting me out into the street."

Her eyes slitted in anger, the duchess gave Teresa a malevolent glare. "It's true I feel no loyalty to you. But I would suffer even your presence if it will safeguard Sarah's future as a viscountess."

"I'm surprised you'd settle for such a lowly title. Why not dangle Lady Sarah a little longer? Who knows she may catch an earl or even a duke." Teresa couldn't keep the bitterness from her voice.

Vivian patted her flawless coiffure. "Really dear, jealousy does little to enhance even your charms."

"Just get to the offer," Teresa said through gritted teeth.

"You may stay on at Perth House in the same

manner as you are now until after Sarah's marriage to Viscount Linley."

"I hadn't realized he'd offered for her."

A sly smile crossed the duchess' face. "He hasn't yet, but he will."

"And what do you want in return for allowing me to live here?"

"You will keep your suspicions regarding Sarah's parentage to yourself. If the slightest whiff of scandal touches her, I won't hesitate to destroy you."

Since she had no intention of ever revealing such hurtful information, Teresa didn't hesitate to agree. "Done." She stood. "Now if you will excuse me, I'd like to dress and attend to my experiments in the greenhouse."

Vivian rose, her nose wrinkled in distaste. "No wonder every eligible man in the *Ton* treats you like the pariah you are. Men don't like women who grub about in the dirt like pigs digging for truffles." She swept from the room before Teresa could respond.

"Oh, I hate that woman, aunt or not," Teresa exclaimed to the empty room.

She walked to the clothespress to retrieve one of the older gowns she wore when working with her plants. Her hand closed around a yellow muslin dress faded to the color of parchment from age and wear.

Suddenly, the duchess' last words rang in her ears. *"Men don't like women who grub about in the dirt..."* Could that be why Montayas had refused her? Yet his kisses told of his desire. Or was that a merely a ploy to gain her confidence? And then there was his claim of wanting her. But surely that meant nothing. Many men wanted to enjoy a woman's charms with no more motive than lust to drive them on.

Why did she feel so confused? She tried to

examine her relationship with Montayas much the same way she would her various experiments: with an analytical mind. Taking only facts into account with no room for her own hopes of what the results would be. Each time she tried to apply the same methods of reasoning, everything became hopelessly tangled with her feelings for the man.

"Are you expecting that gown to attack you?"

Teresa jumped at the sound of Betsy's voice. The maid stood in the doorway, her arms filled with fresh linens for the bed.

"What?"

"The dress, child. You've got that sleeve in a death grip. Keep it up much longer, and I'll have to send it downstairs to have the wrinkles removed."

Feeling unaccountably foolish, Teresa smoothed her hand over the sleeve down to the frayed cuff. "It's the duchess. She makes me so angry sometimes."

"Most of the time, I'd say." Betsy dropped the clean laundry on the bed and closed the door. "What has she done?"

"She's allowing me to continue living here at Perth House."

"How very gracious of her," the maid muttered as she laid the yellow gown on the bed and gestured for her charge to turn around.

****

Teresa pushed open the greenhouse door, afraid of the state her plants would be in. The smell of earth and blooming flowers rushed to greet her. The heavily perfumed air gave her hope. She'd neglected them for far too long.

Setting the few books she carried on a nearby table, she hurried between the rows of wooden tables covered with a profusion of greenery. Her steps slowed as she approached a smaller table set apart from the rest.

They had to be all right. Violets had always been Mama's favorite flower. Teresa grew them year round, picking bunches and filling her mother's room with the delicate blossoms. Her fingers fluttered over the deep purple petals, the fragile stems, and green leaves. A sigh of relief escaped her. They were as hardy as ever. She stuck a finger in the dirt to check for moistness. A smile curved her lips. Betsy or one of the other servants must have been more diligent than she had been lately when it came to keeping the plants watered.

With one last brush of a fingertip over the velvet softness, she turned away and began taking stock of the numerous plants lining the tables. She plucked a few dead leaves and withered blooms here and there but overall, they were thriving despite her long absence. She must remember to find out who cared for the plants and thank them.

Finally, she cleared a small spot on one of the tables she often used for transplanting new seedlings and sat down to make a few notes on the ideas she wanted to try with a new variety of ivy. The sun streamed through the upper portion of the large glass panes that made up the wall. It warmed her and made her feel slightly drowsy. She laid aside her quill pen, careful not to overturn the bottle of ink, and reached for the small book she'd brought as an afterthought.

If pressed, she wouldn't have been able to explain why she'd done so. She traced the faded gold letters with the tip of her finger. "Why did Montayas give you to me?" she asked the weathered tome as she carefully opened the worn leather cover.

Mindful of the deteriorating binding, she turned the first few pages. "I can't even read it. Of all the languages I have mastered, unfortunately Spanish isn't one of them."

She tried to use her knowledge of French,

Greek, and Italian to pick out at least a few words where she might be able to guess at their meaning. A sudden sound in the quiet room drew her attention to the door.

"Mateo—um Montayas!" She leapt to her feet, knocking the bench over in her haste.

He looked as dashing as ever in polished Hessian boots, black trousers, and waistcoat. The deep blue of his topcoat made the white linen of his shirt appear stark in comparison to the darkness of the rest of his attire.

His lips quirked at her use of his given name.

"I didn't expect you." She closed the book and tried to slip it unnoticed under her notebook.

He came forward and righted the bench. "Did I not tell you last night I would pay a call on you this morning?" He raised an eyebrow in inquiry. "Or didn't you hear me in your haste to vacate my carriage?"

Teresa felt her cheeks heat with embarrassment. "A gentleman would not remind a lady of her indiscretions."

He grinned. "If you recall, I do not claim to be a gentleman."

"As you are so fond of telling me. Do you have a purpose for this visit or have you come just to torment me?"

Mateo leaned against the wooden table and brought her hand to his lips. "After your most interesting proposal of last evening, do I need another reason?"

Teresa snatched her hand away. "A gentleman would not even refer to it."

"Not a gentleman?" He laid a hand over his heart. "I'm wounded."

"No more than you will be if you persist in mocking me over something I deeply regret and wish never happened." She wandered away from the table and gazed out the window.

The well-trimmed yew hedges offered little in the way of a view. "Someday I will better rule my impetuous nature instead of letting it rule me," she said more to herself than to him.

She wasn't aware that he approached until his hands warmed her shoulders. "Never regret coming to me last night. I meant no offense in teasing you. I find myself deeply honored that you would offer me something as precious as your virginity."

Teresa shifted uneasily under his touch. "Apparently not as precious as your family heirloom."

"No, not as precious. Even more so. Do you have any idea how difficult it was for me to let you go?" His voice deepened. "The woman who haunts my dreams was suddenly before me in my bedchamber asking me to make love to her." He paused for a moment, tightening his hold. "But for all the wrong reasons."

Turning in his arms, she looked at him in amazement. "I haunt your dreams?"

"Me tientas a mas no poder," he whispered, lowering his mouth to hers.

Teresa met him halfway. She yearned for his kiss, hungered for it in a way she would never have dreamed possible. If her father had had the same effect on Mama, then she could understand her mother's devotion a little bit better.

Mateo feathered teasing kisses against her mouth. He traced her lower lip with his tongue. Teresa gasped at the sensation and he took advantage by deepening the kiss.

She slid her hands over his chest. He shuddered and pulled her closer. She ran her fingers through his hair. It was as silky as she had imagined.

She opened her eyes to find him watching her, the velvet blackness of his gaze dark and intense.

Feeling awkward, she touched the nape of his neck before stroking his throat. "You're not wearing a cravat."

Instead of the usual length of cloth tied into an intricate knot, he wore a thin black strip of what looked to be a ribbon around his collar and tied in a bow.

He touched it briefly before resettling his hand on her waist. "This is what we wear in Spain. I hate to wear your English cravats. I feel as though I am being strangled."

She smiled and ran her fingers down the bronze column of his neck. "I like this better," she whispered and brought his head down to hers.

His hands roamed over her body, seeming to be everywhere at once, skimming down her back to the curve of her buttocks. Sliding upward to cup the fullness of her breasts all the while never stopping the torment of his lips.

Mateo urged her back against the glass wall. She felt the hard length of him burning through the layers of her clothes, bringing her to her senses. "Stop," she panted.

He growled deep in his throat and continued to kiss the throbbing pulse at the base of her neck.

"Montayas..." His name whispered away on a sigh as he thumbed her breast.

"Mateo," he said.

"What?" Sensation clouded her thoughts.

"You called me Mateo before, say it now." He slanted his lips over hers, his arms going around her to work at her buttons.

She caught his hands and held them in her own. "No."

"No?" He rested his forehead against hers, fighting to regain control.

"We can't. Not here. Someone could walk in at any moment."

He gave her a devilish grin and nipped at her earlobe. "We could lock the door."

"And what good would that do, the walls are made of glass. Oh, my God." She covered her mouth with her hand and whirled around to face the wall they had just been pressed against. "What if someone saw us?"

"No one did," Mateo said in a calm tone that did nothing to quiet the fear clamoring within her.

"How can you be sure?"

"If someone saw us, wouldn't they have burst in here to defend your honor?"

"I don't know." She bit her lip. "They may have decided to report to the duchess instead." How could he stand there so calm when her reputation may be in ruins?

"Teresa, look at me." Mateo forced her to turn and face him. "No one saw us. The hedges outside grow too close to the building for anyone to pass between them, and they are too thick for anyone to see through them. Isn't that why you have no plants along this wall?"

"Yes. I've been after the duchess for years to have the bushes removed, but I think she leaves them there to spite me." She stepped around him, straightening her clothing as she moved.

Mateo hoped his words were true for both their sakes. Now that he had calmed her fears, he was glad he neglected to mention that they could still have been seen through any of the other walls. He supposed this was why people didn't actually live in glass houses—a distinct lack of privacy. He would have to take care in the future to keep a tight rein on the madness that compelled him to throw aside his usual cautious nature whenever he was around her.

"What did you say before you kissed me? You spoke Spanish."

Mateo glanced at her and gave a self-depreciating shrug. How could he tell her that she tempted him beyond reason when he already regretting telling her she haunted his dreams? "It was nothing."

"Nothing?"

This time it was her turn to look skeptical.

"I just said how beautiful you look."

"Oh."

"You sound disappointed."

"No. It just sounded so much prettier in your language."

Mateo cast his gaze around the room eager to find some way to change the subject before he lost his head and took her in his arms again. He reached for the two books lying forgotten on the table. "What were you working on when I came in? Another of your experiments?"

Teresa scooped up the books before he had a chance to do more than recognize the smaller tattered volume.

She clutched them to her chest. "Yes. Yes, I was updating some notes. Jotting down ideas I would like to try in the winter garden."

"A winter garden? You have months before winter sets in."

"One must plan ahead."

He rubbed his jaw. "I see. And what would the story of Don Quixote have to do with gardens of any sort?"

Mateo watched in amusement as she flushed a fiery red. It amazed him that she could be bold enough to slay a man with words, break into her friends and neighbors' homes, and yet become embarrassed and tongue-tied over the mention of a mere book.

"I believe you have indeed come here this morning to torment me." She tightened her hold on the books.

"Not at all. I actually came to offer you a modified version of your bargain."

Teresa groaned. "I thought we agreed to forget that dreadful turn of events."

"Come, sit down." He gestured to a corner illuminated by sunlight where a small iron bench sat.

He grasped her hand and led her to the cushioned seat. Taking the books from her unresisting hold, he set them between their bodies, creating a respectable distance. "I propose that we search for the *Pequena* together."

"Together?"

"We are already searching the same houses. We have the same group of people whom—"

"Except for my father," Teresa interrupted.

"Perhaps I have revised my original theory about Sir Darlington."

She clasped his hand in both of hers. "You mean you no longer believe he is a thief?"

"No, I mean I am reserving judgment instead of condemning him outright. That maybe he didn't act alone or was framed to look guilty."

Teresa jumped up from the bench. "This is wonderful. I had given up trying to convince you of Papa's innocence."

"Let's wait until we find the *Pequena* before we start celebrating the innocence of your father."

"Of course." She waved away his cautionary words. "Whose townhouse shall we search next? Have you eliminated anyone from your list yet?"

Mateo laughed at her sudden enthusiasm. "If you come sit with me and stop flitting around the room like a butterfly, I'll tell you."

Teresa perched on the edge of her seat with an air of expectancy.

"First, you have to promise me you won't

continue searching alone. And no matter where we find the *Pequena*, we deal with the consequences together."

"Agreed."

"Within the next two days, Laurence Crenshaw will be leaving London on a short business trip to Calais."

"Papa's man of affairs?" Teresa frowned. "Surely you don't believe he did it? The man has been afraid of his own shadow since he returned with Papa from his last war campaign."

"Looks and mannerisms can be deceiving. After all, I am living proof of that."

"Very well. When shall we investigate his quarters?"

"*We* won't be. I will." Mateo braced himself for the coming outburst.

"You just said we would—"

"I know what I said, but Crenshaw lives in a less than savory part of town. I'd rather not worry about your safety."

"What could go wrong? I'd be with you."

Mateo dropped a quick kiss on her nose. "Your confidence in me is flattering, but I won't be swayed. You *will* stay home and out of harm's way. Promise me that."

Teresa huffed her displeasure. "I promise. Will you come and tell me what you find?"

"As soon as I leave his lodgings." He picked up the small book and held it in front of her. "Now will you tell me why you have this with you if you can't read it?"

She took it from him and studied the cover. "I was trying to pick out a few words using my knowledge of other languages." She hesitated for a moment. "And wondering why you'd given it to me. You never have properly explained."

He shrugged. "I can't explain it. The story was a

favorite of mine when I was a boy. My father would read me parts of it every night before I went to sleep. After," his voice hardened, "after the disappearance of the *Pequena*, our family's good fortune came to an end. We suffered one financial loss after another. Our social standing became nothing more than a joke to the villagers. They believed we had lost the grace of God when that damn jeweled box went missing. We no longer had the respect due a member of the *aristocracia*."

"*Aristocracia?*"

"The closest meaning is the equivalent of a member of the *Ton*." He shifted restlessly on the bench as painful memories tumbled through his mind.

"What happened?" Teresa asked as though sensing his need to talk.

"We were able to keep the debt collectors at bay at least while my father was alive. A mere two days after his death, the money hungry scavengers descended upon us. In the end, the creditors left nothing of the slightest value behind."

"I'm sorry you suffered at the expense of others' greed." Teresa laid her hand over his.

Her touch soothed away old hatreds. But nothing could make him forget the humiliations suffered by his *madre*. He turned his palm upward and closed his fingers around hers.

"That," he gestured toward the book, "was the only thing of any value I was able to retain."

She carefully turned it in her hands. "I hate to admit that I would never have guessed it to be worth more than any other well-read volume."

"It is more sentimental than monetary." He touched a corner where the leather had torn away. "We have been through many adventures, Don Quixote and I, both real and imaginary."

Teresa looked up at him, her manner hesitant.

153

"Would you read some of it to me?"

"Now?" He stalled for time, unsure how to react to her simple request.

Sitting here together, bathed in sunlight, made him wish for things that could never be but if he read aloud to her...it would create an even greater intimacy between them.

"Just a few pages," she pleaded.

Unable to resist her, he took the book she offered and opened to the first page. At first, he felt awkward. His words were stilted as he translated the sentences into English before reading them aloud but after a few moments he found a comfortable rhythm.

Teresa moved closer, settling in against his side. He lifted an arm and rested it at her waist as he continued to read. Soon he lost himself in the story of a poverty-stricken man who lived his fantasy of being a gallant knight defending his fair maiden's honor, fighting windmills that he saw as giants, seeking new quests to win her love.

As he began to turn another page, she stopped him. "Would you read a few lines in Spanish?"

"But you won't understand it."

"Please."

Her amber-colored eyes drew him in, making it nearly impossible to deny her anything. He flipped the page and began speaking in his native tongue.

"It's so beautiful, almost musical," she whispered, as though not wanting to interrupt him but unable to keep from voicing her thoughts.

Mateo smiled and continued to fill the room with words.

Teresa laid her head on his shoulder. He shifted position to make her more comfortable.

Time passed unnoticed until he realized the sun had left them and moved on to another part of the room. He stared down at the sleeping woman nestled beside him. He wasn't sure when he became aware that she'd fallen asleep, only that he was loath to disturb her.

Setting the book aside, he touched the stray wisps of hair that had come loose from the coil at her neck. He longed to remove the pins and run his hands through the honey-colored softness. Even more importantly, he wished he were worthy of her.

With gentle fingers, he caressed her cheek. Perhaps he had found his own Dulcinea.

Chapter Fifteen

Teresa paced between the dressing table and the balcony doors. Each time she came to the opening, she looked out.

A few tree branches rustled in the breeze, but other than that nothing moved in the garden below. Moonlight and darkness battled for supremacy. The grounds would be illuminated only to be cast into shadow moments later as clouds moved overhead.

Where was he? The clock had struck three long ago. Had he forgotten his promise to come and tell her how he fared in his search of Crenshaw's lodgings?

Teresa grew more restless with each passing moment. A growing sense of alarm pushed her toward the iron balustrade. A mere whisper of a wind raised the fine hair on her arms. She shivered and tightened the belt on her pale blue satin dressing gown.

Leaning over the railing, she scanned the dark pockets along the hedges and ivy-covered stone walls surrounding the property. Unable to wait any longer, she ran to the clothespress, grabbed a woolen cloak, and hurried from the room.

Her feet flew down the stairs as though they barely touched them. She skirted the empty foyer and slipped inside the library. Once beside the ornate French doors leading to the terrace, she hesitated. Was she making a mistake? What if while she waited outside in the garden, Mateo awaited her in the bedchamber? Oh why hadn't they discussed a meeting place for all this intrigue?

She would stay in the garden only a few minutes. If he failed to arrive, she'd return to her room. Her decision made, Teresa settled the cloak over her shoulders and walked out into the night air.

The cold from the flagstones seeped through her thin slippers. She had brought the cloak only as a means to hide the light color of her dressing gown. But now, she was grateful for the warmth. Creeping along the edge of the terrace, she searched the grounds for anything out of the ordinary.

After a few minutes, her shoulders slumped and a sigh escaped her. Her toes were fast becoming numb. It was time to return to her bedchamber. She turned away just as a slight movement caught her eye. Swinging around, she scanned the near wall, certain whatever she'd seen hadn't been her imagination.

A figure dropped to the ground, stayed in a crouched position, then rose.

Mateo! He came. She knew he would keep his word.

As she started forward, ready to call out to him, he suddenly staggered. He braced a hand on the stone wall, legs apart, his head hanging forward.

Something was wrong.

Teresa crossed the grassy expanse with no thought to the wet dew that clung to her hem and ruined her slippers, her whole being intent on him. He took great gulps of air. His chest heaved as if he'd run the distance to Perth House.

"Mateo?" Concern pushed her forward.

His head swiveled around at the sound of her voice. The moonlight chose that moment to win the battle against the night. It shone down on him, making it easy to see the pain etched on his face. His eyes were blacker than she had ever seen them.

"What happened?" She grabbed his arm as he swayed.

157

He cried out at her touch, and she released him instantly. His sleeve had felt warm and wet. Teresa looked down at her hand. Blood.

"You're hurt."

"Really, I would never have known without your brilliant observation," he ground out, his injured arm hanging limp at his side.

She raised her brows at his remark. "But apparently not too badly as you still have your sarcastic tongue. You should sit down." She turned in a small circle, looking for the nearest stone bench.

The greenhouse caught her eye. "Do you think you can make it to the greenhouse?"

He glanced in the direction she pointed and nodded. "After getting over that wall, anything else has to be easier."

Teresa wrapped his uninjured arm around her waist, ready to take his weight should he need to lean on her. Instead, he shook her off and with a deep breath, trudged onward. She stayed by his side, watching him carefully as they traversed the lawn.

Mateo ignored her hovering presence, focusing on the glass house looming in the darkness. After what seemed a lifetime, she pushed the door open and guided him to a nearby table, helping him to straddle the bench alongside. He leaned back against the wall, never so relieved to sit down. At least he was saved the indignity of falling on his face while trying to get to this infernal place.

The room tilted crazily. Mateo closed his eyes in an effort to stop the motion. Blood coursed down his arm, dripping from his fingers to the carefully swept floor. Making his way to her had taken more out of him than he realized until this very moment.

"Where is Eduardo?"

Teresa's voice seemed to come from a great distance. Soft and gentle like the hum of a bee. He forced his eyes open. She stood no more than a few feet away, a burning candle in one hand, and a small wooden case in the other.

"Eduardo?" He frowned. Why did she ask for his cousin?

"Yes. Isn't he with you?" She took off her cloak and sat beside him, placing her items on the table.

"No, I didn't want to risk drawing attention by taking a carriage into East London at this time of night."

"He doesn't know you've been hurt?" She arranged a bunch of empty clay pots around the candle.

"Not unless he's suddenly developed second sight." He gave the pots a puzzled glance. "What are you doing? I dare say this isn't the time to be fiddling about with your plants."

She looked away, but he caught sight of her slight smile. "I'm only protecting the flame and ensuring none of the leaves are too close to it. Now, you mean to say you came here without a care to yourself first?"

Mateo shrugged, then groaned as pain streaked down his arm. "Had a promise to keep."

Teresa shook her head and reached for his shirt, slipping the buttons free. As she pulled it off his shoulder, Mateo shifted to allow the material to fall down his arms.

Her sudden exclamation told him she had uncovered the wound. He saw his pain reflected in her deep brown eyes. Turning his gaze away, he examined his arm, seeing the slash ranging across his biceps for the first time.

"How?"

"Your Mr. Crenshaw isn't nearly the coward you think. He didn't hesitate in the slightest to attack an unarmed man."

"Crenshaw! He was supposed to be out of town." She took a square cloth from the box, folded it, and pressed it to the wound.

"Apparently, he returned early."

"You said 'unarmed.' You carry no weapon though you stressed to me numerous times the danger of East London?" Teresa peeked under the cloth. Satisfied the bleeding had stopped, she laid it aside.

"I didn't expect to be on the street long enough to meet up with anyone. Nor did I expect to run into Crenshaw."

"He attacked you without warning?"

"He had his reasons considering I was rifling through his belongings."

Teresa probed the laceration. "This will need to be closed with needle and thread."

"Can you do it?" Mateo tried to ignore the throbbing ache pulsing through his arm.

"Me?" Teresa shook her head. "I'm afraid my skill with a needle is abominable. A drunken sot could sew straighter stitches than I."

"No matter." He eased the shirt onto his shoulders. "It will heal regardless."

"No, wait." She put a hand on his chest and took a deep breath. "I'll do it."

Teresa pulled the wooden box near and sorted through the contents, placing a length of black floss in her lap.

"Do you always keep medicinal supplies among your plants?"

"Betsy insisted on it after I cut my hand on a broken pot last year." She threaded the small sewing needle. "Are you certain about this? I have no spirits to help lessen the pain."

Mateo nodded, closed his eyes, and waited for the first prick of the needle. When none came, he opened his eyes to find Teresa staring at a point over his shoulder, her breathing shallow.

"Teresa?"

She met his gaze with a wan smile. "I find I am a bit queasy."

"Leave it then. I'll have Eduardo see to it on the morrow."

"No. I said I would do it and I will." She moved closer, positioning his arm on the table.

Mateo subsided against the wall. He flinched at the first pull of thread through his skin. Sweat beaded on his forehead and upper lip. With each stitch, the fire in his arm built. Nausea washed over him in waves. He gritted his teeth against the pressure of the floss binding his skin together, determined to make it through the ordeal without a sound.

She must have noticed the effects her ministrations were having on him for she hesitated. "Shall I stop for a bit?"

"Keep going." His voice was both hoarse and gruff all at once. He wouldn't be able to take it if she stopped only to start again.

"Just a few more."

Sure her words were meant to be encouraging, Mateo tried to concentrate on her nearness rather than the pain clawing at him. He tried without success to capture the muted scent of roses she always wore. The damn room was filled with flowering plants each vying with the other to perfume the air.

"Done." Teresa laid the sewing implement aside.

Mateo wasn't certain which of them heaved the bigger sigh of relief and wondered if he was as pale as she.

Taking a length of cloth, she quickly bandaged his arm. She moved in close and gave him a quick hug. "I'm sorry."

As she made to stand, he pulled her into his embrace, his uninjured arm sliding down the satin of her dressing gown to rest at her hip. His lips hovered above hers.

He drew a ragged breath. "Don't be sorry. You did what was necessary, no more, no less."

"I'm afraid that offers little comfort at the moment," she whispered.

"We all do what we must whether we like it or not. You think I like being a thief, risking my life by coming to England with false papers? No, but I had little choice if my family was to survive and if I am to restore honor to the Montayas name."

Her expression wary, Teresa leaned away from him. "And is that how you view time spent in my company? A necessary and unenjoyable task on your journey to regain respectability?"

"I wouldn't say unenjoyable." He stroked her arm. "Your kisses are so much more than that."

She flung his arm away and stalked from the bench. "You are the most odious man I have ever had the misfortune to meet. I should have left you out there to bleed everywhere, but it would have probably killed the ivy." She disappeared into the night, slamming the door behind her with such force it seemed as if every pane of glass in the entire structure rattled.

Confusion, disappointment, and something close to satisfaction warred within him. How had his attempt to tease her into not regretting her actions degenerated into this? He meant no real harm with his words. Or had he?

She was becoming too important to him. Before tonight, he'd never felt so vulnerable to another, not even when he was a child reduced to stealing to feed his family. It was something he could ill afford to feel. Perhaps without even being aware of it, he had chosen his words with the purpose of driving her away.

Time was passing and he was no closer to his goal. Eduardo and Tia Elena were growing restless, missing their homeland. Each day carried greater risk that he would be discovered for the fraud he was. Soon, his time in England would be up, and he would have to return to Spain. He vowed it wouldn't be empty-handed.

****

Teresa rolled over, trying to avoid the clutching hand that was determined to shake her awake.

"Teresa!"

The urgent tone finally registered and she forced her heavy eyelids open. Betsy stood near the bed, Teresa's wrapper in her hands.

Alarm skittered through her. She sat up with a start. "What is it?"

"Your robe." Betsy thrust the garment forward. "There is blood on the sleeve and here," she turned the fabric, "along the side." In the next instant, she whipped the blankets aside. "Where? Where are you hurt?"

Teresa caught the older woman's hands. "I'm fine. Truly. It's not my blood."

The maid's body sagged with relief. "You wouldn't lie to ease my concern, would you?"

"No. Besides, it would be pointless, wouldn't it? You see me unclothed every time you help me dress."

"If it's not yours, then whose?"

Teresa pulled the bedclothes to her chest. She had hoped to avoid a confrontation. Betsy liked Montayas no more than before. It's because she doesn't know him, Teresa told herself, and then she remembered his words of last night. Perhaps she didn't really know him either.

"Well," Betsy prompted.

"Montayas."

"How?" The maid sat on the corner of the bed. "Did you run into him during your searches for his family's heirloom?"

"He came here last night to give me some

163

information on Papa's former man of affairs. He was injured in a scuffle." Teresa hoped the explanation was enough to keep any further questions at bay.

"Why would he tell you anything if he is determined to ruin the Darlington name?"

Teresa bit her lip then blurted out the truth. "We're searching together. I was having no luck on my own and he, well, he didn't want me hurt again." She touched her throat remembering the squeezing pressure of the earl's hands as he attempted to choke the breath from her body. "I can't say I relished the idea myself."

"Are you sure that's the only reason?"

"What other reason could there be?" As soon as the question left her lips, she wished she could recall it. It hung on the air in the silence of the room.

"What indeed?" Betsy left the bed and gestured to a nearby table. "I've brought you a light meal to break your fast."

"Thank you," Teresa said in a subdued tone.

She didn't want to even contemplate what Mateo's real reasons might be in suggesting they join forces. No, she wouldn't believe ill of him. Not now. Not when he had at last opened his heart to her and told her of the suffering his family had endured all due to the loss of the *Pequena*.

He'd gained her trust in so many ways. He had kept his word not to slander her father unless it was proven beyond all doubt that Robert Darlington was involved with the theft. He had helped her escape being caught during her forays into various townhouses. He had even helped her cover up the injuries she suffered at the earl's hands.

His words from the night before suddenly came back to haunt her. What if his ulterior motive was to gain her trust? But why? She had no more knowledge of the *Pequena's* whereabouts than he. She would have to take care he didn't learn that he had accomplished this particular goal.

"Will this do for today?"

Teresa shook away the painful thoughts to concentrate on the tea dress Betsy held up. The soft bronze-colored gown always made her feel beautiful and right now, she needed all the confidence she could muster. She had the strange feeling the Count de Montayas would be paying a visit today. "That would be perfect."

After dressing and allowing Betsy to pull her hair into a twist at her neck, Teresa quickly downed a cup of hot chocolate and left the house. The greenhouse beckoned like a beacon to a ship on a fog-shrouded night.

She pushed through the glass door. The heady scent of blooming flowers filled the humid air. She walked to the table where she had tended to Mateo's arm.

Everything was as before. The box of bandages, thread, and other supplies was back in its original place on a nearby shelf. The only sign that he had even been there was a few small drops of dried blood on the floor. She bent, her fingers grazing the rust-colored spots.

Had she been too quick to take offense at his words? Did he manage to make his way home without someone to help him? Once more she cursed her impulsive nature. Why was she always given to acting first and thinking later?

At the sound of the door opening, Teresa rose and turned around. Relief mingled with disappointment as she smiled a greeting at her cousin. "Good morning, Sarah."

"Did you lose something?"

"What?" Teresa glanced at the floor then moved so the hem of her dress covered the blood. "Not at all. Just checking for signs of rodents." She dusted off her hands. "Didn't find any."

"That's good." Lady Sarah gave the room an uneasy glance. "I came to beg a favor of you."

Gesturing for the younger girl to a seat at the table, Teresa wondered what Lady Sarah could possibly need from her. "Surely you know you have no need to beg. I would be more than happy to grant any favor you need."

Sarah fidgeted with the folds of her satin gown. "In this, I'm not sure." She raised her head to meet Teresa's questioning gaze. "I would not ask it of you if there were any other way."

Fear clutched at Teresa's heart. Had Sarah stumbled into some kind of trouble? "What is it?"

"Would you accompany Viscount Linley and me to the Havenhurst ball?" Sarah asked in a rush.

Teresa stared at her, dumbfounded. "Is that all? I was afraid it was something much more serious."

"I know how large gatherings of people unnerve you so, but Mother has decided to attend another engagement this evening and I have already accepted Lady Havenhurst's invitation. It would be a great insult were I to cry off now." Sarah clasped her hands together. "Please say you'll come."

"But why must I attend if you are going with Viscount Linley?"

"Mother insists I have a proper chaperone."

Teresa's brows rose. "I don't think the duchess considers me exactly proper."

"Of course she does. Why, she has allowed you to act as chaperone many times. Do you not remember accompanying Linley and me to the opera and on outings to Hyde Park?"

"Yes, I remember. I am only four years your senior. I don't think I'll be in my dotage for, oh, at least another few months." A smile crossing her lips, Teresa looked at her cousin's earnest expression and knew she would grant Sarah's request.

"Oh, I didn't mean to offend you," Sarah said in

alarm.

"You didn't. I was teasing you and yes, I will go to the ball."

"You will?" Sarah hugged her. "Thank you. We need not stay long." She jumped up from the table. "I must send a message to Linley right away." With a wave, she hurried to the door.

"Sarah."

Her hand on the door handle, she turned back. "Yes?"

Teresa hesitated then plunged ahead with the question that had plagued her for weeks. "Are you genuinely fond of the viscount, or are you encouraging his attentions because it's what the duchess wishes?"

"I am so much more than fond of him." Sarah's eyes sparkled with happiness. "And I believe he feels the same."

"I'm glad." Teresa watched her cousin disappear through the opening. Perhaps despite the duchess' machinations to ensure her daughter a title, Lady Sarah would marry for love after all.

Chapter Sixteen

Teresa cast a jaded eye around the ballroom and told herself for the hundredth time that for Sarah's sake she could endure a few more hours of the subtle digs and insincere condolences regarding her mother's death.

At a sudden stir in the crowd, she craned her neck to see who had caused the whispers that increased in volume. A number of widows worked their way toward the entrance to the grand room followed by the latest group of debutantes being pushed along by fortune hunting mothers.

Unable to see through the crush, she left her seat along the side of the dance floor under the pretense of fetching a glass of lemonade. Not that she would actually drink the ghastly stuff. Weaving her way around the milling throng, she caught a glimpse of him at last.

Mateo.

What was he doing here? And who was the beautiful woman with hair the color of flame and a scandalously low cut gown clinging to his side like the ivy that grew along the garden wall?

Jealousy flashed hot and furious. Teresa quickly turned away hoping he wouldn't notice her among the crowd. Now, at least she knew the truth. His words of last night had been all too telling. She was no more than a diversion to him. A means to find his family's jewel box and nothing more. A sudden ache lodged itself in the region of her heart.

Well, she would use him in just the same manner. She would continue to search for his

wretched *Pequena* with him and in the process prove
her father had nothing to do with its disappearance.

And he said he was starting to believe in Papa's
innocence. Ha! It was just one more way he had
lured her into trusting him. She had been
unbelievably naïve but no longer.

With a swish of her skirts, she marched back to
the stiff-backed chair next to an old woman that had
introduced herself as Mrs. Ford. Teresa wrinkled her
nose as she resumed her seat. She'd forgotten the
woman apparently didn't believe in bathing. The
stench of her body odor overpowered even the strong
perfume she wore. Shifting her chair a little further
away, Teresa sighed and prayed she could leave
soon.

In an effort to make the time pass more quickly,
she watched Lady Sarah dance with Viscount Linley
and a few other gentlemen. Though it was obvious
she preferred her escort's company, society
demanded she dance with others as well. Sarah
looked lovely in a deep blue gown, her hair pulled
into an elegant coil and dressed with small white
blossoms.

Teresa sighed once more and smoothed the skirt
of her own pearl gray dress. Not exactly the color of
mourning, but Sarah had insisted it was a proper
shade for one who had lost her mother recently.
Indeed, it had been only a few short weeks. She,
herself, thought that it was a bit too soon to be back
in society, but she had been unable to turn away
from Sarah's pleading gaze to act as her chaperone.

Her foot tapping in time to the music, Teresa
inadvertently allowed her fan to slip from her lap to
the floor. She bent quickly to retrieve it when her
field of vision was filled with a pair of black trousers.
Lifting her gaze, she felt no sense of surprise to find
Mateo standing before her. For she knew it was he
by the sudden pricking at the nape of her neck,

almost as if her body sensed his presence before she saw him.

"Miss Darlington. It is a pleasure to see you again." He bowed over her hand, one eye sliding closed in a wink.

Teresa barely resisted the urge to snatch her hand back. How dare he look so devastatingly handsome? Dressed all in black except for a snowy white linen shirt and cravat, he looked more like her masked stranger than the aristocratic count.

She wondered if he was purposely baiting the *Ton* into making the connection between himself and the thief who had broken into so many of their homes. Although, she smiled to herself, many of them were still completely unaware that their properties had been searched rather thoroughly.

"Ah, I see by your smile, you're happy to see me."

Mateo's voice broke into her thoughts.

Teresa arched a brow. "You are presuming too much."

He smiled a wickedly dashing grin that only enhanced his dark looks. "I'm afraid you are not the first lady to tell me such."

"That I find all too easy to believe."

Mateo took her hand and pulled her from her chair. "Dance with me."

Stricken by his lack of propriety, Teresa glanced around. They had garnered the attention of nearby matrons who had given up watching their charges for this much more fascinating exchange.

"I cannot. I'm not here as an invited guest."

Confusion flashed across his face. "Then why are you here?"

"I came as Lady Sarah's chaperone."

"You a chaperone?" His laughter brought a few more stares.

Teresa alternated between wanting to stomp on

his foot or jamming her hand over his mouth. At this rate, he wouldn't have to publicly name her father as a thief to ruin her reputation. His actions tonight would more or less have the same effect if he didn't leave her be to attend to her duties.

"Be quiet," she hissed.

He leaned closer. "Why?" he asked in a loud whisper.

Out of the corner of her eye, she saw Mrs. Ford staring at them all agog.

"Will you please leave me be before we are the talk of the entire room?"

"I have never been one to care what the gossips say, so I fear I cannot go away without a dance."

He may not care what the gossips say. He was leaving for Spain while she would be stuck here with the consequences.

"Fine. One dance." She grabbed his arm and practically dragged him into the center of the floor, amid the other couples.

"See, I knew you were eager to join in the festivities." Mateo took her in his arms and moved in time to the music.

Teresa held herself stiff, refusing to allow his nearness to overcome her defenses. "I am only eager to stop wagging tongues though I fear it is impossible now. Why didn't you mention you were invited when we last spoke?"

"Are you feeling slighted that I didn't ask you to accompany me?" With a finger under her chin, Mateo tilted her head to meet his gaze. "Is that the reason for your foul mood?"

"I am not in a foul mood. I just don't like to be made a spectacle of. And I notice you didn't answer my question. You're quite good at that."

"Appearances, my dear. Appearances. I am here only at the behest of Lord Pendleton. It was only this afternoon that he insisted I attend. I still have to make the pretense of being an emissary to my king believable while I conduct my searches."

"Then why did you seek me out?"

"Because you are by far the most beautiful woman in the room."

Teresa felt her pulse speed up at the warm glow in his dark eyes. Reminding herself of her vow to keep her distance, she looked away. When the music finally came to an end, she breathed a quiet sigh of relief.

"Join me for a walk in Havenhurst's gardens. They are supposed to be unequalled in grandeur." Mateo's voice was husky as he whispered his request.

His breath fanned her neck and she shivered. She stepped back, hating to return to her chair along the edge of the room. "You forget that I am supposed to be—"

"Yes, I know. Chaperoning. Do you honestly believe your cousin needs to have a person hovering over her at every moment?"

Before Teresa could answer, Lady Sarah touched her arm. "Excuse me for interrupting." She curtseyed to Mateo who accepted her address with a nod of his head. "Teresa, Linley insisted I tell you that we will be joining Lord & Lady Havenhurst on a tour of the formal gardens."

Without giving Teresa a chance to respond, Sarah turned away and was quickly swallowed up by the crowd.

"Now you have the perfect excuse to join me outside," Mateo said, a hint of satisfaction in his voice.

"I do?"

"Yes, you do have to keep an eye on your charge, do you not?" He offered his arm. "Shall we?"

Rather than argue, Teresa placed her hand on his arm and allowed him to lead her out into the night.

Chinese lanterns swung in the slight breeze, their candle flames sending flickering shadows on the flagstone path.

"Now, admit it. You needed a breath of fresh air."

Teresa halted instantly at his words then turned around and looked back into the ballroom teeming with bodies.

"What's wrong?" Mateo watched her carefully, his gaze going back and forth between her and the entrance to the ballroom.

"Air," she whispered. She couldn't believe it. Never before had she been so unaffected by a crowded room.

"Air?"

"Yes. I walked through that crush of people. I even danced on a crowded floor and not once did I feel as though I couldn't breathe." She knew without a doubt it was due to the man standing at her side. His mere presence had made everything and everyone else fade from her mind. So preoccupied with him, she hadn't even given the large assemblage of people a second thought much less worried that they were taking up all the air in the room.

"I'm sorry. I wouldn't have coerced you into dancing with me if I had known you suffer from a fear of large gatherings."

Teresa gave him a quick smile. "You didn't know." She turned toward the gardens. "Why did you insist we come out here?"

He put a finger to his lips and led her to a secluded corner near the stone railing. "I thought you would like to know what I found at Crenshaw's townhouse."

"You mean other than the edge of a blade?" Teresa grinned.

Mateo touched his heart. "I see your tongue is as sharp as ever."

She instantly felt contrite. "I'm sorry. That was unnecessary and cruel."

"But true all the same. Other than giving Crenshaw an opportunity to practice his skill at wielding a dagger, the search was a complete waste of time."

"Then you learned nothing to exonerate my father?"

He shook his head. "I'm afraid not."

Her shoulders slumped in defeat.

"Don't feel so disappointed. I didn't have enough time to search much more than a few drawers."

"Then you plan to try again?"

Mateo ran a hand over his jaw. "I'm not sure. I have heard a few rumours from Pendleton regarding a Lord Stansfield that have aroused my interest."

"*Stansfield*?" Teresa looked out over the garden absently searching for a glimpse of Lady Sarah.

"Do you know him?"

"No. I have heard the duchess mention his name from time to time, but I've never actually met him."

Mateo leaned against the railing, his arms crossed over his chest. "Pendleton told me of Stansfield's rather unique estate located just outside of London. Perhaps, you'd like to join me while I investigate these tales being bandied about."

Teresa turned to face him, adrenaline rushing through her. "When do we leave?"

Mateo smiled, his teeth flashing in the darkness. "First, I think we'll have to come up with a suitable excuse why you would suddenly leave town for an overnight excursion."

"Overnight?" Her voice came out in a croak. She cleared her throat and tried again. "Why overnight?"

Mateo reached out and touched a soft curl of honey blonde hair that rested above the swell of her breast. "I hardly think we can enter the estate without being seen during the day. We would have to wait for the cover of darkness."

Teresa stepped away from his hand. His touch was sending the strangest feelings coursing through her, clouding her mind. "Yes, of course. How foolish of me."

He slid across the rail, closing the small distance she'd just created. "Do you think you can be ready to leave in two days?"

Teresa bit her lip. What reason could she give the duchess for the trip that wouldn't sound completely fabricated?

She touched the small locket at her throat. It had belonged to her mother and was the only thing Teresa had been able to bring herself to remove from Sophia's rooms.

Even now, everything remained the same as it had been the day of Mama's death.

Almost as though her return was expected at any moment. Teresa knew she would have to tackle the heart-breaking task of sorting through her mother's belongings, but she couldn't bring herself to do it.

"My mother."

"Pardon?" Mateo looked at her, his expression one of complete confusion.

"My mother had a friend who lives in a small village not far from here. It was the only correspondence that she kept up after Papa died."

"What does your mother's friend have to do with the Stansfield estate?"

"If I tell Aunt Vivian that I am going to visit Mrs. Tompkins and to take her a few of Mama's things that she wanted her to have…"

"Then she would have no reason to doubt you." Mateo clasped her head in his hands and pressed a quick kiss to her lips. "Did anyone ever tell you

you're brilliant?"

Teresa laughed. "Only in the most insulting manner possible."

"Then you've been surrounded by fools."

A tide of happiness swept over her. Mateo admired her intellect instead of deriding her for it like so many of the male members of the *Ton*. She gave him a dazzling smile. "It's too bad that only you and I know it."

He pushed away from the balustrade. "We had best go inside. I have plans to put into motion, and people will be wondering where you've disappeared to."

"Don't you mean where *we've* disappeared to? And the entire room was already whispering about us before we even came out here."

"That's because you were causing a disturbance by refusing to dance with me." Mateo placed his hand on the small of her back, guiding her toward the open French doors.

Teresa stopped dead. "I was causing a disturbance?"

He dropped a kiss on her nose. "That's what I said."

She stepped out of his grasp. "You are the most arrogant—"

"Yes, I know. Insufferable, odious. Let me see what else have you called me. Ungentlemanly." He looked up at the sky. "Hmm. I'm sure there were more but I can't recall them."

"And every word describes you perfectly," she snapped, incensed by his teasing attitude when she knew she would have to suffer the knowing glances of every gossipy person in attendance. She brushed by him and headed for the ballroom.

"Enjoy the rest of the ball from your chaperones' corner," he drawled.

Teresa turned, ready to shoot him a murderous

look, but he had disappeared into the night.

"Pompous windsucker," she muttered. With an angry twitch of her skirts, she strode into the crowded room.

Chapter Seventeen

Teresa shifted the hat she wore for the umpteenth time in the last hour. She cast a baleful glare at Mateo's back. She understood his demand to wear the hateful thing, but couldn't he have found a smaller one that didn't keep falling over her eyes? One in a boy's size perhaps.

She quickened her steps to keep up with him, her gaze traveling over him. Dressed in coarse wool clothing and a hat like her own, he could easily be mistaken for a man who worked in the village now on his way home after a day's work. The satchel of tools he carried completed the illusion.

As she trudged along beside him, she noticed how quiet the night had become. The only sounds were those of chirping crickets and the occasional animal scurrying through the underbrush. How much farther was it to Lord Stansfield's home? It'd grown darker since they had left the small inn where Betsy waited for their return.

Pushing her hat up again, she cleared her throat, then fell silent. Mateo was still angry with her, though heaven knew why. She hadn't said anything to him at the Havenhurst ball that she hadn't said before.

Maybe that was the problem. Perhaps he was growing tired of being insulted every time they were together. She didn't mean to treat him in such a manner, but he always seemed to trigger her temper more than any other person she knew.

He hadn't said a word that wasn't absolutely necessary since his departure from the terrace two nights ago. Eduardo had delivered Mateo's plans regarding tonight with instructions to burn the missives in the hearth after reading them.

She sighed and yanked the cap from her head. It was hot, itchy, and she was tired of fighting with it. With her hair darkened with soot and midnight fast approaching, no one would be able to recognize her, not that she knew anyone in the area anyway.

She sighed again and crumpled the hat in her hand, feeling suddenly close to tears. It seemed nearly everyone she considered important in her life was angry with her.

Betsy was less than pleased with Mateo's scheme to break into the Stansfield estate. And even less happy about his involving Teresa. But she had finally come around and agreed to accompany Teresa as her abigail on the supposed trip to visit Mama's friend.

Even Freddie, who'd come by to see Betsy, had been frustrated by Teresa's refusal to give up her search to find the jeweled box. She had been so sure he would understand how important her family's reputation was to her. After all, everyone he came in contact with treated him badly because of his own lack of a family name. Yet, she couldn't make him see past his fear for her safety to realize she just couldn't stand idly by while her father's name was sullied by rumours of thievery. In the end, he had given up trying to change her mind and left with a sad shake of his head.

"Put your hat back on." Mateo's quiet order broke the silence.

Tightening her grip on the object of contention, she met his gaze. "No."

She ran her fingers over the back of her hair. It hung loose to her jaw then gathered into a braid, which Betsy had tucked up under her hairline. "With my hair done as it is and the late hour, I doubt anyone would think I am anything but a young boy."

Mateo halted in the middle of the lane convincing Teresa they were about to have yet another argument.

He gave her a hard look, then walked away. "I suppose you are right."

Her mouth gaping open in surprise, she stared at his retreating back. Gathering her scattered wits, she hurried to catch up. When she reached his side, he held out his hand. Happy that he was no longer angry, she slipped her hand in his.

He looked at their joined palms and grinned. "I was offering to take your hat so you wouldn't have to carry it."

"Oh." Feeling like a complete fool, she started to pull away.

Mateo tightened his hold. "I like your idea better."

She met his smile with one of her own. As they continued down the road, Teresa didn't mind the silence any longer. For now, it was one of companionship instead of anger. She took his good humor to heart. He had forgiven her after all, and for some reason, that was enough to make her happier as well.

At the end of a gradual bend in the lane, Mateo ushered her into a thick copse of trees. Overhead, broad branches blotted out the sky. Not a star could be seen. The night suddenly seemed darker, more menacing.

Fear touched her like a cold, bony hand. She edged closer to Mateo, gripping his arm as she tried to shake off the eerie feeling.

He pressed a finger to his lips and pointed to an unseen path through the trees. Reluctantly, she released him. Mateo started off, holding branches aside, allowing her to pass unhindered.

Unease followed her like a shadow, forcing her

to keep stealing glances back over her shoulder. She saw and heard nothing out of the ordinary, yet she couldn't quell the niggling feeling of fear.

Trying to put her mind to other things, Teresa asked one of the many questions plaguing her. "How do you know we're headed in the right direction?" she whispered.

"Eduardo scouted the area a few days ago." Mateo didn't look up as he helped her over a thick root protruding from the ground.

"Why didn't he look for the *Pequena* while he was here?"

"Because I am a much better thief than he is. His skills lie elsewhere."

Remembering Eduardo's treatment of Freddie the night she was attacked by the earl, she could just imagine what those skills were.

"Are you regretting coming along?" Mateo asked as he stopped and looked around.

"I wouldn't describe it as regret. I keep getting a strange feeling as if we're about to walk into danger." She tried to make light of her concern. "Just my luck, I choose now to decide to suffer from vapors."

"Don't make light of what you're feeling. Your instincts are telling you to beware for a reason. My own have saved my neck more than once." He moved past her and waited near a huge oak tree.

"Then let's go back to the inn. My whole being is telling me to turn around." She no longer cared if he knew how frightened she was.

"I can't. The *Pequena* is too important."

"But you don't even know if Stansfield has it in his possession. You've nothing but rumours to go on."

Mateo crossed his arms over his chest, his stance unyielding. "And what if, for once, the tales are true."

"More likely they're not." Didn't he feel the malevolence emanating from the forest?

He ran a hand through his hair. A sign of frustration she knew all too well. "I'll go on while you wait here. Don't wander off, and you should be fine. I'll be as quick as I can."

"Stay here alone?" Teresa glanced about the gloomy path. That didn't bear thinking about. "But what if you need my help? Your arm is not quite healed from your unexpected meeting with Crenshaw." She moved closer. "I'm not trying to be difficult."

He ran the back of his hand down her cheek. "I know," he whispered. "I shouldn't have brought you with me."

Teresa took a deep breath and gathered what was left of her courage. Though if she could measure it, she doubted it would fill a teacup. "But I am here. Shall we get this done before dawn breaks and I'm still standing here trying to convince you to return to the inn?"

He gave her a quick hug, then led her on a winding path in and around so many trees she started to wonder if they weren't walking in circles. Teresa hoped he could find the way back. If it were up to her, they would most definitely be lost.

At last, they came to a clearing. Teresa started forward, glad to be out of the oppressive closeness of the forest. Mateo pulled her back into the shadows as she uttered a small sound of surprise. The sight left her breathless.

Stansfield's ancestral home was no manor house. It was a huge, looming fortress cloaked in eddying swirls of mist. Medieval knights would have lived, fought, and died here only a few hundred years ago. Teresa shivered and wrapped her arms around her middle. She glanced back at Mateo.

He met her gaze with raised brows. "Not exactly

what I expected," he said.

"Eduardo said nothing about it?"

Mateo shook his head. "I didn't ask for information beyond how to reach the grounds undetected." He held out a hand. "Shall we storm the castle?"

****

Mateo lit a small candle and held it aloft. A nearly soundless whistle escaped his lips. He couldn't believe his eyes. With one look at Teresa, he knew she felt the same sense of awe.

Silk curtains hung at the windows, their ample folds flowing gracefully to the floor. Mahogany chairs inlaid with ebony flanked a white marble fireplace ornamented with a scrolling ivy design. A large desk took the majority of the room but seemed insignificant compared to the grandeur surrounding it.

Giving himself a mental shake, he crossed to the desk. He carefully slid each drawer open only to be disappointed by the sight of numerous ledgers and account books and nothing more.

Closing the last one, he scanned the room. Teresa stood at the hearth, her fingers seeming to caress the mantelpiece. For a moment, he wondered how it would feel to have her hands skimming over the surface of his skin. With regret, he pushed the thought aside. "What are you doing?"

Teresa looked over her shoulder, her face a study in concentration. "Checking for a hidden compartment."

"I think you've been reading too many books."

"I didn't say I expected to find one. But if there actually are such things, this place would be sure to have them." She continued to examine the ivy design without turning around.

"Very well." Mateo picked up the candle from the desk and crossed to the door. "I'm going to search the rest of the rooms. Stay here."

Teresa swung around, her eyes huge in the dim light. "What if someone comes?"

He hesitated. Certainly, he could check the rest of this floor faster if he were alone. He knew the typical places one used to hide valuables and illegal gains. What were the chances that the staff would be up and about at this hour if their master wasn't in residence and hadn't been for some time?

"I think you'll be safer here. If anyone comes, hide behind the draperies and above all else, don't forget to blow out your candle. If they find one burning where one shouldn't be, they'll raise the alarm."

"I wouldn't forget about the candle," she said, indignation burning in her eyes. "I'm not completely addle-brained."

Mateo smiled at her scowling expression and left the room. Perhaps he should have told her he'd warned her not because he thought her muddle-headed but because he, himself, had been guilty of leaving a burning candle behind in the past.

Admittedly, he'd only done it once or twice when he had first turned to thievery to help his family. Back then, the fear of capture and a subsequent life in prison had chased any thoughts from his mind except those of escape.

****

Teresa walked to the door, shook her head, and turned away. Mateo said to stay in this room. But what was taking him so long? It seemed she'd been stuck here for hours. Her candle stub had long burned out. Thankfully, the moon cast enough light into the room to allow her to discern the furnishings. The last thing she wanted was to upend a table or some such. The resulting noise would be sure to bring the servants running.

She approached the door, her worry taking

control. What if he had encountered someone and was in trouble or worse—hurt? With a deep breath, she turned the handle and peered into the darkened hall.

There were no sounds of movement. It was as though she was the only person in the entire building. Leaving the door ajar, she crept down the hall, her ears straining for some sign of Mateo behind the closed doors she passed.

She rounded the corner and froze. At the other end of the corridor, stood a figure. Torn between running back the way she'd come and remaining where she was, she took a shallow breath and prayed the shadows were enough to hide her from sight. Her fingers curled into her palms, she tried to control her racing heart. Surely, the servant would cry out to other members of the staff.

Instead, the person remained as still and unmoving as Teresa herself. Puzzled, she inched forward. Perhaps it was Mateo waiting for her to join him. No, that couldn't be. He would have made some sign to let her know it was he.

Now half the length of the hall away, Teresa realized it was a woman carrying a large object. She stood near a pedestal of some sort. Had the maid not called to the others because she was stealing from Stansfield? Determined to brazen it out instead of cowering in the shadows, Teresa strode forward hoping she projected at least some measure of confidence.

The woman never broke her stance. She stood there waiting for Teresa as if she hadn't a care in the world. It was her unnatural stillness that struck Teresa as odd.

Stopping a few feet away, she nearly laughed out loud. She covered her mouth to hold back the laughter that threatened to escape.

It was no servant who stood before her. It was a

clock. A clock! A carved figure of a woman resting against a pillar while holding a clock face in her arms.

Teresa reached out to touch the cool stone face. She shook her head, glad no one had witnessed her ridiculous reaction to a piece of furniture. Her imagination was getting out of hand, turning her as jumpy as a spinster in a roomful of gentlemen.

Though she tried to make light of her fears, she recalled her near demise at the Earl of Leighton's estate. It was beginning to color all of her experiences and was probably the reason why she felt so frightened back in the forest. If she didn't get herself in hand, she'd become nothing more than a terrified little mouse.

With one last look at the timepiece, Teresa headed down a corridor that branched off to the right. Here, the wall sconces were lit, illuminating the way to a door at the end. She glanced behind her then pressed her ear against the door. No sounds emanated from within.

Turning the handle, she slipped inside. She gazed around the room, unable to believe her eyes.

A bed of mahogany and bronze overpowered the space. Deep red and black silk covered the bed before spilling onto the floor in satin puddles. The ceiling was painted the blue of an evening sky. Decorative motifs of the night were carried out through the room. Gods and goddesses frolicked among the stars while owls and what looked to be bats flew overhead.

It was obvious the room had been set up for seduction. This was the last place she wanted to be. What if Stansfield and his amour came in before she could leave?

She fumbled with the doorknob in her haste to leave. Not bothering to close the door behind her, she sped from the room, crashing into the hard, unyielding planes of a male chest.

Hands closed around her arms. Terror clawed at her. Images of an iron grip tightening around her throat flashed through her mind. She struggled to break free, gasping for air.

"Teresa. It's me."

She struck him a glancing blow as his words impinged on her fear.

"Mateo." She sagged against him, taking solace in his nearness.

"What happened to frighten you so?"

"Please, can we just leave?" Now that she stood in the safe haven of Mateo's arms, she was starting to feel foolish over becoming frightened so easily. And over something so innocuous as a room's décor. "It was nothing. You know how we females are prone to hysterics."

Mateo stared at her with an unreadable expression. "Some women yes, but not you."

"I don't think we should be lingering here. There's too much light. I don't wish to be discovered." She tugged on his arm in an effort to get him moving.

"As you wish. But you will tell me what upset you."

"Later." She all but dragged him back toward the clock figure.

"Why did you leave the study? I told you to stay there where you would be safe."

She dropped his arm, swinging around to face him, her hand held out in front of her. "No lectures. I don't think I could bear it right now. If you insist on pressing the subject, I shall turn into a wet-goose and—"

"A wet-goose?"

Teresa almost laughed at the sight of his confused expression. "It's a person who is extremely emotional. Tears, crying, carrying on. Surely you've seen someone being a wet-goose at least once in your life."

"No," Mateo said with a slow shake of his head. "And I don't think I would like to."

Teresa smiled at his response.

He cocked his head then turned toward the sound of voices approaching. Without a word, he pushed her through the nearest door and closed it quietly behind them.

But this was no ordinary room. The length of a ballroom with coffered ceilings, and a door at the far end, but it had no windows. Statues and busts on pedestals lined the walls. Burgundy colored curtains hung in long lengths behind the statuary. With the exception of strange chandeliers suspended from the ceiling, there wasn't a single piece of furniture in sight.

Teresa left Mateo at the door and moved further into the room. Every statue seemed to be Greek or Roman and larger than life. Each one stood on a base no higher than a stair step, yet she had to crane her neck to examine their faces.

Mateo crossed to her side in three quick strides. "I think the servants we heard in the corridor are coming in here. We have to get out of sight."

"Where?" Teresa scanned the room. There wasn't enough room to crouch behind the pedestals.

Without answering, Mateo doused the candles and hurried her to the opposite end of the room. He slid along the wall to stand in a corner filled with shadows.

Teresa had to admit it was an ideal spot...as long as the room remained dark.

"Do you intend on passing yourself off as one of your marble counterparts?"

Teresa looked in the direction she had last seen Mateo. "What?"

"A statue. Do you plan on standing there hoping you'll be mistaken for a statue?"

"Of course not."

"Then I suggest you take my hand before that door opens."

Teresa groped in the darkness; her fingers brushing across his hand one minute then held in a firm grip the next. Trying to keep her balance, she half walked, half slid through the narrow opening between the base of the sculpture and the wall.

"There's not enough room for us both," she whispered as she realized Mateo stood with one leg on each side of the corner of the platform.

With surprising swiftness, Mateo clasped her around the waist and swung her in front of him and up onto the flat table-like base.

She shivered and this time it wasn't from fear. His hands rested at her waist, holding her close. Teresa stiffened and stepped forward gaining herself only a few precious inches of space between them. She could feel the warmth of his body, his breath as it whispered across her cheek. Soon she found herself relaxing against him more and more until she leaned against him fully.

"You smell wonderful," Mateo said, his voice low and husky. He nuzzled the side of her neck.

The room faded away as all thought disappeared from her head. A sigh of pleasure escaped her as her eyes fluttered closed. She tilted her chin to allow him better access to the sensitive skin.

His hold tightened as she turned her face to meet his lips with her own. He brushed his mouth over hers in a light tantalizing caress once, then twice, before taking her lips in a heated kiss.

Teresa laid her hands over his as she moved to face him. He stared at her in the darkness. Neither of them said a word as she slid her palms up his shirt reveling in the sensations of linen over silken skin.

He shuddered, his hands moving reflexively, but

he didn't stop her as she explored the hard planes of his chest and width of his shoulders.

She liked standing like this—on a level that brought her even with his height. Wanting to make him feel as carried away as she did, Teresa ran her tongue along the seam of his lips.

Mateo jerked her against him, meeting her mouth with greedy, plundering kisses. He rubbed his hands along her back, each stroke ending lower until he swept over the curve of her buttocks, urging her closer.

Teresa went where he led willingly. The hard ridge of his arousal pushed at the juncture of her legs as she stood between his muscled thighs.

"*Dios*," he muttered raising his head to scan the room. "Why, *mia hechicera*, do you pick this place, this time to grow amorous?"

Teresa stiffened as the words penetrated her passion-fogged brain. Whether he intended it or not, his words had the same effect as plunging her into an ice-cold pond. In her haste to get away from him, she stepped off the edge of the platform and toppled backward to the floor.

"What's wrong, *mia hechicera*?"

She scrambled to her feet and practically ran the length of the room to the door. For a brief moment she waited, listening for the voices of before, all the time aware that Mateo was coming closer.

She couldn't bear it if he were to touch her now. How could she have humiliated herself once again? When would she learn not to let her emotions take control? The questions chased themselves around in her head. Teresa opened the door, flew through the maze of corridors to the study, out the window, and down the black-colored rope they'd used to climb into the second story of the mansion, ever mindful of Mateo's stalking presence behind her.

Climbing up, she had needed his help, but now

so intent on putting as much space between them that she could, she had no trouble getting to the ground. She scrambled to her feet and ran across the vast open space, never once looking back. She didn't know where she was going; she just needed to get away from the source of such constant mortifying embarrassment.

Reaching the edge of the forest, she rested a hand against a tree, the rough bark cutting into her palm. Her breath came in great shuddering gasps, and she longed for the privacy to burst into tears.

She lifted her head, sensing Mateo behind her seconds before he grabbed her arm and spun her around.

"Why do you run from me?" Anger burned in his eyes. "Have you suddenly remembered who I am, what I am?"

She swung free of his grasp. "And what is that?" she asked, her own temper beginning to burn.

"A lowly thief well beneath your touch. Do you admit it?" A muscle pulsed in his jaw as he waited for her response.

"I can hardly condemn you as a thief since you are convinced my father was one as well. Don't think I will apologize for my actions when it was you who insulted me. In fact, you may be insulting me every time you call me *'mia hechicera'*..."

"It's an endearment. I insulted you?" Surprise softened his expression before it hardened into a tight mask. "How? By responding so ardently to your caresses?"

"It was you who instigated those caresses and then you make me feel like a..." she faltered, "...a tart when I take pleasure from them."

"A tart?"

"Yes, a tart. When it's you who can't keep your hands off me, not the other way around."

"I can't keep my hands off you?"

"You're always touching and kissing me."

"I am always touching and kissing you?"

"Will you stop repeating everything I say like some blasted echo?" Teresa wanted to stamp her foot. She'd always thought women who resorted to such displays were spoiled and childish, but now it seemed the perfect outlet for her raging emotions.

"What if I tell you I believed you wanted those kisses, those touches, that you found ways for us to be alone so I could bestow them upon you?" He cast an appraising eye up and down her body. "How many other women would wear men's clothing that showed off their many curves to such advantage?"

"I wear this," she gestured to the shirt and trousers she wore, "because it's a damn sight easier to climb through a window or off a rooftop in them than a gown and petticoats. As for maneuvering you into isolated places, I recall it was you who practically forced me into going out on the terrace with you at the Havenhurst ball."

"And I recall it was you who led me to your intimate little greenhouse in the middle of the night." He ran his hand down his shirtfront. "And all but tore my shirt from my body," he added in a silky tone.

"That was to care for your arm, nothing more," she hissed.

"Was it?"

"Your arrogance knows no bounds. I should have left you there in the garden. It is you who can't keep his hands to himself. You know I speak the truth."

Mateo leaned a shoulder against the tree, one foot crossed over the other. "I think you just can't admit you want me as much as I want you."

Teresa turned away. "I refuse to continue this ridiculous conversation any longer."

"I'm right and *you know it*. Shall we make a wager to prove it?"

Teresa faced him, her mind calculating the odds. There had to be a way to use this to her advantage because heaven help her if he found out that he was right—that she did want him and worse yet that she feared she was falling in love with him.

She chewed on her bottom lip. He watched her with a knowing grin on his face.

Then it came to her. "Fine. You must refrain from touching or kissing me for three days." She held up a hand before he could speak. "But you cannot avoid me during that time either."

"And if I lose?"

"If you lose, you swear to never breathe a word to anyone, anyone at all, regarding your suspicions of my father."

"Done." He pushed away from the tree, moving toward her until he stood scant inches away. "During those three days, you must attend at least one ball where I will be present."

"That's all?"

"Oh, no, *mia hechicera*. You must dance every dance and never with the same partner."

"That's all but impossible."

He smiled his devil's grin. "Do you not think the task you set me is the same?"

"But it's unfair. I can't ask men to dance with me. It isn't done. And you know how I react to large gatherings of people."

Mateo cocked his head and looked at her. "Very well. As I am certain I shall be the victor of this little wager, I will be magnanimous."

"How decent of you," she said dryly.

"You don't have to attend a ball. Instead, if I pass the next three days as you instructed, I win."

"And if you win?" Teresa asked.

"*When* I win...you shall have to give me three kisses—one for each day."

Teresa felt her body go limp with relief. If she

did lose, it would be no great threat to her family. Yes, he would still hold the upper hand by believing her father was the thief. As long as she could prove that he wasn't, and there hadn't been anything implicating him yet, the Darlington reputation was and would forever be intact.

"Don't look so relieved. I do not mean a kiss one would bestow on a family member or a friend. But a kiss a man gives a woman, one given between lovers."

Teresa swallowed. A frisson of excitement mingled with a touch of anxiety ran through her body. Lifting her chin, she held out her hand. "Agreed. Shall we shake hands over it like gentlemen?"

The warm grip of his hand closed over her palm. His gaze rested on her lips, breasts, and hips before meeting her own. "I would never mistake you for a man. Let's seal our agreement with a kiss instead."

She pulled free and stepped back, coming up against the broad trunk of an oak. "I think not."

Mateo sketched a small bow. A smile lurked at the corners of his mouth. "As you wish. It's good to know one's weaknesses."

"Weaknesses! You flatter yourself, sir."

"Not at all. But I shall let you keep your illusions for now."

Teresa opened her mouth to respond with a cutting remark. Instead, she closed it with a click and stomped away through the trees muttering about a certain overbearing Spanish count, Mateo's laughter ringing in her ears.

Chapter Eighteen

Teresa stared out the window and wondered if Mateo would refuse her invitation to tea. She'd sent it early this morning by messenger, but perhaps he had already accepted another engagement. She worried her bottom lip with her teeth as uncertainty gnawed at her. It was the second day of the wager, and Mateo had yet to even attempt to touch her. She had been convinced he would have done so by now. Not that she was by any means irresistible but... Had she put her self-respect in danger to save her family's reputation for nothing?

Teresa grimaced as she remembered how Mateo had outwitted her at Lady Sheridan's sixtieth birthday party last night. More than the usual whispers regarding her strangeness had set tongues wagging after she all but forced Lord Sheridan to escort her to Mateo's side.

Expecting him to take her hand as was proper and thus lose the bet had been foolish. She should have given him more credit for his intelligence. After all, he had managed his family's survival with his wits and cunning for years. Instead of bowing over her hand, he had greeted her with a dip of his head and a compliment on her gown. All the while, his eyes danced with laughter.

Turning away from the view of the empty drive, Teresa took in the pile of gowns lying on Sophia's bed. If she would let herself admit it, this was the reason she wanted him to come. She felt as if she were invading her mother's privacy even if she was no longer among the living.

Teresa felt like the thief Mateo was constantly accusing her father of being, pawing through the mistress of the house's belongings looking for valuables.

If only Mateo would come and give her the excuse to avoid this task for one more day. But she knew it couldn't be put off. The duchess had started making subtle hints about moving Mama's things soon after her death. Now, the hints had become outright orders to vacate the suite of rooms. Just days ago, Vivian insisted if Teresa didn't do it soon, she would have the servants give everything to charity.

Tucking a wayward curl behind her ear, Teresa surveyed the rows of slippers lined up alongside the bed. Like so many of the beautiful gowns of satins and silks, many of them had never been worn.

Betsy entered the room with a quiet knock. "You have a caller. A certain Spanish count. He's been shown to the parlor."

Teresa sagged onto the corner of the bed. He came. She didn't know if she felt thankful she'd have a few hours respite from the sad chore before her or anxious about what she had planned now that he'd arrived.

"Thank you. Would you tell him I'll be right down? Also, please have tea and some of Cook's pastries brought to us in ten minutes."

"I'll see to it." Betsy turned to leave.

"Are the duchess and Lady Sarah still out?" Teresa crossed her fingers and prayed for an affirmative response. It was imperative that she and Mateo take tea alone if she was going to put her scheme into play.

"Yes. I believe they aren't expected back for some time. Would you like to be informed when they return?"

"No." Teresa took a deep breath. "Betsy, I'd like

you to take these items," she gestured to the dresses and shoes, "to the servants' quarters for the maids." Her voice grew quiet. "Unless you think they won't want them."

"Are you sure?"

Teresa nodded, determined to hold back her tears. She took a gossamer soft shawl made of the finest weave of lace from the pile. "Except this."

"I'm sure they'll be honored to have them."

"Thank you," Teresa said with a watery smile. Clutching the shawl to her chest, she headed to her room.

Once inside, she laid it carefully over the back of a chair and checked her reflection in the looking glass. If she wanted to win this wager today, she couldn't go downstairs looking weepy. She smoothed her hands down the lavender silk day dress she wore and combed the wayward strands of honey blonde hair back into place with her fingers.

Taking a moment more, she closed her eyes and mentally pulled herself together. When she opened them again, the light of battle gleamed in the brown depths. If all went well, she would have secured her family's reputation by tricking Mateo into touching her, and he wouldn't know how it happened until it was too late.

A few minutes later, she entered the parlor.

Mateo stood, took one look at the hands she stretched out in greeting, and smiled. "I'm afraid you must forgive my rudeness in not greeting you properly." A rakish eyebrow raised as she dropped her hands to her sides. "Surely, you didn't expect to win so easily?"

Teresa waved him to a chair and laughed at her own obviousness. "One can always hope."

"You didn't invite me to join you this afternoon just for my company, no?"

Thinking of the task awaiting her, she wanted to

reply yes, that was the reason. That she needed his strength to lean on. That she wished he would take her in his arms and wipe away the sadness tearing at her heart with each trunk she packed and item she gave away.

Instead, she forced a smile to her lips and sat down. "Whatever do you mean?"

Mateo watched her take a seat opposite him, her voice all soft innocence. She was clever, but it was her lack of guile that gave her away at times like this. It was one of the many things about her that fascinated him so. Whenever he was in her presence, the very air seemed to vibrate with life.

Though he didn't want to probe the feelings she aroused in him too closely, he knew he would miss her when he returned to Spain. For some reason, the thought of leaving England made him inexplicably sad. Pushing the somber feelings aside, he flashed her a questioning look just as a maid entered the room carrying a tea tray.

He waited until the servant left before speaking. "You realize you only have one more day before I claim my kisses."

Teresa seemed not to hear him as she poured the liquid into two cups, but the betraying tremor of her hand gave her away.

Mateo took a seat across from her.

"Do *you* realize that there is only one more day before my family's good name is safe from scandalous rumours?" She pushed a cup and saucer toward him. "Cream, sugar? Or perhaps you would like honey instead?" She dipped a spoon into the pot and brought it her mouth. "Mmm." She closed her eyes as though relishing the taste. "I do so love wild honey."

Mateo shifted uncomfortably at the sight of her sensual enjoyment of the sweet. In his mind's eye, she was no longer sitting before him taking tea but warm and willing beneath him. His manhood stirred to life. "Sugar," he blurted in a hoarse voice.

Teresa looked up at him from under her lashes. "Are you sure you wouldn't like to try this?" She held the spoon before his mouth for a brief second then brought it back to her own, sliding it across her lips before rubbing them together.

Mateo followed the spoon with his body, leaning toward her. His tongue slipped out to lick suddenly dry lips. He placed a hand on the low table between them, upsetting a plate of teacakes. The sudden clatter brought him to his senses.

Teresa looked from the overturned china and teacakes scattered across the tray to his hand. "Oh. You didn't hurt yourself, did you?"

Grabbing a napkin, he glanced at her. A small smile played about her lips. "Not at all. I fear I seem to have case of clumsiness today."

"How strange. I don't ever recall you being clumsy before."

Now he knew for certain she was up to something. "You are...how do you say...leading me down a garden path, I think."

Teresa ran her tongue over the spoon. "How ever would I do that? You are far more worldly than I."

"You, with your gracious airs, try to make me believe you are an innocent, yet the way you caress that spoon leaves me to think otherwise."

She leaned over the table as though to impart a secret. "Perhaps I am merely trying to entice you."

If she only knew how well she was succeeding. His resolve not to touch her drained away a little more with every breath. "If you keep doing that," he gestured to the spoon, "you'll entice me to do much more than you're bargaining for."

"Really, my lord? You, the most mannerful of gentlemen?" She laughed, a light musical sound.

"I have a tendency to forget my manners when it

suits me, as you well know."

"And does it suit you now?" she asked breathlessly.

With great care to avoid even minimal contact, he plucked the spoon from her grasp and set it on the tray.

Teresa frowned in displeasure, then licked a spot on her fingertip where the honey clung like a lover. Unable to tear his eyes away, he felt his body harden and his breath quicken. Her tongue swirled over her finger then drew it into her mouth.

He imagined the rasp of her tongue gliding over his chest and down his body. His hands clenched on the arms of the chair. With a shaky breath, he shook the image away.

Unable to stand the torment a second longer, he jumped up. "I have to go. *Si*. I have another engagement. Good day to you." He escaped the room and then the house as quickly as possible.

As he headed the phaeton toward Grosvenor Square and home, he castigated himself for acting like an untried lad instead of the experienced man of the world he was. But if he had stayed... If he had stayed, he would have taken her right there among the teacups with the parlor door open, uncaring of the servants or anyone else that may have passed by.

Perhaps he was wrong about her lack of deviousness. Now that he was away from the sensual spell she wove, he was certain Teresa knew exactly what she'd been doing. And by leaving in the manner he had, she was bound to know how close he came to succumbing to her charms. He groaned and slumped down in his seat. How would he get through another day without touching her?

****

Mateo watched Teresa from across the crowded ballroom. He had purposely asked that she and her aunt's family be invited. By the way she gazed around the vast room at its gilt and glittery ostentatiousness, he guessed she hadn't been to Carlton House before. But then she and the Prince Regent didn't exactly mingle in the same social circles.

Upon arriving home after leaving Teresa's seductive tea party, he sent Eduardo to Carlton House requesting an audience. It was then that he asked that Teresa, the Duchess of Perth, and Lady Sarah be included on the guest list.

The only problem was that he hadn't the slightest idea why he pressed the issue when confronted with an unwilling regent. His gaze strayed to the corpulent leader of England. The man was too given to childish whims to run a country.

Instead of being decisive as a king should be, Prinny had pouted and whined that the invitations had been sent out weeks ago.

Sensing the Regent's hesitancy in making a decision, Mateo pressed his advantage. "But this ball is being held in my honor, is it not?"

"Yes, of course. But this is no ordinary soiree. It's to celebrate your stay in England before you begin your journey home to Spain."

"I'm not leaving for another fortnight at least." Mateo hung onto his patience when what he wanted to do most was shake the imbecile.

"Wouldn't you like to invite someone else, anyone else?" Prinny wheedled.

"Why?"

"Well," the Prince Regent examined his beringed fingers, "the Duchess of Perth." He looked up at Mateo. "The woman has the most vicious tongue."

Mateo tried to hold back a smile. The future king of England was afraid of the barbs slung by a woman. "So I've heard," he said in what he hoped was a grave tone. "But if you think I shouldn't invite the duchess, I would be willing to have only Miss Darlington attend."

Prinny gave a negative shake of his head. "Can't. She's a nobody. It just isn't done."

Mateo stiffened at the insult as if it had been directed at him. "You are the ruler of England. You can 'make it done'."

"I'm afraid not. The *Beau Monde* is very discriminating. Think of the position you are putting me in. Would you ask your own king to invite a mere commoner to a royal event?"

I'd be lucky to get within shouting distance of my king, Mateo thought. "Then I shall have to insist on inviting the duchess and her family. After all, I'm sure you wouldn't want such a minor thing to strain relations between our countries," he finished silkily.

"Not at all. Not at all," Prinny stammered. "You may invite anyone you wish. But I shall make it known that that viper of a woman is here at your request."

Mateo smiled at how easily manipulated the man was. "Thank you."

A light touch on his arm brought him back to the present and the garish ballroom with a start. He covered his surprise at finding Lady Sarah and the Duchess of Perth beside him by bowing over each woman's hand. "I hope you are enjoying the ball."

"Oh, yes," Lady Sarah breathed, her eyes filled with excitement. "I, we, wanted to thank you for including us. It was very unexpected."

"Yes, very," the duchess added in a suspicious tone.

"You...both have been very kind during my stay," Mateo said.

"If you'll excuse me, I see Lady Havenhurst and I must have a word with her." The duchess stepped away fully expecting Sarah to follow. When the younger girl made no move to do so, she turned back.

"Sarah, it's unseemly to pursue a conversation with a man who isn't a family member."

Sarah's face flushed with mortification at the public rebuke. "Pray excuse me, Count de Montayas," she whispered.

Mateo took the tips of her gloved hand. "Please. You would do a great kindness to honor me with your presence for a few minutes more. You see, this ball may be in my honor, but I know few of the people in attendance."

"It would be my pleasure," Sarah said with a shy smile.

"Not long, Sarah. People will talk and I'm sure Viscount Linley would be most upset," the duchess warned before striding away.

Now that he had rescued Sarah from the duchess for the moment, Mateo didn't know what to say. He jumped into the awkward silence. "Have you danced this evening? The musicians are quite remarkable."

"Yes."

He waited for her to continue, but she kept quiet. He cast about for something else to say. His gaze flew to Teresa. She remained in the same place as before. She seemed to be hovering by the twin marble columns that led to the gardens. "Has Teresa danced as well?"

"Oh, Teresa rarely dances."

"Why? Is it because of her fear of large crowds?"

Lady Sarah tilted her head to one side. "Maybe. But I think it's more because she isn't asked."

"She isn't asked? Are all English men blind? She's beautiful. How can they not want to be in her arms?" Mateo clamped his mouth shut at Sarah's speculative look.

"She *is* very pretty."

Teresa was so much more than pretty. Tonight she wore a silver gray gown with matching gloves.

Her hair was pulled into an intricate knot woven with miniscule silver flowers. Tendrils of honey blonde hair had been left loose to curl around her face, neck, and shoulders. Dressed as she was, she looked like a star from the heavens. Feeling Lady Sarah's eyes on him, Mateo forced his gaze elsewhere.

Sarah lifted her fan to hide her mouth and said, "I think they are afraid of her."

"Afraid!" Mateo burst out laughing. "Why?"

"Surely you are aware of Teresa's intelligence and fondness for science."

"Yes, but—"

"I think the men are frightened that she may be smarter than they are. Shall we join her? She looks a bit lonely, and she hasn't had a chance to thank you for our invitations."

Mateo was certain he caught a glimpse of calculation in Sarah's eyes before she glanced away. Deciding it was safe to speak to Teresa with Lady Sarah present to act as a buffer, he offered his arm and allowed her to lead them across the room.

"Hello, Teresa. The Count de Montayas was just asking about you. How are you faring among the crush?" Lady Sarah asked as they approached.

"Lady Sarah. Senor Conde," Teresa responded, her eyes sparkling with laughter.

Mateo knew she was remembering their last encounter and his ignoble exit. "Miss Darlington."

"The count was wondering if you had danced yet? Isn't the music wonderful?"

"The music is very good." Teresa looked at Mateo with a mournful expression. "No, I haven't been asked."

Mateo remained quiet knowing she was angling for an offer.

"Oh." Lady Sarah turned to Mateo. "I know this is very forward of me, but you could dance with

Teresa. You don't seem to be intimidated by her."

"I would love to dance." Teresa added.

"I...I can't." Mateo felt trapped.

If he could refrain from physical contact during the ball, he would claim the victory in their wager. He didn't care so much that he would win but that she would lose. After the torment of the last three days, he yearned for her kisses. He refused to forfeit them now when in a few short hours she would touch her lips to his.

He scanned the room, his gaze lighting on his host. "I must speak with the Prince Regent on a very important matter." He spun on his heel and walked away.

His self-disgust threatened to choke him. He had thought it amusing that the leader of England was afraid of a woman's words. Now here he was running as fast as he could from a woman himself. If Eduardo ever found out, he would never live it down.

Chapter Nineteen

Teresa rolled onto her side and counted three sonorous bongs as a clock somewhere in the house struck the hour. It was well after midnight. She had lost.

Now, she would have to give Mateo three kisses. It wasn't that she dreaded the idea; in fact if she were honest, she became breathless just thinking about it. It was that in losing, she had lost so much more than a mere wager. Certain she would have been the winner, she deliberately named the one thing that had been her downfall in the end—Mateo's word he wouldn't sully her father's name.

Teresa saw now that as driven as he was to regain his own family's honor, he would have never allowed himself to be anything other than the victor of the wager. But at the time, it had seemed a sure way to safeguard the Darlington reputation from scandal.

She tucked a hand under her cheek and stared at the candle she'd left burning on the bedside table. His arrogance had been irritating before, now it was certain to be unbearable. The flame danced as though disturbed by an unseen draught of air.

Teresa sat up just as a black clad figure entered through the window. Mateo. It would be no one else.

"What are you doing here?" she asked in a hushed whisper.

He closed the window and turned toward the bed. "I've come to collect my kisses."

"Now? You couldn't wait until tomorrow?" She clutched the sheet to her breasts. Dressed in only a thin night rail, she felt vulnerable and exposed.

He stood at the foot of the bed. "It is tomorrow. And I could wait no longer, *mia hechicera*..."

"But surely the Prince Regent's ball isn't over yet. You'll be missed."

"No more than you were. Did you think I wouldn't notice you left soon after midnight?"

"I...I felt tired," Teresa said, remembering how she had pled fatigue and graciously accepted Lord and Lady Havenhurst's offer to see her back to Perth House.

Mateo tilted his head as though contemplating her flimsy excuse. "No. I think you were afraid."

"Afraid?" She hadn't been afraid when she made her escape earlier in the evening. She just hadn't been able to face the fact that the midnight hour had come and she had lost the wager.

"Yes, afraid I would claim my kisses the moment yesterday became today when I was no longer bound by our agreement not to touch you."

"And would you have?"

"Kissed you then? No." He sat on the edge of the bed. "I would have liked to dance with you."

Teresa stared at his profile, feeling she had hurt him in some way. "And that's why you're here? Because I left before we were able to share a dance?"

"No. I'm here because now I can trust myself to be alone with you. You will no longer try to tempt me into touching you."

Teresa smiled, his hasty retreats from her presence these past few days running through her mind. "Was I really so much temptation?"

"More so. Now, I believe I'd like the first of my three kisses."

"Right here?" Teresa croaked, clutching the sheet higher.

"No." He raised her hand to his mouth. "Right here," he whispered against her fingers.

She shuddered at the touch of his lips beneath her sensitive fingertips. She stared into his midnight eyes. His face was devoid of expression. Teresa had the fleeting impression he was waiting for her to refuse him.

Without giving her a chance to respond, he released her hand with a small smile. "Even though I am the winner, I have lost," he murmured.

He started to move from the bed.

Teresa laid a hand on his thigh. "What of your kisses?" She leaned in and brushed her mouth over his.

His hands came to rest on her waist. He made to pull her closer but instead rested his forehead on hers. "Do you truly want to give them?" he whispered.

"Yes." Her answer was no more than a breath of air.

It was then that she realized she'd been waiting for this moment as much as he during the past few days. Dare she tell him she feared she was falling in love with him?

Mateo closed his eyes and tried to control the sudden racing of his heart. She placed her hands alongside his jaw and lifted his face. The soft pressure of her lips slid over his. He felt the gentle tug of her teeth on his lower lip followed by the glide of her tongue. His body stirred in anticipation.

Teresa shifted closer, the sheet forgotten around her waist. Any thought about her lack of proper attire drifted away. Her hands explored the hard contours of his chest through his linen shirt. Mateo pulled her hands away, holding them tightly as he searched her gaze.

Thinking she had offended him somehow, Teresa cursed her inexperience. "Did I do something I shouldn't have?"

He didn't answer. Instead he took off his shirt,

then lifted her hands to his chest. "I want you to touch me," he said before slanting his mouth over hers.

He eased Teresa down onto the mattress. She turned her head away and rolled to the side.

Mateo pushed to a sitting position. "Have you changed your mind?" he asked, his voice hoarse.

"No. But I'm supposed to be kissing you, not you kissing me."

Mateo raised an eyebrow. "As you wish." He lay back on the mattress, his hands folded under his head.

Teresa stared at his muscular chest, arms, and shoulders. The light sprinkling of dark hair that arrowed down to disappear beneath his waistband intrigued her. She traced the same path with her finger. Mateo inhaled sharply but didn't move. She glanced at him before pressing her mouth to his.

Afraid she would end the kiss, he slipped his tongue between her lips. Expecting her to pull away, he was surprised by the hesitant touch of her own in response. Lifting her mouth, she left a trail of burning kisses down the side of his throat and onto his chest.

Sensation pooled in his loins. Her touch swirled through his senses making a mockery of his self-control. Mateo thrust his fingers into her hair, kissing her with a hunger he hadn't felt in many years. The honey blonde mass flowed over his hands like a waterfall. He slid his hand down to cup the fullness of her breast through the thin lawn of her nightgown. She gasped as he rubbed his thumb over the pebbled tip.

Following his lead, she trailed her fingers over his nipple before touching her lips to the sleek muscle. Mateo groaned, reaching for her. She evaded his hands, her own sliding to his hips. Teresa followed the ribbon of chest hair down to his navel with her mouth. Lying between his legs, she felt the hard ridge of his arousal pressing against her stomach. It filled her with a sense of feminine joy that she could bring him such pleasure.

She lifted her head and looked at him. He lay with his eyes tightly closed as if he were in agony. She'd never felt so daring in her entire life. The excitement of breaking into townhouses paled in comparison. Still watching him, she ran her tongue around the rim of his navel.

"*Dios!*" Mateo's hands clenched the sheet as his hips pressed upward.

His control long depleted, Mateo rolled her beneath him and sealed her lips with his. Easing down the thin straps of her nightgown, his fingers slid over satin shoulders.

Teresa sighed in pleasure as his hands traced her collarbone followed by the erotic touch of his mouth. She couldn't suppress a gasp of shock as his hand covered the bare skin of her breast. He blew over the hardened crest of her nipple, then touched it with the tip of his tongue before pulling it into his mouth. Teresa shivered and held him closer, her fingers tangling in his hair.

Mateo kissed her, his tongue slipping between her lips to dance with her own. He whispered endearments in Spanish between his kisses.

"English, tell me in English," she sighed into his mouth.

"Beautiful. You are so beautiful." He slid his hand up the silken length of her thigh.

Teresa stiffened. Her pleasure in the sensations he aroused vanished in an instant.

He strained against her. "Please," he groaned, his lips hovering above hers. "Let me make love to you."

Oh, how she wanted to. But they had spoken nothing of the future. What kind of woman would she be to give herself to a man who had not so much as uttered a single word of love? And yet, she yearned for his touch.

As though sensing her indecision, Mateo kissed her and with each caress of his mouth and hands, he washed away her misgivings, drawing her into a whirlpool of sensation.

Without her being aware of it, he rid her of her night rail before shedding the rest of his clothes. He stroked her secret places, causing the fire burning within her to rage out of control.

Poised between her legs, he exerted an iron hold over the pulsing demands of his body. "Teresa, tell me if you don't want me to. Tell me now."

She ran her hands over his broad back. "Don't stop. Please, don't stop."

"It will hurt a little. Are you sure?"

"Yes."

Mateo kissed her and with as much gentleness as he could muster, pushed into her. She clutched at his shoulders, her eyes filling with tears.

He fought the urge to move. "I'm sorry. I'm sorry." He kissed her eyelids, cheeks, and mouth, giving her time to adjust to him.

With slow, careful strokes, he began to move. The velvet heat of her body surrounded him as he struggled to maintain an even tempo.

Teresa gave a moan of pleasure as sensation radiated toward the center of her being. She trailed her hands over his body, delighting in the feel of him. He began to speed up the rhythm. She strained upward, feeling as though she was reaching for something just out of sight.

Mateo slid his mouth over hers, pushing deeper. Sensation exploded across her senses in a flash of white heat. She shuddered, her fingers digging into his back. He surged into her twice more before finding his own release. Mateo laid his head on her breast, his breath fanning across her skin. Wrapping her arms around him, she wished they could stay like this forever.

Mateo gave her a gentle kiss before withdrawing. She protested faintly. He pulled the sheet over them, lay down, and curled her into his side. He rubbed his chin over her hair.

"*Tienes mi corazon,*" he murmured.

Teresa looked up at him, her chin resting on her hand where it lay on his chest. "What does that mean? It sounds beautiful."

You have my heart. His soul answered her question while his mind hesitated.

Mateo decided it was time to put aside the past. What his family had suffered at the hands of her father no longer seemed so important. From this point on, nothing mattered but the future. "It means—"

Teresa jerked toward the sound of the door opening.

"Teresa, I—" The duchess stood in the entrance, her hand still on the door handle.

Teresa cast Mateo a horrified look, then dropped her head into her hands. He moved to cover her, but there was no doubt to what they had just done.

Almost as though she decided to brazen it out, Teresa lifted her chin and stared back at her aunt's disapproving figure.

"I'll see you both downstairs to discuss marriage settlements," the duchess said, her mouth curling with distaste before turning on her heel and slamming the door.

Marriage settlements. The words echoed through his mind. A terrible thought dawned—had this all been just a means of keeping him from bringing scandal to the Darlington name? He looked at Teresa's stricken face. No, she wasn't capable of such deception.

As if released from an invisible hold, Teresa stumbled from the bed, taking the sheet with her. "Oh, my God." She covered her mouth with her hand, tears glistening in her sad, brown eyes. "Oh my God, what have I done?"

Mateo stepped into his pants and quickly fastened them. "Don't regret this. Promise me you won't regret this." He moved to take her in his arms but she turned away.

"She'll ruin me. With one single word, my life will be ruined."

He tried to calm her fears. "She can't say anything without bringing scandal to her own house."

Hope flared in her eyes. "You're right. And after we're married, it won't matter."

Mateo stiffened, his doubts crowded into his head once more. "Marriage?"

"We are getting married...aren't we? What of the duchess?"

"How convenient that she came to your room tonight."

"What are you talking about? You think I planned for her to find us like this?" Teresa gestured to the sheet wrapped around her nakedness.

He closed the space between them. "I think that forcing a marriage between us may have been part of some scheme all along."

With each step he took, she backed up a little more. His eyes were flat, expressionless pools of obsidian, frightening her more than his words.

"What man would revile the memory of his wife's father by announcing to the world that the man was a thief?" Mateo shook his head in disgust.

Unable to comprehend how he could think such a thing of her, Teresa didn't know what to say in her own defense. "I didn't...I wouldn't." Tears gathered in her eyes and clogged her throat, but she refused to let them fall.

"I should have realized what you were about when you all but seduced me into your bed during that ridiculous wager."

Anger burned away her hurt for the moment. "I never set out to trap you into my bed or into a lifetime with me. My only intention in all of this was to—"

"Protect your precious Darlington reputation," Mateo sneered. "And now you think you've succeeded, but you forgot one very important thing. I'm not free."

"You said you had no wife," she whispered. Oh God, had she committed adultery among all her other sins? Did some woman pine for him back in Spain?

"The lack of a wife doesn't always mean one is free to marry."

"I don't understand."

"I'm not free until the Montayas name has been restored." Mateo stuffed his arms into his shirt. "You claim your sole reason for our acquaintance was to protect your family name at any cost. I, too, had a purpose for our friendship. When I came to England, I vowed I would accomplish two things. One was to recover the *Pequena*, the other was to destroy Robert Darlington's family as he had destroyed mine."

Teresa sagged against the wall feeling as if she had suffered a physical blow. He didn't love her at all. He didn't even like her. Everything, all of it, had been nothing but a form of vengeance against a dead man. And the worst of it was, she had been a willing participant in her own destruction.

"This," she gestured toward the bed, "was all part of your revenge, wasn't it?" She turned away. "How could I have forgotten? The night we met at the Pendleton ball, you spoke of your hatred for the English."

"Not all of them," he drawled.

His nonchalance tore at her. She whirled around. "Of course. Just one family in particular. I suppose I was good enough to spread my legs and be treated like a whore because by my being English you would have never offered me anything more."

A flash of anguish passed over his features before disappearing so quickly, Teresa was sure it was nothing more than her imagination.

He closed his eyes for a moment as if he were fighting for control. With a sigh, he turned away and walked toward the window.

And then, without a backward glance, he was gone.

Teresa willed her frozen limbs to move. She ran to the window, catching sight of him moving through the garden as the moonlight illuminated him from above. Her whole body felt like it would burst into tears, but she stared dry-eyed out the window as her heart shattered into a million pieces.

Long after he'd gone, she stood there. How had something so wonderful ended so terribly? And now there was the duchess to deal with. Teresa left the window and pulled on the first dress she touched. Somehow it seemed fitting that it was the black mourning dress she'd worn to her mother's funeral.

Her gaze strayed to the rumpled bed. How ironic that in the process of trying to protect her family's reputation, she had succeeded in bringing scandal to her own. A harsh sob escaped her as she forced her eyes away and dragged a brush through her hair.

Crossing to the door, she took a deep breath and released it slowly. She couldn't, wouldn't let the duchess see how badly Mateo had hurt her. Squaring her shoulders, she left the room and headed toward the study.

Teresa raised her hand to knock, then changed her mind. Twisting the handle, she walked into the book-lined room. A small fire crackled in the grate, but the very air chilled her to the bone.

Vivian turned from her contemplation of the portrait over the fireplace. Perhaps it was the glacial coldness in her aunt's gaze that pervaded the room. Teresa glanced at the painting of her uncle, the former duke. He died so long ago. Had his early death caused Vivian to become the bitter woman she was today?

"Where is your lover?"

"He's left. There will be no marriage." Teresa strove to keep her voice even.

"How can you do this to me?" Vivian raged. "To Sarah? I've fed you, sheltered you, and this is how you repay me? By bringing disgrace to this house and ruining Sarah's chances of a good match."

"This has nothing to do with Sarah and everything to do with your own precious position in society." Teresa curled her hands into fists at her sides. "You feed and shelter your servants as well. You have always considered Mama and I to be little better than your hired help all because Mama married a man born without a title. It doesn't matter in the slightest that he spent his life in service to the king."

Vivian leaned toward Teresa. "We all spend our lives serving the king in one form or another."

Teresa could smell the stale scent of champagne on her breath. Swallowing back the bile rising in her throat, she refused to step back. Even that small movement would lead Vivian to believe she had her cowering in fear.

"You will be out of this house by the end of the week." The duchess turned away and examined the large blood-red ruby on her hand. "Your maid may stay or go. I don't care, but I won't provide references. And one from you will be worth nothing." She swung back to face Teresa, a sly smile curving her lips. "Perhaps, she should stay with me. After all, you will be lucky to provide for yourself on the pittance left to you by your father."

"I would rather *die* than leave her to be ill-treated by you," Teresa shouted and left the room. She fled past gawking servants to her bedchamber, unsure how much longer she'd be able to keep her tears at bay.

Teresa slammed the heavy oak door closed on the prying eyes of those waiting for a bit of gossip just as the first tears escaped her lashes.

"What's happened? The duchess has awakened the staff and demanded that your trunks be taken out of storage immediately."

Teresa crossed the room and sank into Betsy's arms, crying freely now. "Oh Betsy, I've been the biggest fool. I tried to keep Mateo from destroying my life, and I've done it myself."

Chapter Twenty

Within three days, her disgrace had sped through the *Ton* like wildfire. Teresa was sure the duchess fanned the flames. Determined to carry on as though her life hadn't crumbled into ashes, she tried to fit in her normal activities between packing her and Betsy's belongings as well as sorting through the remainder of Mama's things.

When she arrived at the weekly meeting of the Ladies of Scientific Interests, she'd been made aware she wasn't welcome. Everywhere Teresa went she was given the cut direct more times than she could count. Ladies of the *Ton* crossed the street to avoid her, held their skirts so they wouldn't brush against her own, or stared through her as if she no longer existed.

And she quickly learned the gentlemen of the *Beau Monde* were in fact disgusting lechers. She had received more indecent proposals than she wanted to acknowledge. The worst of it was some had come from men she'd never even been introduced to. She cringed in embarrassment each time she recalled yet another offer of protection. But unfortunately humiliation wasn't fatal, so she simply bestowed a steely-eyed glare and walked away, leaving the gentleman in question standing in the entryway.

Teresa pushed the plaguing memories away and fastened her blue pelisse. Luckily, she'd been able to purchase a small cottage without draining her limited funds. She would be leaving for Surrey in two days' time. If she wanted the latest journal article on plant studies, she would have to brave the 'good' people of London and visit the bookseller.

Tying the ribbons of her matching bonnet, she tried to quell the churning of her stomach. She wouldn't slink away like some criminal. She would hold her head high today if it killed her.

"Are you certain you want to do this?"

Teresa turned to find Betsy in the doorway. "Yes." She took in the maid's light wool cloak. "Has the duchess sent you off on another fool's errand?"

Betsy fingered the edge of her sleeve. "I thought perhaps you'd like some company."

"I'd like that very much," Teresa said softly.

"Then Freddie has his coach outside to take us wherever you need to go."

"I thought he washed his hands of me."

Betsy shook her head. "Come along before he leaves us for a paying fare."

Teresa stepped outside into the bright sunlight and suddenly wanted to run back to her bedchamber. Could she face another day of censure?

Betsy continued on, unaware of Teresa's change of heart. Freddie helped her into the coach then turned and waited for Teresa to join them.

As though sensing her desire to withdraw from the outing, he bounded forward. "Tess." He bowed over her hand then tucked it in the crook of his arm before leading her to the carriage.

Teresa smiled. "My, what a gentleman you've become," she teased, her apprehension fading away.

"Naw. I just knows how to greet a lady. I seen enough of them rich coves do it when they're trying to impress their lady friends." He blew his brown hair out of his eyes.

"Well, thank you but I'm not a 'Lady.' I'm not even a proper miss anymore."

She started to enter the carriage when Freddie pulled her back. "You are a lady. You always been. Don't let anyone say you ain't. If they do, I'll set them straight." He slapped his hand with his fist.

Touched beyond words, Teresa squeezed his arm. "Thank you," she said in a barely audible whisper.

"Are we going to sit here drawing flies, or are we off to the book lender's?" Betsy demanded, sticking her head out the coach window.

"We're off." Teresa allowed Freddie to assist her inside and settled against the worn leather squabs.

A few minutes later, she was thankful for the frayed curtains that hung limply from the windows. At least she was shielded from the knowing glances sure to be directed her way as they moved at a snail's pace through the congested streets. Finally, they pulled to a stop. Freddie opened the door and helped them alight.

Clinging to her courage the way a frightened child hangs on to its mother's skirts, Teresa lifted her chin and headed for the small bookshop sandwiched between two milliners. She opened the door, catching the scent of old books, paper, and ink and instantly felt calmer. Books had always soothed her and did no less this time.

Teresa started down the aisle toward the newest books on gardening then stopped as the whispered conversation of two women at a nearby table caught her attention.

"Sir Robert Darlington, a thief?"

"That is the rumour. Delicious, isn't it?"

"Does immoral blood run in the family?"

"Well..."

One of the women sidled closer to her companion, and Teresa found herself straining to hear.

"Mere days ago his daughter was caught in a most compromising position. And rather than hide her shame, she's flaunting her new status as a fallen woman by continuing to go about in society as though she hasn't a care in the world."

"Oh, my," the other woman tittered.

Teresa started forward, seeing the two malicious gossips through a red haze of anger when someone grabbed her dress and yanked her backward.

"They're not worth causing a scene. You'll only give them more talk to spread about," Betsy hissed in her ear, her face flushed with outrage.

With a curt nod, Teresa turned away, her jaw clenched tight to prevent the words she longed to hurl at the two women from escaping. She made her way to the far corner of the small room, intent on finding what she wanted and leaving before she was noticed. Directing Betsy to start at the nearest towering bookshelf, she headed to the opposite end.

Her fingers reached for a rich brown leather-bound book just as the import of what the first tallow-faced gossipmonger had said sunk into her brain. *Robert Darlington, a thief?*

Teresa's hand closed around empty air. She stood staring at the numerous volumes on various gardening techniques yet saw nothing. Had Mateo not only taken her virginity but spread the falsehood about her father as well? Had she really been no more than a means of revenge? If so, he had succeeded beyond his wildest dreams. She was no longer welcome anywhere in London.

The portly owner of the shop passed behind her, his hands taking full measure of her backside. She inhaled sharply and whirled to face him.

"I have something in the back room I'm sure you'd like, Miss." He winked at her and leered at her bosom.

"I'm sure I would not. How dare you speak to me in such a manner?" Teresa nearly shouted. In her anger, she forgot her wish to make her purchases and leave unnoticed.

"Don't be so high in the instep with me. I've

heard the rumours. Holding out for a rich pigeon, are you?"

Betsy hurried forward and tried to drag Teresa away from the odious man.

Teresa shook her off. "And what rumours would those be? That all book lenders are lecherous old men with foul-smelling breath and stomachs larger than their nether regions?" she asked in a clear, loud voice for all in the shop to hear.

The man turned bright red and mumbled something under his breath. Without another word, Teresa stormed out of the shop leaving Betsy to scramble after her.

Freddie took one look at her face and jumped to the ground. He hurried forward and opened the door to the coach. Teresa sailed inside without a word, quickly followed by Betsy.

"Take us back to Perth House," Betsy instructed before pulling the door closed.

The carriage bounced and swayed as Freddie resumed his seat. In a few moments, the horses set off at a steady pace.

Betsy pressed her lips together and gazed around the shabby interior. She burst into laughter. Teresa sent her a murderous glare.

"I'm sorry, dear," Betsy said, wiping tears from her eyes.

"You sound dreadfully sorry—laughing like a lunatic." Teresa crossed her arms over her chest.

"Did you see his face when you mentioned his nether parts being smaller than his stomach?" Betsy's laughter echoed around the enclosed space.

"Yes." A grin tugged at Teresa's lips. "I just meant it as a set down. I didn't realize it would be true." She gave a small laugh, then sobered. "Will I ever be treated with respect again? Or will I always be considered little better than a lady-bird?"

Betsy reached across the seat and clasped

Teresa's hand in her own. "Don't talk like that. You will never be a woman of easy virtue. One night with a man doesn't make you anything but a woman who made a mistake. Remember that. Besides in Surrey, no one will know what happened here."

"I don't know if that's altogether true. It's one of the reasons I purchased a cottage on the outskirts of Surrey instead of in the village." Teresa paused. "Do you think I should pass myself off as a widow?"

Betsy sighed. "I feel as though I've failed you. Why didn't I realize you'd fallen in love? All the signs were there, but I was too blind to see them." She touched Teresa on the cheek. "You've always been like a daughter to me."

Teresa gave her a tremulous smile. "And you've been like a mother to me."

"Together we shall deal with what comes as it comes. No sense planning for the worst."

"The worst seems to be all that is happening to me lately," Teresa murmured.

Upon arriving back at Perth House, Teresa went to her room, shed her bonnet and pelisse, and headed toward her mother's suite of rooms. If she kept herself busy then she wouldn't have time to think and if she didn't have time to think, she wouldn't have time to dwell on all she'd lost in the span of one night. She opened the door leading to the bedchamber and froze.

The emptiness of the room assailed her already raw senses, making the loss of her mother as fresh as if it had occurred yesterday instead of weeks ago. The bed had been stripped, the wardrobe and bureaus stood empty, and the credenza was devoid of the many portraits of her father. Those same paintings now lay in a trunk surrounded by tissue and Sophia's jewel case.

Teresa couldn't help but feel she was burying her mother twice. First in the cold, unforgiving earth, and now in a silk and paper lined trunk.

She moved further into the room, trailing her hand over the window seat cushion where Sophia spent so many hours waiting for her beloved to return to her. "Oh Mama, I wish you were here. I miss you so."

Wiping away the tear that slid down her cheek, Teresa crossed to the small connecting parlor. This room too was nearly empty. Mama had rarely used the space for anything other than storing the items of her married life. All that remained were a few odd volumes of poetry and military history on the bookshelves and Robert Darlington's large oak desk she had refused to part with.

Teresa collected the first row of books and put them into an old weathered chest sitting nearby. One by one, she emptied the shelves, leaving only a few traces of dust behind. She closed the lid, brushed off her hands, turned, and nearly collided with Lady Sarah.

"I'm sorry," Sarah reached out to steady her cousin. "I wanted to...I...How are you coping with all the..." she let the words trail off.

"The scandal. You can say the word, Sarah. I won't hate you for it."

Lady Sarah colored and looked away. "Do you regret it?" she asked in a quiet voice.

Teresa moved to the settee and gestured for Sarah to join her. "Do I regret giving myself to the man I fell in love with, whom I thought loved me? Would you believe me if I said I don't know? Ask me instead if I hate the gossip, the way my name is bandied about. Then my answer is yes. But you see it's not the words so much as the whispers I can't bear."

"Have you..." Sarah hesitated then seemed to decide there was no ladylike way to pose her question and plunged ahead, "have you received any word from Montayas?"

"No." Teresa brushed back an errant curl from her cheek. "If I'm honest, I don't expect to."

Sarah looked at her aghast. "How dare he leave you to suffer your fate alone. I shall pay him a call and tell him so. Or perhaps, I will ask Linley to call him out. He feels you've been taken advantage of by an experienced rake and being that you have had little contact with men, you didn't realize what you were doing."

Teresa took both of Sarah's hands in her own. "Please don't do anything. I just want to try and forget everything about that night. The last thing I want is for Mateo to think I'm pining away for him."

"But you are, aren't you?" Sarah asked in a concerned tone.

Teresa avoided meeting her cousin's gaze. "Perhaps," she admitted softly.

"He has taken so much from you and yet you do nothing to make him repay what he's stolen from you." Anger snapped in Sarah's light blue eyes.

"He hasn't stolen anything from me. Everything I lost—my honor, even my reputation though at the time I didn't know it—I gave freely. I have no one to blame but myself." Teresa felt her tears hovering close to the surface.

Lady Sarah cleared her throat and changed the subject almost as if she was aware how taxing the conversation was on Teresa's vow to shed no more tears over the Count de Montayas. "I didn't seek you out to upset you. I wanted to be sure you didn't need any help making arrangements to have your things taken to Surrey."

"I don't need any help, but thank you for the offer. Other than finishing this room," Teresa waved her hand around the nearly empty space, "I believe Betsy and I are ready to set off on our new lives."

"Do you..." Sarah trailed off once more, her

finger tracing the brocade pattern of the settee, then started again. "Will you have enough money?"

Of this, Teresa knew she could put her cousin's mind to rest. "If we're careful, we shall be able to live comfortably."

Sarah raised her head, her gaze troubled. "Are you certain? I have no funds of my own, but I do have this." She released the clasp on the brooch she wore near her shoulder and held it out.

It was an exquisite piece in the shape of a flower. Sapphires formed petals set on a slender golden stem with a tiny spray of leaves made of emeralds.

Teresa shook her head. "I couldn't. Viscount Linley gave that to you. Don't worry." She tried to give a reassuring smile. "Betsy and I won't live like paupers. It'll be different than what we've become accustomed to, but we'll manage."

Sarah reached out and pressed the brooch into Teresa's hand. "Take it. Promise me you'll pawn it should you ever find yourself in need of funds."

Teresa didn't know what to say for fear of bursting into tears.

"No. Don't refuse. You've done so much for me, shielding me from the worst of Mother's temper, playing the chaperone so I could go on outings with Linley. Let me do this. Promise you will use it if you need to."

"I promise." Teresa closed her fingers around the elegant pin. "I fear I have something to ask of you after all." She hesitated for a moment. "If you are certain it will do no damage to your reputation, I'd like to write to you once Betsy and I are settled."

Sarah smiled. "I'd like that. And don't worry about my reputation. I'll make arrangements to receive your letters secretly if I have to. I'm sure a certain hackney driver would be willing to deliver our missives to one another."

Teresa looked up, a movement in the hall catching her eye. It was the duchess. She closed her eyes and felt her spirits deflate a little more. Gathering her composure, she waited for the inevitable scene to come.

She wasn't disappointed.

The duchess strode into the room, her hands jammed at her hips, towering over them in her disapproval. "Sarah, you are to stay away from Teresa." She spoke as if the two of them were the only ones present. "If she approaches you, especially in public, you are to give her the cut direct."

Sarah stood. "No, Mother, I won't. She deserves our support, not our scorn."

Vivian grabbed Sarah by the elbow. "You will do as I say."

Sarah yanked her arm free. "Not anymore."

"Do not cross me in this or you'll regret it. A word in a certain viscount's ear will bring you to heel."

"Sorry, Mother, but you don't control me any longer. Viscount Linley has spoken to the new Duke of Perth, Father's heir and nephew. Surely you remember the man who so kindly let us continue living in Perth House after Father's death. He has given his permission for Linley and me to wed. The betrothal will be announced at a grand ball to be held at the end of the month."

"What?" the duchess screeched. "Why was I not informed? Why was I not present at this so-called meeting?"

"The duke is aware that you approved of the match. You all but crowed over your coup of landing your daughter an heir to an earldom as if Linley and I had no say in the matter. It was decided that it would be best if the duke told you the news. Was there not a letter from him in today's post?"

"You will not marry that sniveling bastard. How

dare he go behind my back. I shall forbid the marriage."

"As much as you like to believe you control my fate, you don't. After all, as a woman, you have no more power in these things than I do. Linley has offered for me, and the duke has accepted. The marriage settlements have all been arranged." Sarah turned and headed for the door.

She stopped and looked back as she reached the threshold. "Oh, and Mother, I told Linley all about you and what you're capable of." She grabbed the door handle and slammed the door as she left.

Teresa stood in shock, her mouth agape. Gone was the pale, submissive ghost of Lady Sarah. In her place was a confident young woman who, secure in the love of her intended, had finally found the strength to stand up to her mother's bullying.

Giving herself a mental shake, Teresa quickly followed Lady Sarah from the room in no way eager to take the brunt of the duchess' wrath.

****

Unable to bear the thought of sitting across the table from the duchess for the evening meal, Teresa had asked Betsy to have a tray sent to her room. And even then, she found she had no appetite and only picked at the chicken swimming in wine sauce, unable to do justice to the fine repast. Finally giving up the pretense of eating, she finished packing her remaining gowns, leaving only enough garments for the next two days hanging in the clothespress.

A few hours later, Betsy returned to collect the tray and to help Teresa undress before she retired for the night. She bustled about moving bandboxes and stacks of books from one side of the room to the other while Teresa checked items off a list of things still to be done.

"I've spoken to Freddie," Betsy stated, setting one last book atop a stacked column of scientific tomes.

Teresa looked up from the list, her quill poised over the sheet of vellum. "Please tell me he didn't go back and accost that wretched bookseller on my behalf."

"I don't believe he did. His knuckles didn't look any worse than usual. Though I must say, it would have served the repulsive scoundrel right if Freddie had." Betsy waved the air as if dispelling a particularly unpleasant odor. "Freddie asked me to tell you he called in a few favors owed him and has arranged transportation for our possessions to be taken to the cottage. He will, of course, take us himself as promised."

Teresa stared at her in dismay. "But I've already made arrangements to have everything except two bandboxes to be sent in the morning. A Mr. Tibbles will be arriving, expecting payment."

"I know. I've taken care of that. Mr. Tibbles won't be here in the morning." Betsy attempted to look innocent, but she failed miserably, blurting out, "I sent a note stating we would no longer be in need of his services and signed your name."

Teresa jumped from the bed, the sheet of paper fluttering to the floor. "Betsy, you didn't. I could ill afford to pay his fees. How will I manage to pay twice that amount to Freddie's companions?"

"I see I've forgotten to tell you the best of the news. They require no payment but a pint of ale at the nearest tavern."

"Truly?" Teresa calculated the money she would save. While they had more than enough to last several years, she intended to limit additional expenses to as few as possible.

"I knew you'd be pleased," Betsy beamed. "Would you like to retire for the evening, or shall I return later?"

"Now, I think." Teresa retrieved her list from

the floor and laid it on the small desk in the corner of the room. With care not to spill it, she capped the ink and began pulling pins from her hair.

Betsy came around behind her and unfastened her gown. "Would you like to rise early on the morrow? Freddie and the others will be here before the noon hour to begin loading the coaches and wagons, and I'm sure you'll want to double-check that nothing has been missed."

Teresa ran her hands through her hair, massaging her scalp. "Yes, I would. I want to be able to watch the proceedings to ensure the duchess doesn't try to interfere. I don't expect any unpleasantness but…"

"But one can never tell what her grace will do," Betsy finished. She helped Teresa out of the gown then dropped a clean white night rail over her head.

Teresa pushed her arms into the sleeves. "I'm sure she'll be glad to be rid of us."

"I know I won't miss her," Betsy muttered under her breath.

Teresa smiled and turned around, tying the slim pink ribbons at her throat. "What would I do without you to help me keep my good humor in spite of all that's happened?"

"You'll never find out. When you embarked on this path, I promised to stand beside you regardless of the outcome. I mean to keep my word," the maid responded, folding Teresa's discarded dress and petticoats over her arm. She moved to the table and picked up the untouched dinner tray. "I'll bid you good night."

Teresa opened the door, and Betsy stepped out into the hall with one final warning. "Don't stay up too late reading your journal articles. The morning will come soon enough."

Teresa closed the door, crossed the room, and climbed into bed. With the sheet pulled up to her waist, she leaned back against the headboard, hugging her knees to her chest. She hadn't the heart to tell Betsy she seemed to have lost the ability to concentrate on her studies since Mateo's fateful visit that night.

Mateo. Where was he at this moment? Was he in a club like White's or Boodle's proclaiming to all within hearing that Robert Darlington was a thief with a daughter of easy virtue? Or was he at home in his barely furnished townhouse on Grosvenor Square plotting the next step in his carefully orchestrated plan of revenge? Or perhaps, having gotten his revenge, he didn't think of her at all. Of the three scenarios, Teresa wasn't sure which she hated the most.

How had she, a woman of intellect, allowed herself to be taken in so completely? *Because*, whispered a voice in her mind, *you fell in love with him...* "And became a willing pawn in his game," she said aloud.

Her gaze strayed to the window. He had climbed into her heart with as much stealth as he employed to climb into her room on so many occasions. Pushing back the sheet, she padded across the floor, the wooden boards smooth under her bare feet.

Teresa opened the window and looked out. The moon hid behind a bank of clouds. Gazing out over the gardens, she could see nothing but an inky blackness below. She didn't understand the compulsion that drew her to the window. There would be no more midnight visits from the masked intruder who had stolen her heart.

Her eyes closed as a soft breeze teased her hair bringing stray tendrils to brush against her cheeks like a lover's touch. She replayed all the times Mateo had kissed her, touched her, and seemed to care for her.

Teresa opened her eyes with a shake of her head

and leaned against the window frame. "How could I have been so wrong?"

Feeling more alone than she ever had, she contemplated pouring her hurt and anger into a letter to Blaine. His last letter waited on the desk for a response. She dismissed the idea almost as soon as it formed. What was done was done, as Betsy liked to say. By telling Blaine, she would only cause more pain. She knew he would rush back from France and force a confrontation with Mateo in an attempt to defend the honor she no longer possessed.

With a sigh, she turned away from the window. Knowing she wouldn't be able to sleep anytime soon, Teresa headed to her mother's former sitting room and one of her father's dusty volumes on military history. Surely that would enable her to fall asleep and escape her sorrow for a little while.

Lighting the candle she left on the desk, Teresa noticed all of the trunks and boxes had been removed save one. It sat on her father's desk. Betsy must have had the others taken downstairs to be placed in the coaches on the morrow. She opened the trunk, glad to see it was one she had packed full of books. Reading each title as she came to it, she soon had a precarious stack of rejected tomes.

The Horse and the Battlefield. That seemed like a dry enough subject to put anyone to sleep. Teresa set the book aside and began replacing the others into the trunk. Knocking the pile with the side of her hand, she sent them toppling to the floor. She cursed her own clumsiness and dropped to her knees to retrieve the books. Gathering them in her arms, she gripped the edge of the desk as she gained her feet.

A quiet click and the sound of a cupboard door opening held her motionless. Looking around the side of the desk, Teresa gazed into the gloomy recesses of a hidden compartment. She dropped the books into the trunk, grabbed the candle from the desktop, and sat back on her heels in front of the opening.

Had Papa known about the hidden panel when he purchased the desk? With hesitant fingers, she reached in and pulled out an oilskin packet whose seal had long been broken. Scanning the sheets, she realized they were missives sent to her father from his superiors during his tenure in the military. It seemed he had indeed known of the hidden compartment. She replaced the papers in the packet and set it aside.

Next, she removed letters that had been tied together with a faded blue ribbon. Opening the first, she recognized her mother's handwriting. Love letters. They were love letters from her mother to her father. Teresa retied the fraying ribbon with care and set them next to the oilskin packet. The space was empty now save for a small wooden box.

Teresa pulled the candle closer to her from its position on the floor. Settling the box in her lap, she lifted the lid. There, nestled among white velvet folds, sat a gold box encrusted with jewels, a large ruby in the center. It was half as long as her hand and nearly as wide.

The Pequena.

Chapter Twenty-One

Teresa stared at the precious stones glimmering in the candlelight. "Oh Papa, Mateo was right," she whispered.

Dropping her head into her hands, she closed her eyes against the proof of her father's thievery. Everything she suffered had been for nothing. Strange though that her father's betrayal left her feeling only numb, whereas Mateo's tore at her heart.

Carefully closing the lid, she laid the wooden box near the candle, replaced the packet of military orders into the cupboard, and shut the panel. As much as she dreaded it, she knew there was only one thing to do.

She had to return the *Pequena* to Mateo. Loathe to even consider his reaction, she gathered up her candle, love letters, and the wooden box. Teresa glanced at the book she'd set aside to take back to her bedchamber and left it where it lay. It wouldn't be needed. She knew, regardless of the boring reading material, she would get no sleep this night. On leaden feet, she slowly made her way back to her room.

Closing the chamber door, she slipped the packet of letters into the last remaining trunk. Though she would never read the letters, they were a symbol of her parents' love. She would treasure them always. She crossed the room and crawled onto the mattress. The box sat in the center of the bed, yet she couldn't bear to look at it. Pride had cost her so much. Not once had she considered Mateo's accusations to contain even a grain of truth.

A sound of anguish broke free from her heart. How naïve she'd been, blindly believing her father could do nothing wrong. In truth, he was responsible for the destruction of an entire family. All because he coveted something that belonged to another. But why? Why would he risk all to steal the jeweled box only to hide it away for the next twenty years, never revealing his secret even on his deathbed?

Morning dawned, leaving her heavy eyed and withdrawn. Disillusionment hung over her like a shroud. She found no answers in the long hours of darkness.

Betsy entered the room, placed a tray of tea and toast on a nearby table, and pulled back the curtains, allowing the early morning sunlight to filter into the room. She turned toward the bed and gasped in surprise at finding Teresa sitting fully clothed in the middle of the wide expanse. "Gracious. What are you doing sitting in the dark?"

"Sorry. I didn't mean to give you a fright. Do you think Freddie would be willing to take me to Grosvenor Square after our things are loaded for transport?"

Betsy raised her eyebrows. "Grosvenor Square? Where a certain count resides?"

Teresa examined the fine ribbon threaded through the lace at the end of her cuff. "Yes."

"You're not going to do something you'll only regret later, are you?"

"I'm afraid where the Count de Montayas is concerned, I have nothing but regrets."

Betsy sat down on the edge of the bed. "Then why pay a call on him? Why cause yourself more pain?"

Teresa looked into her maid's concerned gaze. "I need to right a wrong that has been left too long undone."

****

Teresa stepped down from the coach and stood staring at the imposing entrance of the townhouse, unconsciously gripping Freddie's arm.

"Tess? You certain you're wanting to go through with this here visit? You look whiter than Betsy's hair."

She smiled, knowing Betsy would have a word or two to say about his comparison. "I can do this," she said more to bolster her courage than to convince Freddie. "Would you accompany me to the door?"

"You don't think I'd a let you go in there alone, do you?" He brushed off his shabby black jacket and pulled at the worn cuffs.

Teresa took a deep breath and clutched the small wooden box she carried a little tighter. "Shall we?"

Freddie led her to the door and knocked twice. He looked down at her and winked, trying to make things better for her just as he always had. Though he was no relation by blood, Teresa considered him the best brother one could have hoped for.

The door opened. Eduardo filled the doorway, his scowl fading away into surprise.

"We're here to see the count, and we ain't leaving 'til we do." Freddie stepped forward, ready to force their way into the building.

Instead of refusing, Eduardo stepped back and allowed them to enter. "*El Senor Conde* is entertaining. If you would wait here, I will see if he's willing to receive other guests." He turned and started down the hall when the woman Teresa knew as Tia Elena rushed from a nearby room, a flood of Spanish pouring from her lips.

Eduardo responded in his native tongue. "I must..." he looked at his mother then looked back at Teresa as though searching for the English words to convey his meaning. "You wait." He turned and let the other woman lead him away.

"I hope this don't take long. I already sent Tom and Paddy ahead to Surrey with the wagons," Freddie said.

Teresa gave a wan smile and looked about the foyer. She had no desire to linger here anymore than he did.

Sounds of male laughter drifted down the hall. She leaned forward, concentrating. Mateo was in that room. She'd know his voice anywhere. She also discerned one other.

Sir Charles Astley. He must have returned to Town. He'd left on sudden urgent business the day after he had accosted her on the terrace at the...funny, she couldn't remember what ball it was. But then after all that had happened, it seemed oh so long ago. And yet, that night changed her life. It was the first time she met Mateo, though with his face masked she hadn't known it was him at the time.

Teresa started forward.

"Tess, where you goin'?" Freddie whispered. His voice seemed loud in the empty foyer.

She pointed to the door along the hall on their right. "Montayas is in there, and I mean to speak with him." She picked up her skirts with one hand and headed toward the room.

"All right," Freddie said, his tone registering his displeasure.

Teresa approached the entrance, wondering if she shouldn't have waited for Eduardo's return. She started to knock on the open door when Mateo's next words stabbed at her like a knife.

"I suppose it was the novelty of bedding a Spanish nobleman." He tossed back the rest of his drink and poured another measure.

"I'm sure the rumours that you Spanish blokes are hung like a horse had a lot to do with it," Astley said with a coarse laugh. "I've been trying to bed her myself for months. Look. She's ruined, yet she's come looking for more." He pointed to the open door where Teresa stood, unable to move.

Mateo met her gaze. Shock, anger, and sorrow passed over his face in quick succession. She felt her face drain of color and with a strangled sound, backed away from the opening.

"Teresa, wait," he called over the raucous laughter filling the room.

She turned and collided with Eduardo. His hands gripped her arms to steady her. Wrenching free, she ran to where Freddie stood, Eduardo close on her heels.

Sensing something was wrong, Freddie hurried toward her, his hands curled into fists.

Mateo clattered into the hall. "Teresa, wait."

She turned and shoved the wooden box at Eduardo. Teresa took a small step forward overwhelmed by feelings of hurt and humiliation. She stared at Mateo. "I am not a whore," she said with quiet dignity.

"A whore!" Freddie exploded. He lunged at Mateo.

Eduardo grabbed Freddie, holding him back.

"Bloody bastard," Freddie snarled, struggling to break free. "I'll tear his head off, I will."

Eduardo called to Mateo. The foreign words sounded distinctly like an order. Mateo shook his head in the negative, gestured at Freddie, and answered with what sounded like an order of his own. Eduardo quickly responded.

Mateo raked a hand through his hair and looked at Teresa. He opened his mouth to speak, then turned away and went back into the study, closing the door.

Eduardo released Freddie with a push. "Leave now."

"Like hell." Freddie glowered.

Teresa clutched at his arm. "Please, take me back to the carriage. I want to leave."

He looked at her, then the closed door, clearly torn between his desire to defend her honor and to do as she wished.

"You're right. He's not worth bloodying my fives over." Laying his arm around her shoulders, he drew her toward the front door where Eduardo stood ready to escort them out.

Noticing he held the wooden box she'd pushed at him tucked under his arm, she halted in front of Eduardo. "That," she gestured to the box, "belongs to your family. If you would see that Montayas receives it. There is a letter inside explaining everything. I put it there as I wasn't sure he would see me." She turned and led the way outside.

"Bloody Spaniards. Almost makes me want to join old Boney's forces," Freddie muttered.

Teresa looked back at the figure standing in the doorway. She turned, determined to know the answer to at least one of the questions plaguing her since that fateful night with Mateo. "What does *mia hechicera* mean?" she asked.

Eduardo hesitated a moment before answering. "My enchantress."

Hiding her surprise, she inclined her head. "Thank you."

Without a backward glance, she allowed Freddie to assist her into the carriage. As he started to close the door, she held out her hand. "Would you take us to the cottage instead of Perth House?"

Understanding her need to leave London behind, he nodded. "Sure, Tess."

"But you haven't said a proper goodbye to Lady Sarah," Betsy protested from her corner of the seat. "What happened in there to make you want to leave a day early? I knew I should have insisted on coming inside with you. But no, I let you talk me into staying out here."

"I'm certain Lady Sarah will understand. I'll send her a letter and apologize for my rudeness." Teresa's composure began to crumble. She drew in a shaky breath. "Nothing happened. I just don't think I can bear to stay in London another day."

"Nothing, my arse," Freddie muttered.

"Watch your language," Betsy said.

"Yes, Mum." With a tide of red color staining his cheeks, he shut the door.

Teresa lifted the curtain and stuck her head out the window. "Freddie."

"Yeah."

"Promise me you won't try to defend my honor to the count or anyone else."

Freddie shook his head. "Can't do that. If I get the chance..." He glanced back at the townhouse.

"I'm asking you not to do this."

"You afraid I can't handle myself? Why I been in more tavern brawls than I can remember."

Teresa realized she had insulted his manly pride. Being only seventeen, she was certain Freddie had been called on quite often to prove his manhood. "No, it's not that at all. I just don't want to have to visit you at Newgate."

Freddie's eyebrows rose. "Newgate! Guess I'll do as you ask then."

"Thank you." She dropped the curtain back into place and sat back on the seat. A sigh from the depths of her soul escaped her lips.

As agreed, Freddie headed for Surrey, leaving Perth House, London, and Teresa's former life behind. She pulled aside the thin drape and stared out at the passing countryside. Low moss-covered stone walls divided rolling pastures. Cows huddled together, dotting the landscape.

Teresa watched shadows roll over the ground as

a bank of clouds blotted out the sun. She shivered and couldn't help comparing the action of the clouds to Mateo's presence in her life. With his betrayal, he'd taken the sun, leaving her in a dark and dreary world.

Would she have been better off not knowing what he was about until it was too late to save the Darlington reputation? Even though she had known of his plans, she certainly hadn't stopped the destruction. Nothing had been the same since her father's death and it had only gotten worse as time passed.

Closing her eyes, she remembered happier times when her parents were still alive. Mama's laughter filling the air. Papa's booming voice echoing down the hall. Would life ever be that happy again?

Chapter Twenty-Two

Mateo slouched in the broad wingback chair, his feet stretched before him and crossed at the ankles. Though it was barely noon, he nursed a second glass of Madeira. From where he sat, he watched the rain fall against the window. It was a soft gentle rain, reminding him of a woman's tears. Did even the heavens cry for what he had done to Teresa?

He rose and walked to the window, setting the glass on a nearby rosewood table. Raising an arm to rest against the casing, he leaned against it, rubbing his chin along the back of his hand. It had been nearly four weeks since his return to Spain and the day she had brought the *Pequena* to him.

He'd begun repairing the Montayas name and all that it entailed, yet it meant nothing to him. Nothing. The ceremony given by the Church restoring its blessing to the house of Montayas, the villagers willing to work the lands once more, even being respected by his peers as he had longed for since he was a boy. Still, a beautiful woman willing to risk anything to protect her family haunted him. How could he have not realized that she was so much like himself?

Mateo closed his eyes, shame washing over him. How could he have let her leave that last time without trying to explain? He hadn't meant a word of the horrible things she overheard. Still searching for the *Pequena*, he'd invited those male members of the *Ton* who were known for their ability to ferret out the secrets of others albeit for their own uses. He had hoped with a few well-placed questions, he would learn some clue to the *Pequena's* whereabouts.

When questioned about Teresa, he felt he had no option but to play the rake. Unfortunately, he noticed her standing in the entrance of the study too late. He'd already uttered the damning words. That fool Astley had only made things worse by drawing attention to her and braying like an ass. Instead of smashing Astley in the jaw as he wanted to, Mateo joined in with the laughter. Even now, the memory of her face, the hurt and bewilderment in her eyes, tore at him.

"*El Senor Conde.*"

"Don't call me that," Mateo snarled, turning around to face his cousin. He raked a hand through his hair. "*Dios*, I've grown to hate that title."

"But you are the *Conde* with all the respect due one of the *aristocracia*," Eduardo said.

"And I don't want it."

Eduardo moved to stand beside him. "You've achieved all you promised, but you're not happy. Your title is no longer an empty one without meaning." He eyed Mateo, his head tilted in speculation. "You are here in Spain, but I fear your heart is still in England."

Mateo left the window, crossed to the table, and downed the rest of the wine in his glass. "It was just a slight flirtation to keep her off balance while I exposed her father." His hand tightened around the crystal goblet. "That was all it was meant to be," he whispered.

"But it turned to love." Eduardo leaned against the newly hung silk drapes.

Mateo shrugged and poured another measure of wine.

"Why didn't you say anything these past weeks?"

He turned around with a sigh. "How do I tell you of such things when her father is the cause of the years of hardship and humiliation our family endured?"

"Love rules the heart, not the mind. One has no control over who he falls in love with." Eduardo took the glass from Mateo's hand and set it aside. "I think a trip to England is in order."

Mateo dropped into the chair he vacated earlier. A rising tide of hopelessness threatened to overwhelm him. "How can I ask her to forgive me? How could I have left the way I did, with not a word of explanation, of remorse, or even a thought to her feelings? No, I was only concerned with my own pride and restoring the Montayas honor."

Eduardo sat in the chair opposite. He leaned forward, resting his arms on his knees. "I have an idea. A proposition that will benefit all involved."

Mateo rubbed his forehead. "What is it?"

"Forfeit your right to the title."

"What?" Mateo bolted upright in the chair.

Eduardo held up his hands in a placating gesture. "Let me explain. You see, it's really quite simple."

****

Days slipped into weeks and though Teresa tried to forget Mateo, he haunted her dreams. Even in her waking moments, she found him stealing into her thoughts. It made it easier to keep some small hope alive in her heart.

When her monthly flow failed to appear as usual, an irrational fear that maybe she was in fact increasing preyed on her mind. How would she explain the child with no husband? She nursed a secret hope of a baby conceived during that brief night of love. Then one morning she woke to find blood on the sheets.

Staring at the small spots, Teresa burst into tears. She didn't know if she cried from relief or for the child she would never have. Sinking further into a pool of depression, she floundered through each day. Her studies no longer held her attention. She couldn't remember the last time she'd read any of the journal articles piling up on the hall table.

More than once through the past weeks, Teresa would feel Betsy's concerned gaze as they sat together in the evenings. This night was no different.

Betsy sat near a branch of candles, sewing buttons and repairing hems on a few of their gowns. Teresa stared out the window at the darkness and tried to stifle a sigh. It had become an all too familiar ritual, sitting here gazing at the shadows playing over the small garden as she listened to the pull of thread through fabric.

"I know it's not my place, but I feel I must speak bluntly." Betsy's determined tone broke the silence filling the room.

Teresa looked away from the window. "You, of all people, know you are dear to my heart and can speak freely. You've done it often enough in the past," she added wryly.

Betsy looked down at the seam she'd just finished, then lifted her head. "I'm worried about you. You take no interest or joy in your life anymore. Even your studies seem unimportant now. You're withering away like a flower at the end of summer."

"I'm sorry." Teresa didn't know what else to say. How could she explain that she felt as if she'd lost a part of herself?

"Don't apologize for the way you feel. I just want you to be happy again, to start living again." Betsy folded the gown she'd repaired, her hands smoothing away tiny wrinkles. "You've become your mother," she said so quietly Teresa wasn't sure she'd heard her correctly.

"With the knowledge of hindsight, I think I can finally understand how Mama felt. Except she had the consolation of knowing Papa loved her. Whereas I..."

"Whereas you were taken advantage of by a man who pretended to be something he wasn't."

Teresa shifted position, putting her back to the window, and tucked her legs beneath her. "Oh, but Betsy, it was like he walked out of my dreams, and I didn't even know I dreamed of him until he was there. He was tall and dashing and exciting. We had so many adventures. He seemed to be impressed by my intellect instead of intimidated by it. And he wanted to spend time with me, Teresa Darlington, blue stocking extraordinaire." She looked up at the ceiling. "How could I have believed him?" she asked, fighting the tremor in her voice.

"You were in love. Love blinds you to all but the good things."

"Was I? How could I have been so foolish?"

Betsy set the gown aside and moved to sit beside Teresa. "That's what love does. It makes you throw caution to the wind."

"Then I shall have no more love in my life. I can't bear the consequences." Teresa burst into tears and fled from the room.

She ran to her bedchamber and shut the door. Closing her eyes, she held her breath in an effort to stop crying. She promised herself she would shed no more tears over Mateo. She removed her dress and slipped into bed. The thin blanket clutched in her hands, she prayed for sleep to come.

****

Teresa stared at the dressing table as the birds began to sing, heralding the beginning of another day. She longed to pull the blanket over her head and stay there forever. She considered the idea a moment longer before deciding it would only upset Betsy further. How could she go on each day as if nothing had happened when she felt as if her soul had died, leaving her to be nothing more than a walking shell?

After a preemptory knock, Betsy entered carrying a tray. She set it on the small table near the bed and left without a word.

Teresa eyed the tea service for a moment then pushed to a sitting position. As she reached for the cup and saucer, she noticed a sheet of paper folded in half placed beside the sugar bowl. With a frown of puzzlement, she picked up the note.

It contained a single sentence written in Betsy's hand. "It will get easier, I promise you."

Remembering Betsy's loss of her husband and child, Teresa smoothed the paper flat. Suddenly she felt ashamed of the way she'd been acting. Betsy had not only coped with the death of her family, she'd embraced life by raising Teresa to do the same.

Teresa read the passage twice more, a new determination to push Mateo from her heart stealing over her. No more would she mourn the loss of a love that was on her part alone.

She threw back the blankets, strode to the wardrobe, and pulled on her old brown gardening dress. Twisting her hair into a careless knot at the back of her head, she used a few pins to secure the strands that threatened to cause the whole thing to come tumbling down. Without a second glance at the looking glass, she picked up the tray and headed to the kitchen.

She stopped in the entryway. "Betsy, I'll be in the workroom if you need me."

The maid set a hot loaf of bread on the worn surface of the broad countertop. "Your workroom? I'm so glad, but what made you decide to start your experiments again? I've been trying to get you interested in your plant studies for days."

Teresa set the tray down on the small table tucked into the corner of the room. "I'm tired of holding on to the past. Yesterday is gone. Only tomorrow awaits. I want to change things. I want to be happy again, well at least as close to it as I was before."

A look of relief crossed the older woman's face. "Go on then." She made a shooing motion with her hands.

Taking a cup of tea with her, Teresa wandered down the hall. She came to the room that had been set aside for her studies. It was a long narrow room running the entire length of the rear wall of the cottage. A back door led into what would one day be her gardens. On a much smaller scale than those at Perth House, but hers nonetheless. She pushed the door open and stared at the jumble awaiting her.

Boxes and trunks were piled everywhere. Teresa set her teacup on a trunk that stood on end and moved further into the room. There was enough to be done to keep her busy for days. And for some reason, the thought made her happier. She tied an apron around her waist and set to work.

Various plants covered three long trestle tables. By the look of the verdant green leaves and lush blossoms, it was immediately apparent Betsy had been looking after the plants.

The morning passed quickly, and Teresa found herself humming as she worked. She wrestled a table into the center of the room and set a small bandbox on top when Betsy appeared in the doorway, her eyes dancing.

"I've a surprise for you."

Teresa wiped her dusty hands on the corner of her apron. "Has the post arrived? Is it a letter from Lady Sarah? From Blaine?"

"It's much better than that." Betsy looked out into the hall and made a beckoning motion with her hand.

For an instant, Teresa's heart leapt into her

throat. Had Mateo finally come? No. She knew he hadn't. Betsy wouldn't be nearly so welcoming. She rounded the corner of the table. "Is Sarah here?"

Betsy stepped back and allowed the visitor to enter.

"Blaine!" Teresa rushed forward and threw her arms around him. "Was your trip to France successful? Have you seen Freddie? Does the Prince Regent know—"

"That I've been to France? I don't know though I'm no longer required to have a guard follow me wherever I go. Prinny has asked no questions of me. I'd rather leave it that way." Blaine smiled. "Now for the rest of your questions. Mother's family is settled. Yes, Freddie found me soon after I arrived in England. He is well." He stepped back from the embrace then lifted her face to meet his gaze. "I heard what happened. I came as soon as I learned your direction."

She turned away. "I don't regret it. Not a moment of it."

"Even though it caused you to be banished here? Don't you miss London?"

Teresa heard the disbelief in his voice. But as soon as she'd spoken the words, she knew them to be true. She had the most wondrous memories to comfort her when she grew old and sat dreaming by the fire on cold winter days. And she had to believe that in time her heart wouldn't ache so.

Teresa put the table between them and shrugged with what she hoped was the right amount of indifference. "It's not as though I was vetted by the *Ton*. Any ball, soiree, or house party I attended was because the duchess forced me to, certainly not because I was invited. We both know I was only tolerated due to the power she wielded. That was one of the reasons I was made to attend—to remind the *Beau Monde* of her position in society. And to make me suffer, of course."

His gaze traveled over her. She wished she'd taken more care with her appearance. If he looked too closely, he would see what she did when she looked into the looking glass—a woman with sad eyes and deep shadows beneath them.

In an effort to deflect his scrutiny, she began unpacking the small bandbox. "Will you stay for luncheon?"

Blaine shook his head. "I can't. I'm staying at Serenity, though it brings me little peace these days. I've sent Cyrus ahead to warn the caretaker."

"Serenity, your house here in Surrey?"

He nodded, still watching her closely.

"How is Cyrus? I'm surprised he's still with you."

"He's well. As a manservant, there is none better. And though he threatens to leave every time I'm in a foul mood, I think he enjoys coaxing me out of them." Blaine reached out and took her hands. "You are not nearly as happy as you pretend."

She gave him a wan smile. "And could I not say the same thing about you?"

"Marry me. Perhaps together we can find happiness."

Teresa touched his cheek, feeling the faint brush of whiskers against her palm and shook her head. Why couldn't she have fallen in love with this man? "You pine for a dead woman, and I may as well be. Mateo has returned to Spain."

He covered her hand with his own. "Then what better reason to find solace in a marriage based on loving friendship?"

She slipped free of his hold and took a small wooden box from the trunk and set it on the table. Running a finger over the label that read "Dissecting implements," she sighed and looked into his eyes. "In the space of one horrible night, all my dreams of the future were shattered. I can't express how much it means to me that you offer marriage, but you deserve to be loved for yourself, not used as a substitute for another. I have to do this alone. I've no one to blame but myself."

"You don't have to be alone." He moved to stand beside her, his fingers stroking the leaves of a fern as it sat on the corner of the table. "I'll not take no as your answer. Think on it for a few days then I will ask again."

"I fear my answer will be the same."

"Teresa." Betsy hovered in the doorway, her hands twisting her apron into knots. "He's here."

"Who?" Teresa frowned. She couldn't recall ever seeing Betsy so agitated.

"The Count. He's here."

"Mateo?" The word came out in a whisper. She staggered back from the table. Her hands skimmed over her hair, face, and dress. "Tell him I'll see him in the parlour. No, tell him I'm not here. No, wait."

Her gaze flew around the room. She felt like an animal caught in a trap with no escape. Now that he was here, she didn't know what to say, what to do. For weeks, she longed for him to come to her and now that he had, she wasn't sure how she felt. He abandoned her to the cruel members of the *Beau Monde* without a backward glance and yet, her heart cried for him desperately. "Tell him—"

"Tell me what, Teresa?"

She closed her eyes, savoring the way her name rolled off his tongue.

Blaine moved closer and took her hand. She saw the concern in his eyes and stepped nearer, taking comfort in his presence.

Mateo's expression darkened as he glanced from Teresa to Blaine. "Ah, I see what you hesitate to say. I did not mean as much to you as you claimed." He tossed a bouquet of flowers on the table in front of her. "Perhaps I was right after all. You offered your body only as a diversion to keep me from announcing the truth—your father was indeed a thief."

Teresa felt Blaine's entire body go taut at the insult. She touched his arm before stepping to the table.

"And perhaps," she opened a case of knives, took out the sharpest blade and with a single blow, beheaded the flowers, "you should take joy in your revenge. It was quite complete."

She grabbed the stems, leaving the blossoms where they lay, and pushed them at Mateo's chest with such force, he stumbled backward. Teresa pressed her advantage and continued to move forward until he stood outside the room. She slammed the door shut with as much force as she could muster.

Turning to Betsy, she gave her beloved maid an order for the first time in her life. "See that he leaves at once."

Blaine caught her arm, his gaze stormy. He pointed to the rear door. "This, where does it lead?"

"To the gardens."

He crossed the room, nearly wrenched the door from its hinges, and was gone.

Out of the corner of his eye, Mateo saw the figure charging toward him from around the back of the cottage, but he had no chance to turn and face his pursuer. A hand pulled him around. In a fast blurring motion, a fist connected with his jaw. He staggered back under the blow.

Wiping the corner of his mouth with his hand, Mateo glanced at the smear of blood there with an odd kind of detachment. He raised his head and met Blaine Hobson's steely-eyed stare.

The poet stood in a boxer's stance, his fists clenched. A flare of satisfaction lit his gaze as he saw the blood Mateo felt trickling down his chin.

"For Teresa's sake I won't call you out, but I didn't promise anything else." He landed another jab on Mateo's cheekbone.

Mateo's head snapped back. He made no attempt to defend himself. Didn't he deserve much worse than a sound thrashing? Refraining from touching his throbbing cheek, he turned away. The long walk to the inn where he'd found lodgings on his arrival in Surrey would give him plenty of time to relive his regrets.

"Why do you not stand your ground? Is a mere English poet beneath the touch and notice of a great Spanish Count? Or," Blaine's voice lowered and filled with scorn, "are you a coward?"

Mateo stiffened at the insult, his feet slowing to a stop. He had been called many things in his life ranging from the most despicable names imaginable to the more lofty titles of the *aristocracia*. Most of the names he'd probably earned while trying to keep his family together, but he'd never once been accused of cowardice. Oddly enough, the term hurt more than he expected coming from this man.

He looked over his shoulder. "Perhaps, I deserve all you have said and done." Without waiting to gauge Blaine's reaction to his words, Mateo walked along the narrow ruts caused by the numerous passing of wagons over the years.

"Montayas."

Mateo continued onward. Should he return to Spain? But what would he return to? There was nothing left there for him anymore save the cold graves of his parents. Had he given away his birthright for nothing? Damn these plaguing questions, these insecurities. He hadn't once in all the years since his father's death questioned his decisions and now, it seemed it was all he did.

How could he have let his jealousy overcome him? He'd longed to see Teresa for days. The journey from Spain had been long and difficult. Knowing that she would soon be close enough to touch pushed him onward. He promised himself he would do anything to win her back, and his first words to her were insulting.

The clip-clop of horse hooves and the rumbling noise of a vehicle approaching distracted him from his mire of self-pity. He moved onto the grass alongside the lane and plodded onward, his hands tucked into his pockets, shoulders hunched forward.

A shiny black carriage pulled beside him and kept pace with his every step. Mateo tried to ignore the conveyance, knowing without a doubt who it carried. Several yards later, he couldn't stand it any longer.

He shot the driver an infuriated glare. "Move on." He gestured for the coachman to pull ahead.

The man shook his head. "I've orders to follow."

"Well, here's a new order. Go to Hell."

Blaine's head appeared in the window of the carriage. "One can't go where one already is."

Mateo's jaw turned to granite. He knew that blasted poet was in the coach. Why wouldn't he leave him alone to nurse his injured heart in peace? "What do you know of Hell?" Mateo demanded.

"What do I know of Hell?" The sound of laughter filled the air but the poet's eyes were pools of despair and loss. "I have lived in Hell these last eighteen months, long enough to know it intimately."

"Due to a woman, no doubt." Mateo crossed the lane to stand near the coach window.

The door swung open, and Blaine gestured toward the seat opposite. "It involves a woman, yes."

In the act of entering the carriage, Mateo froze. An invisible band tightened around his heart. "Teresa?" He forced the single word out, dreading the response.

"No."

He released a pent-up breath and leaned back against the well-upholstered seat. His heart began to beat once more, the stranglehold on it gone, only to have it return in full force at Blaine's next words.

"I must warn you. I have asked Teresa to marry me."

"What?"

Blaine leaned forward. "You used her, ruined her, and then abandoned her. She isn't welcome in polite society. She'll spend the rest of her life as an outcast and most likely a spinster. Regardless of what her father may have done, she doesn't deserve that."

"She told you about her father? I never meant for her to suffer."

Blaine rapped on the roof of the carriage, setting it in motion. "She didn't have to tell me a word. It's the talk of the *Ton* even now. There were some that took great pleasure in regaling me with all the salacious details the moment I returned to London. And I find it exceedingly difficult to believe you never intended to take your revenge on Teresa."

Mateo looked away, certain his guilt showed on his face. How could he explain his feelings when he arrived in England and the change they had undergone as he came to know the woman behind the Darlington name? It was time for honesty. It was his only hope to win Teresa back.

He sighed and pinched the bridge of his nose. "Yes, my original plan when I arrived in your country was to have my revenge at any cost, but that changed soon after I met Teresa."

Blaine raised a disbelieving brow. "Then why did you abandon her the moment you took her virginity?"

"I thought it was a trap to keep me from renouncing her father. I was angry. I had no choice. Or at least at the time, I thought I didn't."

Blaine shook his head. "There's always a choice."

"You think I don't know that now? That I don't regret every moment since that night the Duchess of Perth stormed into Teresa's bedchamber?" Mateo turned his face toward the window. "I came to England determined to restore honor to the Montayas name and in the process fell in love with the daughter of my family's greatest enemy."

"Love!" Blaine exploded. "You know nothing of love."

"I know there isn't a moment in the day that she's not on my mind. I think of her, and I can't breathe. I have hungered for the sight and touch of her like no other in my life." Mateo heard the desperation in his voice. He stroked his throbbing cheekbone. "Have you never done something you would give anything to go back and change?"

Anguish crossed Blaine's features before it was quickly erased. "Yes," he said in a hushed tone.

Mateo turned back to the window. "Do you love her?"

"Teresa? Yes."

He closed his eyes at the unbearable pain stabbing his heart.

"But I do not love her as you do. She is no more than a sister to me. Go to her. Explain yourself even if it puts you in an unfavorable light. She deserves an honest explanation."

New determination urged Mateo on. "I plan to. I will not lose her."

Chapter Twenty-Three

Mateo stared at the bloomless stems he held in his hand. It was his third trip in as many days to see Teresa. Each time, she gave him no chance to say a word, pushing him out the door holding only a handful of flower stems. He tossed the offensive bouquet into the grass with a sigh of discouragement.

"She's still angry, I see." Blaine leaned against the door of his carriage.

"Very observant of you," Mateo said dryly. "She beheads my flowers, then refuses to listen to a word I might say. Not that I have a chance to utter a sound."

Blaine laughed then looked contrite. "Sorry, old chap. I'd forgotten how stubborn she can be."

Mateo toed the edge of a stem lying along the flagstone path. "Today, I received the distinct impression she wished it were me under her blade."

"Let me talk to her."

"No. I will not have another man plead for forgiveness for what I've done."

Blaine pushed away from the carriage. "I don't intend to. You must win her back on your own. I'll only try to convince her to allow you time to speak before she shuts the door in your face."

"I'm glad you find this amusing," Mateo growled.

"I do. You're a good man, Montayas. I wouldn't have said that a week ago, but you must truly love her. I can't see any sane man subjecting himself to such humiliation daily. And I have one more word of advice." Blaine walked by him and knocked on the front door.

"Violets," he called over his shoulder as Betsy ushered him into the cottage.

Mateo stared after him. Violets?

****

Upon Blaine's unexpected appearance in the entry of the workroom, Teresa dropped the fragrant blossoms she'd crushed to her face only moments before into the wastebasket and turned away.

"Blaine. What an unexpected delight." She forced the words past the lump of unshed tears threatening to cut off her breath.

A hand gently turned her to face him. "You are as miserable as ever, I see." He brushed a stray petal from her cheek. "Why won't you let Montayas explain himself?"

"I'm quite happy. I have no reason to listen to one word that man has to say." Teresa pushed past him and began watering the various plants around the room.

"You are not happy. And we both know it." Blaine's quiet tone seemed to reverberate through the room.

Teresa set the watering can on the table, her shoulders slumping in defeat. "No. I'm not. But don't you see, I can't let Mateo explain. I was taken in by his lies before. I won't be again."

"He wants to tell you the truth. You risked your reputation when you trusted him before. Now take the chance and risk your heart."

"I did and I lost both my heart and my reputation. Why are you doing this? Why are you defending him and what he's done?"

"I'm not defending him."

Teresa sank onto an old settee, the fabric worn along the sides. "Would you be so ready to forgive if a woman had broken your heart and abused your trust?"

Blaine sat down beside her. "I just ask that you listen to Montayas, nothing more. Or do you wish to be like me—mourning a lost love that will forever be unattainable? A life of 'might have been' is a lonely one."

Teresa touched his cheek. "I'm sorry about Collette."

Blaine eased her head down on his shoulder, his arm resting lightly at her waist. "We aren't talking about me. There is no hope for me. But you, you have a chance at happiness. Don't throw it away."

"I'm scared," she whispered. "Will you be here when he comes?"

Blaine framed her face with his hands and pressed a gentle kiss on her forehead. "I can't. You have to do this without me. I've meddled in this affair far too much already. Just promise me this—listen with your heart, not your head or anger."

"I'll try. But only because you ask it of me."

"Enough of this maudlin topic." He pulled her from the settee. "Come walk outside with me. I will tell you the latest gossip from my last trip to London, and you can tell me your grand plans for your garden."

****

Teresa checked the small walnut clock sitting on the mantel. It was only two minutes later than the last time she looked, yet it seemed like a lifetime. She crossed the room, picked it up, and held it to her ear. Was it working properly? Surely, time couldn't possibly pass this slowly.

Replacing the clock, she moved to the small table where she'd laid the note from Blaine that arrived this morning. Teresa skimmed over the words. Mateo would be calling in the afternoon. Would she please hold her temper and allow him to speak?

A small smile curled her lips. Blaine knew her

too well. Restlessness pushed her into movement. She wandered around the small room, her hands smoothing non-existent wrinkles from her gown and brushing imaginary strands of hair that had fallen loose from her elegant hairstyle.

Determined to look her best, Teresa had taken great care with her appearance. Mateo would never know the heartache she suffered from his cruel rejection. She would not be at a man's mercy ever again.

A knock at the door brought her spinning around and running into the hall. Betsy hurried toward the front door.

"No," Teresa called. "Let me, but promise you'll be close by."

Betsy nodded, worry darkening her brow. She turned back to the kitchen, but not before she shot one more frown in Teresa's direction.

Wiping her suddenly damp palms on the sides of her dress, Teresa took a deep breath and opened the door. Mateo filled the opening, a hand raised to knock once more.

Why did he have to be so handsome? Her gaze traveled over him, remembering his gentle touch, the way it felt to be in his arms. Why did she ever agree to this torture?

Raising her eyes to his, she thought she detected uneasiness there. Could he be as fearful of this meeting as she? More likely, he was afraid of having to deal with a clinging female he no longer had any use for.

With a flourish, he removed his hand from behind his back. "For you."

Teresa stared at the bouquet of...stems. There wasn't a single bloom among the handful of rich green leaves and stalks he held.

"I thought I'd save you the trouble."

Unable to hide the smile kicking up the corners

of her lips, she accepted the unusual gift and led the way into the parlour.

Taking a decorative crystal vase from the end of the mantel, she placed it on a nearby table, her back to her unwanted visitor, and set the stems in it. She felt like the biggest fool as she arranged the thin green stems, but she needed to keep her hands busy less she found herself clutching the lapels of Mateo's frock coat, begging him never to leave her.

Why wasn't he saying anything? Why didn't he just inflict his misery and go? But at the same time, she took comfort in his silence. She had no desire to hear the excuses, lies, and half-truths he would use to rationalize his behavior. What possessed her to agree to this meeting? She truly was going mad. How else could she explain why she stayed in the room, waiting for his words to flay her sensitive heart with the cruelty of a whip?

"Teresa, please look at me. Don't treat me like I'm no more than a piece of horrid furniture to be tolerated at best."

She composed her features into an expressionless mask and turned around. "Forgive me, *Senor Conde*. I was overwhelmed by your magnificent gift." She flung a hand toward the stem-filled vase.

"Sarcasm won't help. This is difficult enough as it is. And my name is Mateo. I'd appreciate it if you would address me as such." Mateo closed the door and came further into the room.

"I agreed to see you, not make this easy for you. And I want the door open."

Mateo laid a hand on her arm as she headed for the door. With a visible attempt to hold on to his temper, he released her. "If you are willing to let an intimate conversation such as this to be overheard, it is your right."

Teresa hated to admit he had a point. She didn't

want Betsy knowing all that had happened since the first night she'd had the misfortune to meet him. No doubt the maid had guessed the worst of it, but guessing and knowing for certain were two different things.

She swung away and stood near the window, gazing out but seeing nothing. "We will not be sharing anything of an intimate nature."

Behind her, Mateo released a deep sigh. "Forgive me. I never meant to hurt you. I didn't mean for you to fall in love with me."

She closed her eyes. With each word, he ripped her heart to shreds. "Fall in love? With you?" A bitter laugh escaped her. "You always were unbearably arrogant." She turned around. "You are obviously misinformed. I've accepted a marriage proposal from Mr. Hobson just this morning." A blatant lie but one that would allow her to salvage at least a little of her pride.

He was handling this badly. Damn it. How could she stand there and lie about marrying another? If he didn't know Blaine Hobson was no more than a friend to her, he might well believe her.

"He doesn't love you." Mateo grimaced as pain flashed into her eyes before being quickly suppressed.

"Why? Am I so unlovable?" Her voice trembled as she continued, "Or is it because I am ruined and no longer worthy of marriage, good for nothing more than to be a man's mistress?"

He moved across to where she stood, leaving a mere foot of space between them though it felt like a yawning chasm. "No. That's not the reason."

He gazed at her soft brown eyes and tried to let all the love he felt for her show in his expression. "No. It's because no one can feel about you the way I do. No one can kiss you like I do. No one can hold you like I do." He laid a hand on her shoulder, his thumb caressing the hollow of her throat.

Teresa shrugged away from his touch. "Don't."

She moved to the far side of the room as though desperate to keep him at arm's length. He folded his fingers into his palm, trying to hold on to the soft feel of her skin. He longed to reach out and touch her once more, but knew if he did so, it would only cause her to push him away and his chance to explain would be lost.

"All my life I've known pain and loss. At times it seemed so hard to bear. Yet, the pain of those past hurts was nothing when compared to the loss of your love." Mateo ran a hand through his hair.

Teresa longed to touch the silky black strands but longings like that are what led her to this place. She had finally learned to control her impetuous nature. But at what cost?

"Nothing means more to me than you. Not the *Pequena*, not regaining the Montayas honor. Nothing."

Teresa looked down at her hands, unwilling to say a word. She would not be taken in by his lies again. She would not.

"Have you nothing to say?" Mateo asked, exasperated.

She planted her hands at her hips, trying to dredge up some of the anger she'd harbored for so long. Anger that dissipated with each word he uttered.

"What would you have me say? I've learned that men will say anything and mean none of it all to get what they want."

"I speak only the truth." He held out a hand to her, his eyes urging her to take it. "I would give all that I own to have you love me again."

Teresa ignored the gesture. If she succumbed to the need to touch him, to believe him, it would destroy her this time when he left. "Even your precious *Pequena*?"

He dropped his hand to his side, defeat settling over his features. "Yes. Even my birthright."

"What do you mean, your birthright?"

"I am no longer *El Senor Conde*, if I ever was. We were never treated as members of the *aristocracia*. Shunned is a more apt term. With the jeweled box returned to its rightful place, I was able to restore the Montayas name to glory, yet it meant nothing. I yearned to be with you but was tied to Spain by my duties as the Count de Montayas."

Teresa shook her head. "I don't understand. What are you saying?"

"Eduardo arranged to have documents forged stating I am illegitimate, thus have no right to the title. As the only living male relative, he became the heir, and I gained my freedom to come to you."

She stared at him in disbelief. "You expect me to believe you willingly gave up the wealth and privilege that accompanies a noble title?"

"There was never any privilege to my title. And wealth, well, there was not much of that either."

"How will you live?"

"You don't think I handed over my birthright with no thought of how I would provide for you, do you? I knew Eduardo coveted the title, but he's an honest man and wouldn't cheat me for his own gain. We came to an agreement of sorts. He is a member of the nobility, and I received funds through the sale of a minor parcel of land and will reap a share of the profits when the family estate becomes prosperous once again."

"Why? Why would you give up all that you hold dear? And to allow yourself to be branded illegitimate..." Teresa shook her head in confusion. "It is the greatest of insults to be called a..." She trailed off unable to voice the vulgar term.

Mateo slid his knuckles down the side of her

face, his accent growing more pronounced. "Have you not been listening? I love you, Teresa. I would do anything for you."

With a quick shake of her head, she turned her back on him. "Don't say that...because you don't mean it. You're just feeling guilty."

Could it be true? He loved her? Loved her enough to give up a life he was born to for her? She wanted to believe him. Her heart wanted to cry with happiness while her head warned her to be cautious.

His hands closed around her shoulders turning her to face him. "Perhaps I am feeling guilty. I will never be able to forget the hurt I caused you. My only excuse is that I was a fool." He brushed a soft kiss over her lips. "But believe this—I mean every word I say. I love you." Cradling her head in his hand, he kissed her with a hunger born of desperation.

The scent of him, the feel of him, the touch of his skin on hers all combined to weaken her resolve. She responded with all the love in her heart. Her fingers slid into his hair at the nape of his neck, her body pressed closer, wanting the kiss to last forever.

Releasing her mouth, Mateo looked at her with hope in his eyes.

Betsy's words filtered through the haze of sensation. Love makes you throw caution to the wind.

"I love you, Mateo. Even when I hated you, I couldn't stop loving you."

Mateo laughed, a sound of joy coming from deep within him. He picked her up, hugged her close, and turned around in a small circle before setting her back on her feet.

Her stomach tightened at his sudden somber expression. "What is it?"

"You will marry me?" he said in a rough voice, taking a wilted violet from his waistcoat pocket.

She drew a fingertip over the tiny petals. Violets. Mama found great happiness in marriage. Perhaps she could too.

Touched by the gesture, Teresa stood on her toes and pressed a kiss to his mouth. "Yes. I will marry you." She cast him a coy look from under her lashes. "I have no choice. You've stolen my heart."

Mateo took her in his arms. "A priceless treasure second to none." A brilliant smile curved his lips. "And I would know. After all, I am a thief like no other."

A word about the author...

A book lover from an early age, the curse (or is that blessing?) of an overactive imagination led Katherine to the natural progression of writing her own stories.

She lives in upstate New York with her family.